A Weekend with Frances

Lois Jean Thomas

Seventh Child Publishing, LLC

This book is a work of fiction. Names, characters, and incidents are the product of the author's imagination or are used fictitiously. Any resemblance between events or persons, living or dead, is coincidental.

Cover design by A. R. Thomas

ISBN: 978-9976445-0-0

Library of Congress Control Number: 2016910632

Lois Jean Thomas, Saint Joseph, Michigan

To my soul sister Margaret, in gratitude for the many years we've journeyed together. Thank you, dear friend, for understanding all of this.

CONTENTS

ACKNOWLEDGMENTS

As always, I wish to thank the members of my writers group for listening to my work, and for providing the feedback that helped to make this novel a better story.

Thank you to my friend Mary Ruth Fox for providing necessary details about the locale in which this story is set.

And thanks to my husband Allen for his patience in helping me format and publish this book.

A Weekend with Frances

FRIDAY MORNING

FRANCES RAFFERTY: Katherine's comin' this weekend. That just tickles me. Edith come over here just a minute ago, remindin' me of that, sayin' we hadta git ready. She said Sam's runnin' up to Indianapolis this afternoon to pick her up at the airport. Yup, I'm so tickled I don't what to do with m'self.

Well, I knowed she was comin' sometime this month. She called a while back and told me that. But I been sittin' here thinkin' it was the next weekend or the one after that. Cain't keep track of time no more.

It's such a treat when Katherine comes. She always brings me somethin'. I s'pose I'm like a little kid when I know she's a'comin', 'cause I just cain't wait to see what all she's bringin' me. Oh, I know I oughta be ashamed of m'self for actin' that way, but I cain't help it.

Coupla years back, she brung me a box of chocolates with some gooey sweet stuff in the middle of 'em. Real tasty, they was. "Sweetheart," I says to 'er, "this here candy's the best dern thing I ever did put in my mouth." So she took to bringin' some every time she comes. She always brings me somethin' else, too. But them chocolates have started bein' a regular thing.

I know I shouldn't be takin' 'em for granted. Mind you, them chocolates ain't the kind of thing you find at the IGA in Bean Blossom. I don't know where my girl gets 'em, but I can tell you one thing, they cost her a purty penny. Never tasted nothin' like 'em in my entire life.

To tell ya the truth, they stick to my dentures somethin' awful. But I wouldn't tell Katherine that. I wouldn't hurt her feelin's like that for nothin' in the world. Anyways, if I said that, she'd stop bringin' 'em, and I wouldn't want that, no siree.

So what I do is take my dentures out and let that chocolate melt in my mouth. After I put on my nightie and take my teeth out of an evenin', I sit in my chair with my Bible in my lap and Katherine's box of candy there on the table beside me. I pop one of them candies in my mouth and then open the good book and read a few verses. And I mean to tell ya, that chocolate tastes like heaven. Makes me feel a little bit closer to God for a minute or two.

Whenever I have a box of Katherine's chocolates, I think about 'em all day long. I smile to m'self whenever they come to mind. Even though I'm hankerin' after 'em real bad, I tell m'self, "Now, Frances, you're just gonna hafta wait till evenin'." One or two a day is all I let m'self have. I stretch them chocolates out as long as I can.

But like I told ya, them chocolates ain't the only thing Katherine brings me. The last time she come—when was it, six, seven months ago? I remember now, it was in the early spring, 'cause it was still a little bit chilly outside. She comes in the spring 'cause she likes to see the dogwood in bloom. That brings her some nice memories of when she was a little girl comin' up in this neck of the woods. Even though she don't wanna live around here no more, she still hangs on to the memories. I'm glad of that.

Anyways, when she come out here last spring, she brung me the purtiest little sweater you ever did see. I says to her, "Katherine, where on earth did you get somethin' like this?" It looked to me like it mighta been crocheted by hand. I know how to crochet some, but not stitches that

fancy. Oh, I know it was made by a machine, but still . . . .
It was the softest dern thing, and the color of a robin's egg.
The yarn had a little bit of sparkle to it. So purty and so
soft. I just hadta hold it up to my cheek and feel it that
way.

I says to her, "Katherine, I'm gonna put this away and
keep it for somethin' special."

And she says to me, "No, Mama, I mean for you to
wear this on ordinary days. You should be wearin'
somethin' purty every day of your life." Then she kissed
my cheek and said, "It'll bring out the color of your eyes,
Mama."

Oh, that Katherine! She got such sweet ways about
'er. When I was a girl goin' to Helmsburg High School,
everybody said my eyes was my best feature. One time,
there was even somethin' said about my purty eyes in
yearbook. Dependin' on the day, they sometimes looked
blue and sometimes green. Katherine knows I was once a
nice-looking young girl with the purtiest eyes in my class,
and it's so sweet of 'er to say somethin' that puts me in
mind of that.

I never raised my three girls to hanker after fancy
things. Lord knows I was never wearin' things like that
sweater when they was comin' up. But after the hard times
we been put through, I'm thinkin' it ain't a bad thing to
enjoy a little somethin' special every now and then. I know
Katherine's thinkin' along them lines, too, and that's why
she keeps on a'bringin' me all these presents.

I wanted to wear that sweater every day, I did. But
then I got to worryin' that I'd wear it out too quick.
Katherine made a point of tellin' me that it hadta be washed

out by hand. It's too fine a thing to go in the washin' machine, and that means Edith would hafta take extra time with it. God love 'er, Edith's got so much on her right now. I hate to think of puttin' anything else on her shoulders. So I decided in my own mind that I'd wear the sweater just one day a week. Of course, it was too warm to wear it durin' the summer. But the past coupla weeks, it's been gettin' chilly, and I told m'self it's time to pull it out again. After Edith helps me with my bath later on this mornin', I'll put on the sweater so I'll have it on when Katherine comes. She'll be so tickled to see me wearin' it.

I hafta tell ya, when Katherine left all them years ago, it liketa killed me. Here we been through them hard times, with her right there by my side, and I got to feelin' like she was my only friend in the whole wide world. Like she was the only one I could count on. Then she up and leaves me.

I thought for sure I lost my baby girl for good. The day she was fixin' to leave, I was sittin' there at the kitchen table, just a'bawlin' my eyes out. But before she went, she bent down and hugged me around my shoulders and said, "I love you, Mama. Don't you ever forget that. I'll be back to see you. I promise."

And you know what? That girl kept her promise. That was . . . how many years ago? Thirty? No, I'd say more like forty. And she been a'comin' back here twice a year ever since then, just to see her ol' mama. Just jumps on an airplane, and in a coupla hours, she's landin' there in Indianapolis. Me, I never been on an airplane, and that ain't somethin' I wanna start doin', not at my age. But flyin' ain't nothin' a'tall for Katherine.

In between her trips back home, she's always a'callin'

me on the telephone, checkin' up on me. I hear from her so much, it kinda feels like she's still right here with me.

Awhile back, she got one of them newfangled phones. One of them little bitty contraptions you carry around with you all the time. That way, she can call me whenever she wants to, even when she ain't at home. She'll be callin' me some evenin', sayin', "Just checkin' in, Mama. I'm on my way to play practice." That girl's always in some kinda play or 'nother. Been doin' that since high school.

Or she calls and says, "Mama, Bryce took me out to the nicest dinner this evenin'." Then she starts a'tellin' me how everything was, what the place looked like, how the food tasted. And 'fore I know it, it starts to feelin' like I done ate that dinner right along with her. She does that 'cause she knows I don't never get to go to any place fancy, and she wants me to share in her good times.

Sometimes, she calls me on her way to the gym. "Why's you always needin' to go to the gym?" I says to 'er. She tells me she needs to get some exercise. Back in my day, nobody never needed to go someplace special to get exercise. We got all the exercise we needed from doin' the house chores and workin' out in the garden. After we was done workin', we was so tuckered out, we was glad just to sit down and take a load off our feet.

Katherine, she don't need to work hard no more. She don't even hafta clean her own house. Once, she sent me a picture of her house, and I tell ya, that place was bigger than anything you ever could think of.

I says to 'er, "Katherine, how on earth do you keep that place clean? It'd take me a year and a day to get through that house, dustin' and sweepin'."

5

And she just laughs and says, "Mama, I don't clean it m'self. I ain't got no time for that. I got a maid comin' in three days a week, and she does all my cleanin'.""

Things is different for Katherine since she left here, that's for sure. But I'm kinda glad she don't need to work hard no more. She done worked hard enough when she was a young girl. In my mind, it's okay if she takes it a little easy now.

She wanted me to have one of them little phones she's always a'callin' me on. Told me I could carry it around with me so's I don't have to strain m'self jumpin' up and runnin' to the house phone every time somebody calls.

I says to 'er, "Now why would I wanna carry that thing around all day long? I'd just lay it down somewheres and forget where I put it."

She says, "Mama, you don't carry it around in your hand. You keep it in your pocket."

She told me to think about it for a while, and I did. But I told m'self that if I had that thing on my body all the time, I'd be jumpin' out of my skin every time it went to ringin'. It'd be scarin' the livin' daylights outa me all day long. So I says to 'er, "No, sweetheart, I don't need nothin' like that. It don't hurt me none to get up and walk across the room when the phone rings."

Yup, things is a lot different for Katherine, livin' there in New York City. She was just a young girl when she left here. A year or so outa high school. She been workin' up there in Bean Blossom at that little family restaurant, waitin' on tables and washin' dishes. She was such a hard worker. Always cheerful about it, too. She was helpin' out her daddy and me, givin' us what she earned so's we could make ends meet. That was durin' the time when Martin wasn't capable of workin' much.

I never knowed it then, but Katherine was keepin' some of that money back for herself. I ain't sayin' that was wrong. It was her money, and she had a right to it. But I had no idea that all along, she was cookin' up a plan with some girl named Sheila over there in Nashville. Sheila and her went to Brown County High School together their senior year. I guess both of 'em got the notion in their heads that they wanted to get out of the county and see the world.

Edith, she went off to college after she graduated high school, over there in Bloomington. She was wantin' to go real bad. I'm thinkin' her daddy put that idea in her head, 'cause he never got the chance to go hisself. But I guess after two years, she decided that kind of thing wasn't for her, 'cause she up and quit and moved back home. She ain't the same type of person Katherine is. She's more of the kind that stays in one spot and put down roots.

The minute Edith come home, that was when Katherine up and left. Bless 'er heart, I think she just wanted to make sure somebody was here to help me out. Her and that girl Sheila hopped on a Greyhound bus, and off they went to New York City. Can you believe that? Two young girls, eighteen, maybe nineteen years old, not knowin' left from right or up from down. They just up and went out to the big city on their own. Lord, I was so scared for my girl. I prayed day and night, beggin' God to watch over her.

Coupla months later, I heard it said that Sheila come back home and was livin' with her folks again. Couldn't make it out there on her own. Purt'near had herself a nervous breakdown.

But not my Katherine. She stuck it out. She's like that. The girl's got grit. I liketa think she takes after me. She was bound to have some rough times during them first coupla years. She never told me nothin' about it, 'cause she knowed hearin' that stuff would git me all worked up. But she got through it, and I hafta say, she made somethin' of herself. Been on TV and everything.

Of course, if I'd a'had my way, I woulda kept all my girls close to me out here on Sprunica Ridge Road. Katherine and Edith, anyways. But I s'pose insistin' on Katherine stayin' here woulda been kinda selfish of me. Katherine's like a flower that don't grow in the type of soil we got around here.

We got a lot of wildflowers growin' in these parts. When my girls was little, they useta go out and pick little bouquets and bring 'em back to their mama. I'd put them wildflowers in a Mason jar and set 'em in the middle of the table, so's we could all look at 'em while we was eatin' supper. There's them blue cornflowers that grow alongside the road. And that purty orange butterfly weed. Of course, you can always find plenty of wild daisies and black-eyed Susans around here.

Edith, she's like a wildflower. Like a sweet little violet you find in some shady patch under a tree. You don't see it at first, and 'fore you know it, you might even step on it. But if you look at it a good long time, you can 'preciate how purty it really is.

Rosalie . . . I don't never think of her like a flower. I ain't gonna say nothin' more about that, 'cause I ain't

8

wantin' to give off the impression that I'm the kind of mother that don't love her own child.

But Katherine, she's like a flower growin' somewheres far away from here in some fancy greenhouse. Maybe an orchid. Somethin' out of the ordinary, for sure.

Even though Katherine's gone, I count m'self lucky that I still got Edith. Sam and her live over there 'cross the yard in the house where me and Martin raised the girls.

It's such a blessin' that we got to keep the house in the family. Martin's granddaddy Rupert Rafferty and his daddy Isaac Rafferty built that house way back in the 1920s. Martin was raised there. Purty much lived there all his life, exceptin' for the time when we was gone for that short spell. Every time I look back, I tell m'self we shouldna left like that. A person gets to thinkin' the grass is greener somewheres else. I'm here to tell ya there ain't no truth in that.

Well, what's done is done. I try not to think on it too much, 'cause it gits me all worked up. My doctor tells me I ain't supposed to let m'self git too upset, 'cause it makes my blood pressure run high.

Martin, he was always proud of that house, even though it wasn't nothin' much to brag about. He always liketa point out to people those great big beams in the livin' room. He liketa tell the story about how his daddy and granddaddy cut them beams from the poplar trees that was growin' around here. Nowadays, people like havin' somethin' like that in their home. Makes it look rustic, they say.

My husband passed away thirty-one years ago. I got to thinkin' the other day that I been a widow-lady for more

years than I ever was married. I stayed on in the house a
year after he died, but to tell ya the truth, I didn't much like
rattlin' around in that place on my own. I'm the type that
needs people around me.

So I talked to Edith and Sam about it, and they ended
up movin' into the house. They raised their own young'uns
there. 'Cause I let 'em have the house, they bought me this
here trailer and set it up in the yard. I hafta say, it's just
about the best deal I could ever think of. I get to be on my
own, but I still got family right here close to me. I got to
watch my grandbabies grow up. Now that I ain't gittin'
around so good no more, I got somebody right here to look
after me. Cain't complain, not a bit.

Yup, I'm so glad we didn't let go of that house. When
we up and left for Greenwood all them years ago, we was
thinkin' along the lines of sellin' the place. But everything
happened so quick, we didn't have time to figure that out.
So we ended up rentin' the place out to my sister Della's
girl for a year.

We wasn't countin' on movin' back here, but it turned
out we had to. Sometimes, I get to thinkin' that the Lord
stopped us from sellin' the house 'cause he knowed we'd
be needin' it again. When we hadta leave Greenwood, it
was such a blessin' to have our own home waitin' for us.

I was hopin' to move back in and pick up right where
we left off. That woulda been nice, if we coulda started
livin' like none of that bad stuff ever happened. But I
learnt it don't work out that way. You're always gonna
have a shadow hangin' over you.

Sam an' Edith got that place fixed up now, to the point
where you cain't hardly recognize it as the same house.

They put on some new sidin'. The old sidin' was wood, painted yellow. Edith said the new sidin' is vinyl, or somethin' like that. She says the color is slate gray. It's purty, but it's a little too dark for my likin'. I cain't get used to lookin' at it after all them years of seein' yellow.

Sam and Edith put on a new roof, too, and then they went and put in some new windows. I says to Sam, "What's wrong with them old windows?" And he told me somethin' about the new windows bein' better at keepin' out the cold. Energy efficient, he calls it. Says they'll be gettin' a break on their taxes because of puttin' in them windows.

Then they went and did a whole bunch of plantin' around the house. Edith calls it landscapin'. They got all kinds of bushes and little trees along the front of the house. And flowerbeds. Don't Edith love her flowerbeds! That girl liketa break her back workin' in her flowers all summer long. I'm always sayin' to 'er, "Hows come you wear yourself out, doin' all that?" She says it's her way of gittin' rid of stress. That don't make no sense to me. Seems like she's just makin' extra work for herself.

Anyways, they got that place lookin' real nice. Best lookin' home around here, I'd say. You know how every so often some folks from up around Indianapolis take a notion to move down this way. They get tired of livin' in the big city, I s'pose. Edith told me just the other day that her and Sam was out workin' in the yard and some fellow drivin' by in a fancy car stopped to look at the place. He said it was just the kind of place him and his wife was lookin' to buy, and he wondered if they ever thought about sellin' it.

Sam told him no, said they wasn't thinkin' about sellin' a'tall. Then that man pulls out some kinda card and gives it to Sam and says if they ever do think about sellin', they should give 'im a call.

Imagine that! Some high falutin' person wantin' to buy me and Martin's old place. It makes me downright proud. But I sure was glad to hear that Sam and Edith ain't thinkin' about sellin'. Wouldn't liketa think about what would happen to me if that was the case.

EDITH CLEMENS: Oh dear God! I'm not ready for this weekend! I should be. Kathy emailed me a month ago, telling me that she and Bryce were planning on coming. I should've put it on my calendar right away. But I didn't, and it just slipped my mind. Kathy called me Wednesday afternoon to let me know what time her flight was landing in Indianapolis, and I was totally caught off guard. I tried to act like I'd been expecting her all along. I told her how much I was looking forward to seeing her. After I hung up, I said to myself, "Oh, Edith, how could you have been so stupid?"

When Sam came home from work Wednesday evening, I told him about Kathy coming. He was upset, having it sprung on him at the last minute. My husband is a creature of habit, and he doesn't like surprises. I asked him if he'd think about taking a vacation day from work so he could pick Kathy up at the airport while I get stuff done around here. That ticked him off, but he went ahead and put in the request for a day off. He's been at his job for so long that they pretty much give him whatever he asks for.

I've been so flustered, running in circles trying to get

everything done. And would you believe I forgot to tell Mom about Kathy coming until this morning? I don't know what's wrong with my mind these days.

When Kathy emailed me about her plans for the trip, I wasn't surprised. She almost always comes out to visit in the fall. It's pretty much a routine thing. Maybe that's why I didn't give it much thought, and then forgot to put it on the calendar. Kathy likes to be here when the leaves are in color. Most of the time, she comes out here alone, but every couple of years, her husband Bryce comes with her. He's been here four or five times, I'd say.

I always get a little nervous when I know Kathy's coming. I do love her, and I always enjoy visiting with her. But all the while she's here, I'm wondering what she thinks about my house. I get embarrassed about how shabby some of our furniture is. We're replacing the old stuff little by little, as we can afford it. It is what it is, I guess.

I'm happy with my home, I really am. Sam and I have put so much time and energy into remodeling it. I'm proud of what we've accomplished. But I know how Kathy lives out there in New York, in her big, fancy house on Long Island.

I've never been out there to see her. Kathy's invited me to come, dozens of times. At least once a year, she says, "Edie, why don't you fly out here and spend a week with me? There's so much I could show you. We'd have a blast." But Sam refuses to go, and I don't have the nerve to fly to New York City on my own.

She emails me pictures of her place. I always feel like she's putting me to shame, even though I know she doesn't mean to do that. She'll send me a picture of some gorgeous new planting her gardener did. It's like all she has to do is snap her fingers to make that kind of thing happen. And I think, *I slave for hours on end in my flowerbeds, and they don't look half that good.* Sometimes, it gets me down, and I start feeling like I want to give up.

Kathy likes to post things on Facebook, like pictures of vacations she and Bryce take. They're always going off somewhere, to Hawaii or the Caribbean Islands or Italy or the French Riviera. Places like that. And here I sit, in exactly the same spot where I was born. I'm sure Kathy thinks I'm a stick in the mud.

I hardly ever travel. When our kids were growing up, Sam and I would take them on little family trips every summer. Like to the zoo in Cincinnati, Ohio. Or to Mammoth Cave. Once, we took them to Abraham Lincoln's birthplace in Kentucky. Fun places to visit that aren't that far from here.

About the only special thing Sam and I do now is to go to the Indy 500 every Memorial Day weekend. That's been our tradition for the past twenty years or so. To tell you the truth, I don't care for it that much. I'm a quiet person, and I don't like dealing with the noise and the crowds.

Every year, the people around us in the stands start drinking and getting out of hand. Sam gets irritated when people act stupid like that, and it puts him in a bad mood. And of course, dealing with all the traffic when we're trying to get out of there makes him mad. He ends up cussing and fuming all the way home. Then he's a real bear to live with for a day or two after that, and I think to myself, *Edith, what's the point of going through all this?*

One year, I suggested to Sam that he might like to take

one of our boys to the race instead of me. He got a hurt look on his face and said, "I thought this was something you and I do together. But if you don't want to go, you don't have to."

So I backed off real quick and said, "Of course I want to go, honey. I was just thinking you might have more fun if you went with another guy."

That was a lie, actually. If someone told me I'd never have to see that racetrack again, I'd jump for joy. But I'll go for Sam's sake, as long as he wants me to.

I'm sure Kathy never goes to places like that. She goes to the opera. I wouldn't mind going to the opera, if I had a way to get there. But I'm happy staying at home, too.

I love living here in Brown County. It's beautiful. Being surrounded by nature makes me feel peaceful. I'd lose my mind if I had to live in all the commotion of a big city. This is the only place I could ever call home. I know Kathy doesn't understand that. She thinks I'm stuck here because I don't have the gumption to get up and get myself out of here like she did. But I've never wanted to leave.

A month ago when Kathy told me she and Bryce were coming, I thought, *I can put them in the upstairs room Sam and I painted this summer. That will give them some privacy.* I've got a double bed in there. I know they're used to something bigger, like a king-sized bed. If there's anything even better than that, I'm sure they've got it. But the room is so tiny, and a double bed is all that will fit in there.

That was my room growing up. It was pretty shabby back then. There were holes in the plaster walls. The wallpaper looked ancient, like it was from the 1940s. It was gray with bouquets of pink and white flowers on it, and it made the room look dark and dingy. The wallpaper was peeling off in places. From time to time, I'd sneak some flour from Mom's canister on the kitchen counter and mix it with a little bit of water to make a paste. Then I'd use it to stick the wallpaper back on the wall. It never worked very well. If I'd manage to get one part to stick, then another part would start peeling off.

Of course, my little sister Rosie didn't help matters. She was nervous when she was a little girl, and she cried a lot. Well, I don't have any room to talk. I was that way, too. Mom used to get on both of us for being crybabies. When Rosie would get punished, she'd be scared to cry in front of Mom. I'd be up in my room, and I'd hear Rosie coming up the stairs, trying to choke back her sobs. She'd come into my room and sit on the floor, sucking her thumb and picking at the loose wallpaper.

I'd let her go ahead and do it, because I knew it was her way of settling herself down. So that wallpaper ended up being a mess. In the spots where Rosie picked away the gray paper, you could see a layer of paper underneath it, a bright coral with blue flowers and white seahorses on it.

Sam and I pretty much gutted that room. We replaced the plaster walls with drywall. Then we painted the room pale yellow. I love the color, and it inspired me to get the room completely fixed up. I bought a new bedspread and some matching curtains for the window. They're a floral print that picks up the color of the walls.

I framed some old family photos and hung them on the walls. The room looks real cute now. Nothing to brag about, but it's homey. Sometimes, I like to go up there and take a nap in the afternoon. It sort of makes up for the shabbiness of the old days.

But wouldn't you know it, when Kathy called me two days ago, she said Bryce wasn't coming. Something came up with his business. I'm not sure what Bryce does. Something to do with investments. Hedge funds, I think they call it. I don't know what that means. All I know is that Bryce makes a whole lot of money. He's got a huge company to manage, and I'm sure there's always something coming up that needs his attention.

I actually felt kind of relieved to know that Bryce wasn't going to be here this time. Sam doesn't like Kathy's husband. He says Bryce doesn't do an honest day's work, and he's always tense when he's around. He didn't like Kathy's first husband that much, either, although he liked him better than he likes Bryce. Rodney was a musician, and that's not the type of guy Sam relates to.

Sam's a hardworking man. That's the kind of life he believes in. He's been working at Cummins in Columbus for more than forty years. They build diesel engines. Sam started out on the assembly line when he was hardly more than a kid. He's worked his way up to a supervisor position.

Cummins has a good man in Sam Clemens. He knows that company inside and out, and he's very loyal. I think that's one reason why he's so stuck on the idea of going to the Indy 500 every year. The Mr. Cummins who started the company a hundred years ago helped build the engine of the car that won the first Indy 500 race. I think Sam feels like he has a personal stake in the race.

When Sam retires next year, there won't be anyone

who can fill his shoes. He hardly ever misses a day's work, even though his poor body is wearing out. He's always complaining about his bad back or his sore shoulder. He can hardly stand being on his feet all day long. I hate that he had to take a vacation day to help me get ready for the weekend. He should be using his time off to rest. Having Kathy come to visit isn't his idea of a good time.

I hate to say this, but Sam doesn't like Kathy very much, either. He thinks she's arrogant and conceited. He says she talks to him like he's some kind of ignoramus. I know Kathy can come across that way, but it still hurts me to hear him say that. She's my sister, and I love her.

My husband's an intelligent man. I don't think Kathy knows that. He's capable in so many ways. There isn't anything that breaks down around here that he can't fix. He did two years of college, like I did. Even though he's spent his life working in production, he's a well-read person. There's always a book on his nightstand, maybe something by John Grisham or an old-time author like Ernest Hemingway. I like to tease Sam because he has an author's name. It's the same as Mark Twain's real name.

Well, I only had half a second to be relieved when I heard Bryce wasn't coming, because as soon as Kathy told me that, she said she was bringing Katrina with her instead. And Katrina's baby girl, Lilly. Katrina is Kathy's daughter by her first husband, Rodney Rosen. Kathy and Bryce don't have any children together.

"I already had the two airline tickets," Kathy told me. "So I asked Katrina if she wanted to come along. Katrina hasn't seen her grandmother in years. She wants Mom to see Lilly. This might be Mom's only chance to see her great-granddaughter. We don't know how many more years Mom will be with us."

Kathy was so excited about the idea of Katrina coming. She said, "Will that be okay with you, Edie?" Of course, I said yes. I never say no to family when they want to visit.

But that changes the whole game plan. I can't put Kathy and Katrina and the baby all in that tiny little room upstairs. And the other upstairs bedroom is a mess. We haven't gotten around to fixing it up yet. It's full of Sam's tools and lumber and paint cans, and God knows what else. I'm just going to keep that door closed and hope nobody goes in there.

Maybe I'll put Kathy upstairs in the small bedroom, and Katrina and the baby in the downstairs room next to our bedroom. Katrina won't want to be running up and down the stairs with the baby all weekend. Anyway, she'll need to be close to the bathroom, so she can clean the baby up when she needs to. I wish I hadn't gotten rid of that old crib. My own grandkids have outgrown it. Maybe it's still in the garage. I'll have Sam take a look.

I don't have that room cleaned up yet. I haven't set foot in there for two weeks, not since the last time my grandkids spent the night. I'll change the sheets and run the vacuum cleaner this afternoon.

I sure hope Katrina's baby sleeps through the night. Sam will be aggravated if she cries and keeps him awake. His ulcer has been acting up again. He needs his rest, and I shouldn't be putting any extra stress on him.

I'm forever and always feeling like I'm stuck between two people I love. I never get myself out of that jam. If

I'm doing my duty by one person, then I'm doing wrong by someone else. If I'm trying to be a loving sister, then I'm not respecting my husband's needs. Some days, I spend the whole afternoon at the trailer, helping my mom out with this and that, and then I don't have time to fix a proper meal for Sam when he comes home from work.

I know Sam's sick and tired of people coming over here. He's sixty-four years old now, and his health isn't what it used to be. He can hardly wait for retirement. I tried to get him to retire at sixty-two. I told him, "Honey, there's no point in killing yourself on that job." But he's trying to stick it out until he's at least sixty-five, so he can get his full Social Security benefits. That's Sam for you, looking out for our future.

Even though I want to protect Sam, I never want to make my family feel unwelcome. Our three children are always stopping by. They're great kids, and we're so proud of them. We managed to put all three of them through college. Brian is a math teacher at Brown County High School. David is an addictions counselor at a clinic in Bloomington. Megan has a degree in English, but right now, she's staying home with her children.

I'm glad we have good relationships with all of them. But Sam and I hardly ever have time to ourselves.

One or two evenings a week, we end up babysitting for a couple of the grandkids. We have eight of them. The oldest is twelve and the youngest is two, so you can imagine that when they're around, things get pretty lively. Sam ends up getting a bad headache from all the noise.

And now this weekend, we're having a houseful of out-of-town guests.

Wednesday evening when I told Sam about Kathy and Katrina coming, he said, "Don't I ever get to have a say in any of this?" Then he said, "I might as well keep on working until I'm seventy, because I sure don't get any peace and quiet around this house."

I felt absolutely horrible. I apologized to Sam over and over. I told him that if he wanted me to, I'd call Kathy and cancel the whole thing. But he said, "No, go ahead with your plans. I'll deal with it."

The last two nights, I've been so nervous that I've had a terrible time getting to sleep. I just lay there worrying about how things will go this weekend. Then, wouldn't you know it, I had one of my dreams last night. They always come around three or four o'clock in the morning, and then I wake up feeling so upset that I can't get back to sleep again.

It seems like every time the stress gets high around here, I have that same dream. Every time Sam gets cranky and hard to live with, I have that dream. Then I can't get it out of my head, and I'm out in La-La Land the whole next day.

Even now, I feel shaky. I can't think straight, even though I need to get all my plans sorted out.

When that dream comes around, it tends to come two or three nights in a row. I hope to God I don't have another one this weekend. I just can't handle anything more.

I should probably sit down and make a list. I need to get over to Mom's. Tidy up a little bit, run the vacuum cleaner. I cleaned her trailer pretty good last week, so it shouldn't take too long. And how much mess can an old woman make? She doesn't do much of anything. She just sits in her chair all day long, reading her Bible or watching TV. But she always wants her place spic and span when she knows Kathy will be visiting.

Oh dear God! It's Mom's day for a bath. Of course, she'll want a bath since Kathy's coming. I hope she won't insist on having her hair washed. My mother's not a small woman, and it's getting to be more and more of a chore to take care of her. My sciatica's been acting up really bad, and getting her into the bathtub is almost more than I can handle.

I always knew I'd be the one who'd take care of my mother in her old age. I wouldn't feel right if I wasn't doing it. But I didn't know it was going to be this hard. I'm exhausted all the time. I pray every day for the strength to do what needs to be done.

I wouldn't say this to anyone else, but dealing with my mother is sometimes like dealing with a small child. She's very stubborn, and she gets ideas in her head that she just won't let go of. There's no talking sense to her. When she's in one of her unreasonable moods, it really tires me out.

Kathy seems to be the only one who can reason with our mother. I'm amazed at what she can talk her into. My mom had hung onto a lot of old clothing she'd had for years, stuff that looked horrible. Stuff she'd had since before my father died, and that's been more than thirty years ago. Awhile back, I tried to talk her into getting rid of some of it. Her closet was stuffed so full that she could hardly get in there to get what she needed. But she wouldn't budge. She argued with me, saying she wasn't a wasteful person, and that she wasn't going to throw out perfectly good clothing. I never win any of the arguments I have with her. So I gave up and let her keep it all.

The next time Kathy came to visit, she brought Mom some new things, like she always does. And before I knew it, she was hauling bags of Mom's old clothing out to our garbage can. She had a disgusted look on her face, like she thought I should've taken care of that a long time ago. And when I went to the trailer to see Mom, I could tell she wasn't a bit upset about letting go of her old things. She did it because Kathy said she should. She trusts Kathy more than she trusts me.

Kathy's actually a lot of help with Mom, even though she lives so far away. She has such a big heart for Mom, and she knows how to do things that bring some sparkle to her life. I'm always afraid Kathy thinks I don't do enough of that kind of thing. She has no idea about the ordinary things I do for Mom on a daily basis.

Rosie doesn't help at all. I understand why. She and Mom can hardly stand to be in the same room together. Plus Rosie has her hands full with her son. Marty's a lot of work for her.

Sam says we should be looking into getting Mom some home health care. I know he's right. I just can't do it all anymore. I'm going to have to work up the nerve to talk to her about it. Mom doesn't take well to strangers, and she's going to pitch a fit about having someone she doesn't know coming into her house. She doesn't have anything of value in that trailer, but she doesn't like people messing with the stuff she has. Nobody besides Kathy, anyway.

What the heck am I going to fix for dinner tonight? This sounds awful, but I hope it's one of those times when

Kathy insists on taking us out to eat. She likes to go to some of those little places in Nashville. She thinks Nashville is quaint. She acts like a tourist coming to town, seeing this place for the first time. Like she never grew up here. Like she never went to school there in Nashville.

Kathy's picky about what she eats, and I'm always afraid I'm going to fix something that offends her. Sam's pretty much a meat and potatoes kind of guy. Kathy doesn't eat like that. She's always talking about the most recent thing she's heard about health food. She says she doesn't want to put anything toxic into her body.

Maybe if she doesn't offer to take us out, I'll ask Sam if we can eat out anyway. We'll foot the bill, even though we can't afford it. Not after what I did last week, anyway. Sam doesn't know about that yet, and when he finds out, he'll go through the roof.

I'm going to have to work extra shifts at Margaret Brown's gallery just to make up for that big check I wrote. Margaret's a good friend of mine. She has a ceramics studio and gallery in Nashville, and sometimes I mind the store on weekends, just to help her out. Well, I do it for myself, too. It gets me out of my little world way out here in the country, and puts me in contact with people.

Margaret wanted me to work this weekend, but I told her I couldn't. I felt bad about turning her down. But I can't do everything everybody wants me to do. Sam tells me that all the time. My mom even says that, even though she's the one who demands the most from me.

Maybe I can figure out a menu really quick. I'll count on eating out tonight. Tomorrow morning, I'll make waffles. I have some blueberries from my garden in the freezer, and I can make some nice syrup to go with the waffles. Kathy should like that, because the blueberries are organic. Sam will want sausage or bacon with the waffles. I won't deprive him just because my sister doesn't believe in eating meat. I have no idea what Katrina eats.

I'll send Sam up to the *IGA* in Bean Blossom before he takes off for the airport. I know I need milk and butter and orange juice. Kathy probably only drinks fresh squeezed orange juice, but honestly, I just don't have time for that this weekend. I'm almost out of eggs. We have some friends who live over there by Fox's Corner. They raise chickens, and always have eggs for sale. Sam can stop by there on his way home from the store to pick some up. That way, they'll be fresher. I can't remember whether or not Kathy eats eggs, but I should have some on hand, just in case.

I wonder if Sam would be willing to pick up a bottle of wine. I'm not much of a drinker, and Sam has two or three beers a month at the most. But Kathy drinks wine with her dinner, and she likes a couple of drinks in the evening.

I try to have wine on hand for her. But I don't know how to pick out good wine, and Sam and I can't afford the expensive stuff she and Bryce drink. Lately, Kathy's been bringing a bottle along with her when she comes. She presents it to me like a hostess gift. No one else brings gifts like that when they visit us.

Sam says she's bringing it for herself, because she wants to make sure she has plenty of booze on hand. That makes her sound like an alcoholic. I really don't think she is. The way I take it is that she doesn't trust me to provide anything decent to drink.

I figure she'll bring some wine along again this time. But I don't want to take that for granted. I guess I'll ask Sam if he'll pick some up. He'll probably say what he always says, that he's not going to spend his hard-earned money to support my sister's drinking habit.

Well, enough of that kind of talk. We'll get by. Kathy always helps out when she's here. She's really good about that.

KATHERINE HUDSON: I'm so excited about this weekend! Even though it's not happening quite the way I'd envisioned it. My original plan was to have Bryce come with me. We haven't gone anywhere together for a while, not since we went to Cancun last spring. And I don't think he's gone to Brown County with me for three or four years.

I thought he was looking forward to our trip. He's been so busy. Recently, he's been at work twelve hours a day, maybe more. I thought he'd be ready for a break. But before he left for the office Wednesday morning, he said, "Kathy, this isn't a good time for us to travel. I think you should call your sister and cancel your plans."

"But, sweetie, I already have the tickets," I told him.

"That's the least of my worries right now," he said.

I don't know what's come over Bryce. He's been so preoccupied the past couple of months. He seems worried. That's not like him. He's always been the most confident man I've ever known.

In the twenty-three years we've been married, we've never allowed ourselves to fall into a pessimistic outlook on life. You know what I've observed? People bring all sorts of misfortune into their lives by their own negative thoughts. Bryce and I aren't like that. We're both aware of the fact that we can exercise control over our lives by what we think and what we say. We expect the best.

Bryce's positive attitude is what attracted me to him in the first place. Whenever I tell people the story of how I met my husband, they say it sounds like a fairy-tale, too good to be true. But it's not. It's the way life actually works. If you keep a positive outlook and stay focused on your hopes and dreams, you will attract good things into your life. That's a law of the universe.

When I first met Bryce, I was going through a rough time, struggling to keep my head above water. Rodney, my first husband, worked as a musician. He played background music in recording studios. It paid pretty well when he was working, but sometimes his gigs were few and far between. We'd been married for fourteen years, and things were starting to fall apart between us.

Rod wasn't a person with a lot of drive, even though he was very talented. He played the guitar and the bass and the keyboard, and just about any other instrument you could think of. I used to push him to better himself. I'd tell him he should put himself out there and try to develop a solo career.

But he told me he didn't have the personality for that. "I'm not a performer," he said. He preferred staying behind the scenes. It seemed to me he was wasting his God-given abilities. I don't understand people like that.

He didn't mind lying around our apartment all day while I went out and earned a living for us. I was starting to feel like I was pulling all the weight in our marriage, taking care of him, myself, and our daughter Katrina.

But I've never been one to let circumstances take me down. I've always believed that if you set your mind to do something, you can make it happen. Bryce and I think alike that way.

I was working as a secretary at the time I met Bryce. I wasn't making much money, and was feeling pretty discouraged. Every morning when I got up, I had to pump myself up just so I could get through the day. "It's going to be okay, Kathy," I'd tell myself over and over again. "You'll find a way to get through this."

One morning, I felt especially bad, and it was all I could do to get myself out of bed and ready for work. Rod and I had argued the night before. I'd told him I couldn't carry all the weight on my own anymore, and that he needed to start hustling and find more work.

"I'm doing the best I can, Kathy," he said. But I didn't believe him.

When I went to the office that morning, I felt totally defeated. I wanted to give up. I hated Rod. I felt like taking my daughter and running away, but I had no idea where I'd go. All I knew was that I desperately needed something in my life to change.

It's amazing how things show up in our lives just when we need them the most. When I went to the break room for coffee, I walked past the employee bulletin board. Something caught my eye, and I stopped to look at it. It was a flyer for a weekend self-help seminar.

As I stood there staring at that flyer, a strange feeling came over me. I knew I needed to be at that seminar. I couldn't afford the cost of it. Our rent was due. It was going to take my entire paycheck plus everything I had in the bank, and that still wasn't going to cover it. I was just hoping and praying that Rod had a little money in his account.

But I couldn't get over the feeling that something was waiting for me at that seminar. I knew I'd miss out on it if I didn't jump on the opportunity. So I didn't hesitate a minute. I went straight back to my desk and picked up the phone and made my reservation.

From the moment I arrived at the seminar that following Saturday morning, I knew I'd done the right thing. The speaker talked about manifesting our destiny and tapping into the unlimited potential within us. I felt something powerful stirring inside of me. His words reminded me of what I'd actually known my whole life: that if I put my heart and soul into what I do, I can create the kind of life I want. I'd started to lose sight of that fact. But the speaker gave me just what I needed. It was as if he was recharging a battery inside of me that had started to run down. He gave me the confidence to believe in myself and to move ahead with my life.

I'd known for years that being married to Rod wasn't what I wanted. I hadn't gotten to the point of filing for divorce, because I didn't have the money to hire an attorney. I knew Rod didn't want a divorce, and that I'd have a fight on my hands.

The longer I sat in that seminar, the more convinced I was that I needed to take the step of divorcing Rod. I had to unload the baggage that was holding me back. I knew it would be hard. But I'd overcome difficulties in the past, and I'd do it again.

At the first break, I was trying to make my way

through the crowd to get a cup of coffee at the refreshment table. The place was packed. Somebody caught me in the ribs with an elbow, and I lost my balance. I fell against the man standing next to me, and made him spill his coffee down the front of his suit.

When I looked up at the man to apologize, I found myself gazing into the most incredible blue eyes that I'd ever seen. They were kind, but I could also see strength and determination in them. The man was tall and very nice-looking. Very sexy, actually. He looked fit, like he worked out in a gym. He had thick, wavy black hair with a hint of gray at the temples. I noticed that the suit I'd ruined when I spilled his coffee was an expensive one.

The universe works in such interesting ways. Sometimes, there's a little humor involved. I was destined to meet that man, to bump into him that day. And I literally bumped into him.

I looked at his nametag. "I'm so sorry, Mr. Hudson," I said.

He smiled at me. Then he glanced at my nametag. "It's okay, Ms. Kathy Rosen. This is what keeps our drycleaners in business." He extended his hand and said, "Call me Bryce."

I told him I'd pay for the cost of the cleaning. He said, "Sweetheart, I wouldn't dream of letting you do that."

Then he put his arm around my shoulders and steered me out of the crowd. When we got to a place where we could talk, he asked, "So what brings a beautiful woman like you to this seminar?"

And we started talking. We continued our conversation at lunch, and the next break, and then over dinner that evening. We talked late into the night. I went home to catch a few hours of sleep, and the next morning, I headed back to the seminar. Mr. Bryce Hudson was waiting there for me, and we sat together. We had lunch and dinner together, and we kept on talking.

The more we talked, the more I knew Bryce Hudson was the kind of man I wanted in my life. I could tell he was someone who took charge and made things happen. He had an amazing confidence, like he knew exactly what he wanted out of life. I knew he'd never let anyone or anything stop him from reaching his goals.

Bryce was obviously well-off financially. I always made a point of dressing my best, but compared to him, I felt shabby. He didn't seem to mind that I didn't have much money. He made me feel at ease in his presence.

For some reason, I wasn't embarrassed to tell Bryce about my humble beginnings. I told him about growing up in the country in southern Indiana. I told him I'd known from the time I was a little girl that I wanted something more out of life. I talked about my childhood dream of becoming a singer and an actress.

He listened to me intently, as if he was truly interested in what I was saying. When I told him how I used to practice my singing and dancing in my bedroom, he laughed and said, "Kathy, you're so precious."

I told him that when I was a teenager, I'd worked as a waitress at a little family restaurant, helping out my parents and saving up every penny I could, just waiting for the day when I could follow my dream. I told him about buying a bus ticket to New York City, not knowing what I was going to face when I got there. I told him how rough it was getting started, living in a nasty little YWCA room and working the late shift at an all-night restaurant so that I could go to casting calls during the day.

I admitted to him that my dream career hadn't taken off. "But I still haven't given up on it," I told him. "When the time is right, it will happen."

He reached across the table and covered my hand with his. With deep feeling in his voice, he said, "Don't give up, Kathy. I don't want you to ever give up."

At that moment, it was like a dam broke inside of me. I started telling Bryce about some of the sensitive issues in my life, things I'd never discussed with anyone else. I told him about my father's mental breakdown when I was a teenager, how devastating that had been for my mother, how hard she'd had to work to carry the entire load while he lay in that hospital bed. I told him how the role of being my mother's primary helper had fallen on my shoulders, and how I'd stuck with her until she didn't need me anymore.

"Right now," I said, "I'm in the same position as my mother was. My husband's barely working, and everything is on me. But I'm not going to let him pull me down."

On Sunday evening, Bryce and I were having our last meal together. I knew we weren't ready to part ways. He'd been taking me to upscale restaurants, and I was already starting to feel like I'd entered a completely different world. Like living in that pitiful apartment with Rod and struggling to make ends meet was already a past chapter of my life.

I'll never forget what Bryce did that night. We were standing outside the restaurant under a streetlight. I couldn't bear the thought of never seeing him again, and I knew he felt the same way. He took my chin in his hand and looked intently into my eyes. "Kathy," he said, "you're one of a kind. You're indomitable. I want you to come and work for me at B. K. Hudson Investments. I need people in my organization with your kind of spirit. Whatever salary you're making now, I'll double it."

See what I mean? If you have faith in yourself and put yourself out there, wonderful things are bound to come your way.

So the way Bryce is acting right now doesn't make sense to me. When I get home, I'm going to have a talk with him. I'll remind him of what we've believed in all these years. Maybe with the long hours he's been working, he's slipped up on his diet. Or maybe he hasn't been going to the gym. I'll call our naturopathic doctor and make an appointment for him. Maybe he could benefit from a new dietary supplement.

EDITH: I can't believe this! Rosie just called me. She said, "Edie, I won't be coming until after dinner tonight. I have to work late."

I was completely caught off guard. Nobody had said a word to me about Rosie being here this weekend. "I didn't even know you were planning on coming," I blurted out.

Then I felt bad, because I knew I sounded rude. I could tell Rosie felt bad, too. She said, "I'm so sorry, Edie. Kathy called me a few days ago and told me what was going on this weekend. She said she wanted all of us to be together for a family reunion. I didn't think I could make it at first, but she insisted, so I canceled my other plans. I thought she'd worked everything out with you. She said she was going to call you."

"No," I said. "She didn't call me about you coming. Well, maybe she did and it slipped my mind. I'm so forgetful these days."

Then Rosie said, "I'm really sorry, Edie. Why don't we just call it off, then? It's not fair to spring this on you. You have enough on your plate with Kathy coming, and I don't want to make any more work for you."

"Please come, Rosie," I said. "It'll be wonderful to have all three of us together. It won't be any trouble at all."

That last sentence was an outright lie. Of course, it will be extra work for me. But I can't turn Rosie away, not after what happened to her all those years ago. I know she hasn't felt like a part of this family for a long time. I don't want to give her any more cause for feeling that way.

"Edie, are you sure?" she asked.

"Yes, Rosie," I said, "I'm absolutely sure."

"Okay," she said, "I guess we'll come. Marty would've been so disappointed if we'd had to cancel our plans. He always looks forward to seeing his Aunt Edie."

Then I realized she was planning on bringing her handicapped son. He's in a wheelchair, and he can hardly do anything for himself. When he's around, there's always extra work.

I figured I might as well throw all my plans out the window, because I knew the weekend was going to be totally out of control.

Of course, I'd never say anything like that to Rosie. I said, "Well, you tell Marty that Aunt Edie is looking forward to seeing him, too."

After I hung up the phone, I sat down at the kitchen table with my head in my hands, trying to think. Then Sam walked into the house with the groceries I'd asked him to get. He said, "What's going on, Edie?"

I lifted my head and said, "Rosie just called. She and Marty are coming, too."

Sam slammed the grocery bags down on the table. "That figures!" he said. "Your family always piles in on us all at one time."

"We're going to have to put Rosie and Marty in our bedroom," I told him. "It's the only room big enough for Marty to move around in his wheelchair. I'll put Kathy in the upstairs bedroom and Katrina and the baby in the downstairs guest room."

"So where are you and I going to sleep?" Sam asked. His face was bright red, and I could tell he was really ticked off.

"I guess we'll have to blow up the air mattress and sleep in the storage room upstairs," I said. "Will you get the mattress out before you go to the airport?"

"Since Rosie's coming," he said, "why don't you have her stop at the airport and bring Kathy down? It would save me making a trip up there."

"Rosie isn't coming until after dinner," I told him. "She has to work late. Kathy and Katrina would have to wait around in the airport for five or six hours. They have the baby with them."

"Hasn't Kathy ever heard of rental cars?" he growled.

"It's not that big of a deal for us to run up to the airport to get her," I said. "It's nice for Kathy to have family waiting for her when she gets off the plane. I don't want to tell her she has to find her own way down here. That wouldn't make her feel very welcome."

Sam shot me a dirty look and headed up the stairs. "What are you doing?" I called after him.

"I'm going to move the stuff in the storage room up to the attic," he yelled back. "I have to clear a space for us to sleep. Isn't that what you want me to do?"

"No!" I said. "Absolutely not! Don't you dare put that junk in the attic! Just push it all over to one side."

I hardly ever talk like that to Sam. I'm not the kind of wife who puts her foot down.

"There's not going to be enough room to lay the mattress down," he said.

"Just pile stuff up," I told him.

Sam stomped up the stairs. I could hear him banging around in the storage room. When he came down ten minutes later, he said, "Well, don't blame me if you get conked in the head by something falling in the middle of the night." Then he went out and jumped into his Jeep and took off for the airport, mad as a wet hen.

I should've thought to tell him to take my car. I don't think Kathy will be comfortable riding in that Jeep.

I don't like upsetting Sam. I know he thinks I'm being unreasonable. But I can't have that attic piled full of junk. I won't allow my father's space to be desecrated like that.

Nobody cares about that room but me. Nobody even thinks about that room, except for me. Well, I guess Sam thinks about it when he needs more storage space, and he's always aggravated when I won't let him use it.

We have two bedrooms upstairs with a hallway between them. There's a door at the end of the hallway, and behind it is the flight of stairs leading up to the attic. When I was a little girl, that attic was a mess. The door was always kept shut, and we weren't supposed to go up there. Mom said it was too dangerous. The stairs were narrow and steep, not meant for a lot of foot traffic. The attic was full of junk, and it was really dusty up there. There were exposed electrical wires, which is hazardous for little kids.

But of course, we sneaked up there to play every now and then. We'd come down with cobwebs stuck to our hair and our clothing. Mom would get so mad at us.

Then one day, Rosie fell down the attic stairs and skinned herself up really bad. That's when Mom lost it. She said if we ever went up there again, she was going to beat the tar out of us. So we decided to listen to her.

It's funny when I think about it. It was always Kathy's idea to go up to the attic when she knew we weren't supposed to. But Rosie and I were the ones who ended up getting in trouble.

But about fifty years ago, that nasty little attic was transformed into something special. I was twelve, I think, so that's exactly forty-nine years ago. That's a long time, but I remember that day just like it was yesterday.

For a couple of months, Mom and us girls had heard my dad working up there in the attic, sawing and hammering and sanding. He was doing everything by hand, because he didn't have power tools back then. We didn't think much of anything about it.

My dad was a preacher. He was a kind person, a gentle soul. But he was also creative. Artistic, I'd say. We were all used to him working on his little projects.

One day, he came downstairs and said to all of us, "Come with me. I have something to show you."

We girls were really surprised when he opened that door at the end of the hallway and told us to follow him up those forbidden stairs. And when we stepped into the attic, I was shocked to see what he'd done up there. Totally dumfounded.

No, I don't think dumfounded is the right word. More like awed. I can hardly explain the feeling that came over me. It felt like I was standing in heaven. That was the first time in my life I ever had that experience.

My father had hauled every bit of junk out of the attic. Then he'd paneled all the walls and the ceiling with cedar boards. It made the space seem cozy, and it smelled so good. He'd sanded the pine floorboards and stained them. Everything was done so nicely. My dad was a perfectionist about things like that.

There were two small windows in the attic, put there for ventilation, one in the front of the house and one in the back. And the most special thing about that attic room was what my father had done with one of those windows.

One of his friends had a stained-glass studio in Nashville. My dad had gone down there to learn how to work with the glass. He loved things like that. My mom would get on his case about wasting his time on frivolous things. "If you want something to keep you busy," she'd say, "there's plenty of stuff to do around here." Then she'd rattle off a list of all the things in the house that needed fixing. She never understood my father's artistic nature, and why his projects were important to him.

That day in the attic, I realized that my father was truly

an artist. He'd taken the panes out of one of those little windows and replaced them with panes of leaded stained glass. The colors were gorgeous.

He'd built a stand, like an altar, and had it sitting under that window. Then he'd laid his big family Bible on it.

I thought the whole room was spectacular. Simple, but stunning. Magical, really. "It's beautiful, Dad," I said. "It's like a little chapel."

He smiled at me and said, "It is a chapel, Edith. It's a place where I can be quiet and listen to God." He pointed to a shabby old desk standing along one wall. "This is where I'm going to sit and write my sermons."

I could tell my mother wasn't impressed. The whole thing seemed to aggravate her. She's always been a practical, no-nonsense type of woman.

"So what do you think, Frances?" my dad asked her. She just scowled at him. Then she turned and went back down the stairs.

To my knowledge, she's never gone up to that room again. Not in forty-nine years. Of course, she wouldn't be able to now. She couldn't begin to make it up that steep staircase anymore. But she never even speaks of that room. It's like it doesn't exist.

I could tell the room didn't make much of an impact on my sisters, either. Something that simple would never strike Kathy's fancy. And Rosie was too little to appreciate the meaning of it.

For my father's sake, I was glad at least one of us was excited about what he'd done. I'm glad he knew that I loved it. I hope he knows that I still love his little room, that I treasure it.

Since he's gone now, I consider the room to be mine. I had to clean it out after Sam and I moved into the house, because when my cousin and her family lived here, they piled junk up there. Now, I go up to the room every couple of weeks to dust and sweep it. I keep it spotless.

Dad's desk is still there. I had Sam carry up an old armchair, so now I have a comfortable place to sit. I have the chair facing the window and the little altar Dad built. Dad's Bible isn't there anymore. I have no idea where it went. Now, I always have a candle sitting on the altar. When my flower gardens are in bloom, I keep a bouquet of fresh flowers up there. Sometimes during the winter, I splurge and buy a bouquet from the Village Florist in Nashville. I do that when Sam isn't around, so that he doesn't think I'm crazy for carrying flowers up to the attic.

When we replaced the windows in our house, Sam wanted to pull out that stained glass and put in something new. He said the house would look better if all the windows matched. But I wouldn't let him touch that window, even though there are a few cracks in it.

Whenever I get overwhelmed with stress, I go up to my little attic room and sit, just to calm myself down. Like my father, I've made that my place for being quiet and listening to God. I always feel my father's spirit in the room, too.

That little stained glass window is truly a mark of my father's genius. It faces east, and in the early morning, the sun shining through the window is the most magnificent thing you've ever seen. In my opinion, you couldn't find a more beautiful chapel anywhere in the world.

When people come to our house for the first time and

stand out front looking at the place, I see their eyes travel up to that stained glass window. They get a strange look on their face, like they're wondering about the meaning of it. Unless they point blank ask me about the window, I never say anything about it. If they do ask, I tell them my father used to work with stained glass, and that the window is a sample of his work. I never tell them about the window being a part of the chapel he created in our attic.

After the first time they see it, people don't seem to notice the window again. I'm pretty sure that Mom and Kathy and Rosie never see it anymore.

But I see it. Every time I'm outdoors, I glance up at the window before I go inside. I do this silly thing every year when I plant annuals in my flowerbeds. I try to choose colors that match the colors in the window. Marigolds match the yellow. Geraniums go with the red. I like using Gerbera daisies, as they come in a variety of colors. Having my flowers match the window makes me feel like two of the things I love in this life are tied together.

I went up to the attic early this morning after I had the dream. I do that every time it comes around. The little chapel comforts me. I lit the candle on the altar and sat there in the darkness for an hour or more. Then the sun started coming up, and it shone through the window like a ray of hope. Like God was telling me everything was going to be okay.

I need to keep that thought in my mind for the rest of the day. Everything's going to work out this weekend. Everything's going to be fine.

At least we shouldn't have much stress this evening at

dinner, since Rosie won't be here. That doesn't sound like a very nice thing to say about my sister. I don't mean anything against her. It's not her fault. But whenever Rosie is around, it puts Mom in a sour mood. She barely speaks to Rosie, and when she does say something, it's usually hateful. Rosie reacts by clamming up. That makes Mom mad, and she goes after her all the more.

Mom's always been outspoken. Maybe too outspoken. The older she gets, the less she watches what she says. I'll try to have a talk with her before Rosie gets here. I'll remind her to go a little easy on her youngest daughter.

KATHERINE: Edie called me on my cell phone just as Katrina and I were boarding the plane. She sounded flustered. "Rosie called me a minute ago," she said. "She told me she and Marty are coming this weekend. I didn't know anything about it."

That Rosie! She's an intelligent woman with a whole string of degrees. You'd think she could remember a detail like calling ahead of time to confirm plans.

I talked with her last weekend. I told her I was flying to Indiana to see Mom. I suggested that she drive down to Edie's place so that we could make a family reunion out of the occasion. We three girls haven't been together with our mother in years.

Of course, Rosie made excuses, like she always does. She said she's really busy at work, and that she hasn't been feeling well. I told her that taking some time off work would be good for her health. I reminded her that we won't have our mother with us forever.

Then Rosie got into her old stuff, whining about how

hard it is for her to visit Mom, and how it always makes her depressed. I can't stand to hear her singing that sad old song. What happened between her and Mom was more than forty years ago, and it's time for her to get over it. If anything really did happen. I've never been convinced that it did.

If there's one thing that pushes my buttons, it's people wallowing in the misery of their past. That's what Rosie does. What a waste of time!

I lost patience with her. "Look, Rosie," I said. "I'm taking the time to fly all the way to Indiana from New York City. The least you can do is make the forty-five minute drive from Indianapolis to Brown County. You're an adult. You can pull yourself together and get through one weekend of being around Mom."

I guess I made my point with her. She said she'd try to come. But I can't believe she forgot to tell Edie about her plans. That's so inconsiderate of her.

Oh. Wait a minute. It might've been me that dropped the ball. Now that I think about it, I remember saying to Rosie, "I'm going to call Edie after I hang up with you, and I'll tell her you're coming." I said it that way because she sounded like she hadn't fully made up her mind, and I didn't want to give her a chance to back off.

I guess I got too distracted by what was going on with Bryce. After I ended the call with Rosie, he walked into the room and started talking to me about cancelling the trip. And I completely forgot about calling Edie.

This morning, Bryce asked me, "Kathy, will you stand by me no matter what?"

"Of course I will," I told him. "I always do, don't I?"

"No matter what happens?" he asked.

"I don't know what you think is going to happen," I said. "We've had our share of challenges, and we've always made it through. We make the best of whatever comes our way."

That's absolutely true. We always have, and we always will. My husband and I make a great team.

After I met Bryce at that seminar, I went to work for him at B. K. Hudson Investments, like he asked me to. I started out as a secretary, making a higher salary than I ever dreamed of earning in that position. Bryce had promised me there would be opportunities to work my way up in the corporation, and that's what I did. Within six months, I was working as his administrative assistant.

I can't believe how fortunate I was to have Bryce enter my life. He was a gift from the universe. He supported me every step of the way while I went through my divorce from Rod. He set me up with the attorney that he'd used in his own divorce two years earlier. Rod and I didn't have a lot of personal property to contest, but that attorney protected me from Rod taking everything I had. Rod tried to talk me into letting him have custody of Katrina, but there was no way I was going to let that happen. My attorney made sure I was awarded custody.

When I moved out of the apartment I shared with Rod, I didn't have the money for a deposit and first month's rent on a new place. Bryce paid for that out of his own pocket.

Three months after my divorce from Rod, Bryce and I got married. At that point, Bryce told me he wanted me to stop working for him. He said it was important to him to have a happy home life, and that he didn't want me bogged down from stress at the office. He said it was time for me to focus on what I really wanted out of life, my dream of singing and acting.

I didn't mind giving up my job. I had no passion for secretarial work. Even though I always gave one hundred percent on the job, it was nothing more to me than a way of supporting myself.

"Kathy," Bryce said to me on our wedding day, "I want to give you everything you've ever wanted. That's my job as your husband. I want a happy wife. If you're happy, then I'll be happy."

And Bryce truly has given me a wonderful life. We've traveled all over the world together. For the past twenty years, I've been involved with my real passion, the theatre, and I've loved every minute of it. I've done a lot of off-Broadway shows, mostly musicals. Recently, I've gotten into directing. Bryce set me up with people who helped me get started in doing TV commercials. I've even done some infomercials for cookware and skin care products.

Why wouldn't I stick with Bryce, no matter what happens? After everything he's done for me, I owe him every bit of my loyalty.

When I was leaving for the airport this morning, Bryce was looking more depressed than I've ever seen him look. "Honey," I said, "you need to get away from the office this weekend. The weather is beautiful. Why don't you play a game of golf? Or go out on the boat?"

"I can't," he said.

"Can't isn't a word in our vocabulary, sweetie," I reminded him. "You can do anything you choose to do."

"I have meetings," he said.

"On a weekend? With who?"

"With my attorneys," he said.

Well, I don't know what all that's about. I don't push Bryce for details about work. He likes a clean separation between his work life and his home life, and that's always been fine with me.

I'm not going to allow my husband's depression to ruin my weekend. I intend to have a nice time with my family, and I'm not letting anything stop that. I can't wait for my mother to see Katrina and our precious little Lilly.

ROSALIE JACOBSON: Going down to Brown County to see Mom is the last thing I want to do this weekend. I've had a stressful week at work, and I haven't been feeling well for the past couple of months. The last time I saw my doctor, he gave me a lecture about slowing down and getting plenty of rest. I don't know why I give in to Kathy's guilt trips. Every time she starts lecturing me about my shortcomings as a daughter and a sister, I cave in. Afterwards, I always kick myself.

Here I am, with a doctorate in psychology, acting like a scared little six-year-old when my older sister starts bullying me. I should know better than that.

I do psychological testing at Riley's Hospital for Children, here in Indianapolis. I'm part of a diagnostic team that assesses children with developmental disorders. At the hospital, I live the life of Dr. Jacobson, a competent professional woman. I'm respected by my peers. And then I get dragged back into the life of poor little Rosie Rafferty. Believe me, I don't like it.

My mother doesn't want to see me any more than I

want to see her. She'd have a better time with Kathy and Edie this weekend if I wasn't around. Sometimes, I ask myself why I don't make a clean break and put this unworkable mother-daughter relationship out of its misery.

Years ago, I gave up on the idea that the problems in our relationship could be resolved. Back when I was working on my master's degree, I tried to initiate conversations with my mother, using the communication skills I'd learned in my training. Those skills are supposed to work wonders. But to be effective, they take two people who want to communicate. My mom's not interested. Every time I tried to talk to her, both of us walked away from the conversation more upset than we'd been before.

My mother is filled with bitterness about what happened when I was a young teenager, an eighth-grader. She can't stop blaming me. She refuses to take a bit of responsibility for what happened.

If she'd ever own up to what she did, I could forgive her. Even though the memories are painful and always will be, I can see her point of view. I've made myself look at things through her eyes. She'll never do the same for me. She isn't capable of that. Or maybe she is capable. Maybe she's just unwilling to let go of the belief that she was the only victim in that situation.

Even if I could put the past completely behind me, I can't tolerate her ongoing condemnation of me. It's there in her eyes, the minute she looks at me. She despises me. Being around her takes me down, lower than I ever want to go. Lower than I can afford to go. I have a demanding career. I have Marty to look after. I can't allow someone to suck all the life out of me.

But something inside of me stays hooked into the idea that a decent person would never completely turn her back on her aging mother. So about twice a year, I make my duty visits. Afterwards, I have to pump myself back up so that I can get on with my life again.

If it was just a matter of seeing Edie, I'd make the trip down to Brown County at least once a month. Having to avoid Mom means I'm missing out on a relationship with my sister. Edie and I have always gotten along well. She tries to understand the problems I have with our mother. She wishes things were better between Mom and me, but she doesn't judge me for how I feel.

It's a lot harder for me to get along with Kathy. She won't listen to my feelings about Mom for a minute. Of course not. She's our mother's dream child. Playing the role of the beautiful princess feels a whole lot different than being the one who gets kicked when she's down.

I feel bad, springing my visit on Edie like this. Kathy told me she was going to call and tell her I was coming. Kathy always takes charge of everything. I shouldn't have taken that for granted. I should've taken a minute out of my busy day to confirm my plans with Edie.

Initially, I wasn't thinking about taking Marty with me. When I stopped by the group home to see him earlier this week, I told him I was planning on driving down to Brown County to see Aunt Kathy and Aunt Edie. Something about the way I said it made him think the two of us were going, instead of just me. His eyes lit up and he said, "Oh, fun! I can't wait to see Aunt Kathy and Aunt Edie!"

I couldn't bear to disappoint him. So I'll take him along, even though it's a lot of work.

Not many people can understand Marty's speech. I can, and the staff at the group home has grown accustomed to his way of expressing himself. For Marty, speaking is a laborious process. Even though he's had a lot of speech therapy, what comes out is garbled and unintelligible to most people. But, bless his little heart, Marty never gives up trying, even though he gets frustrated when he can't make himself understood.

It's hard for people to listen to Marty, to be patient with him while he tries to express himself. It can be hard for people to look at him, too, because of the drooling, the jerking, and the grimaces.

Marty moved to his group home ten years ago. It was his idea, not mine. I would've been happy to keep him at home, utilizing the services of home health aides. He needs twenty-four hour care.

But he's thirty-one years old now. Living away from home makes him feel more grown up and independent. "I can't live with my mom all my life," he told me. "I need to be on my own."

Marty was born with cerebral palsy. He has a pretty severe case, classified at Level V. His poor little body just doesn't do what he needs it to do. He's confined to a wheelchair. Even though we've tried to enhance his mobility in every way possible, he'll never be able to walk.

But he does have some use of his left hand. He can operate the controls on his wheelchair. To a certain extent, he can feed himself, but he needs supervision because of his difficulty with swallowing and the risk of choking.

Marty's IQ puts him in the range of mild mental retardation. He's actually brighter than most people think he is. Because of his profound difficulty with speech, they don't recognize how mentally capable he really is. He takes in a lot that goes on around him, but he's unable to fully express his responses to his environment. It's a constant frustration for him.

My mother doesn't understand Marty's condition. She's never asked any questions that show she's even interested in trying to understand it. She's never paid much attention to him. She loves Edie's three children, and gets all wrapped in up their lives. But not Marty.

I'm sure she thinks my son is God's punishment for all my wrongdoings. Even though having a disabled child has been a challenge, Marty has been a blessing to me. Never a punishment. The little guy is the light of my life.

My mother doesn't see Marty as someone with a soul, a human being with his own thoughts and feelings, his own hopes and dreams. A human being with rights. To her, he's just a messed up body in a wheelchair. Whenever people look at my son in that way, I get furious.

I won't disappoint Marty. For his sake, I'll make the best of our weekend. He and I will have a good time with each other, even if no one else enjoys our company.

Maybe I'll take him on a walk. If I don't make a point of getting my son out in nature, his only outdoor time is sitting in his wheelchair on the patio of his group home. Marty loves going to the Indianapolis Zoo. He gets such a kick out of watching the animals. I take him there several times a year. And both of us love going to the Holcomb Gardens at Butler University. It's so beautiful there. It's my favorite place to replenish my energy when I'm feeling drained.

FRIDAY AFTERNOON

FRANCES: Edith was over here just a bit ago. While she was helpin' me wash up, she says, "Now, Mama, I'm gonna tell you somethin', and I don't want you gettin' upset. Rosie and her boy are comin' this weekend."

All I says to Edith was, "Okay." Believe you me, I wanted to say more'n that. But I didn't, 'cause I ain't wantin' to upset her none. Poor girl's got so much to do. I 'magine she's workin' her little fingers to the bone, tryin' to get ready for company.

But I'm sittin' here now, my mind a'goin' ninety mile an hour. All along I was thinkin' one thing was gonna happen, and now it's somethin' else altogether. Kinda puts a damper on my spirits.

I ain't wantin' to give off the wrong impression here. I love all three of my girls, I really do. I try to be even-handed with 'em. But I hafta tell you that things ain't so easy for me when my youngest is around. Stirs up a whole lotta stuff I'd just as soon forget about.

Sometimes when my mind starts a'wanderin', I get to wishin' that we could all go back and do things over again. Back to the simple times, before all them things happened that turned our life upside down. Lord, how I wish for that old life we had!

My husband was a preacher, you know. Martin, he didn't have all that much schoolin'. Nowadays, they make a man that wants to be a preacher git a lot of trainin', but not back then. Martin didn't need all that fancy schoolin' anyways, 'cause he already had a good mind. Yup, there was a day when he had a mighty good mind, 'fore he started goin' downhill. He was a serious-minded kind of fellow, his thoughts always a'turnin' to the things of God.

A coupla years after we got married, right around the time Edith was born, Martin started preachin' at that little country church just down the road from here. 'Bout a quarter of a mile, I'd say. Strictly speakin', it was a Baptist church, but to the people that went there, what they called it didn't matter none. It was just a gatherin' of folks from around here, wantin' to get together to worship the Lord.

Edith and Sam don't go to that church no more. I wish they did. They go to the Christian Church in Nashville, 'cause that's the church Sam growed up in. Edith let Sam have his way on that. She purty much lets everybody have their way on everything. That girl needs to learn to stand her ground.

I don't go to that little church no more, neither. I'm too old and tuckered out to be gittin' up for church early of a mornin'. But they still think of me as a member. The preacher, Reverend Donovan, comes to see me every now and then. He sits down with me and takes out his Bible and reads a little bit of the holy word. He always says to me, "Mrs. Rafferty, we're prayin' for you." Then he takes a'hold of my hand and says a prayer for me right then and there. That makes me feel real good.

Reverend Donovan, he does a good job, and people think so highly of him. Just like they thought so highly of Martin when he was the one doin' the preachin'. You'd never find a man more kindhearted than Martin Rafferty. Every time somebody was in need, he'd be right there, speakin' his comfortin' words. He was good at that, he was, and everybody loved him for it.

But let me tell you somethin' I learnt. Kind words, they only go so far. The true measure of a man is whether he can stand up to the hard times in life. Whether he can keep on a'goin' when the goin' gits rough. Twenty years into our marriage, I found out Martin Rafferty wasn't capable of that.

Martin, he never raised his voice to me or laid a hand on me. He wasn't that kind of a man. But sometimes, I think I woulda preferred him to rough me up a little bit than to have him lose all his nerve and fall down on the job the way he did.

We didn't have a whole lot during them early years. But we didn't have nothin' to complain about, neither. Bein' a preacher of a little country church don't pay a man much of anything. So of an evenin', Martin hadta work as a janitor at Sprunica Elementary School, which ain't that far from here. That's where my three girls went to school when they was little.

Durin' the summers when Martin wasn't workin' at the school, I worked at that little fruit stand up there in Bean Blossom. I didn't mind that. Nope, not a bit. It was nice visitin' with all them people comin' to buy apples and peaches and stuff. I always kept a vegetable garden goin', and sometimes I'd take my fresh peas and beans and squash up there to sell. It brung us in a little extra money.

If we woulda had to make a house payment like some people do, I don't think we coulda made it back then, not on the little bit of money we had comin' in. Thank the Lord, that house was passed on to Martin from his folks. But we got by. Lookin' back, I'd say them early years of raisin' our family was the happiest time of my life. It don't take a whole lotta money to bring a person happiness.

I hafta mention somethin' here about our little Ralphie. Wouldn't never be right to forget about 'im. Ralph Dixon was his name. The girls, they all said Ralph was an old man's name, so they started callin' him Ralphie.

There was times when things got a little tight for us. There was times when we didn't know how we was gonna keep our tank filled with oil to heat the house. Sometimes, we didn't even have the money to go to the IGA for groceries, and we just hadta make do with what was in the house. But when I was workin' at the fruit stand one day, I learnt about somethin' that helped us out for awhile.

You see, some people come by the fruit stand, and they had a coupla kids with 'em, maybe eight, ten years old. I mentioned how nice the kids was, helpin' their parents carry bags of stuff to the car and all. And them people said the kids was their foster children. I asked how they come by havin' foster children, and they said it was through the welfare department in Nashville. They said they got paid money to take care of 'em.

I went home and said to Martin, "You know, we could take in foster kids to bring us in a little extra money. Did you ever think about that?" Martin wasn't all that keen on the idea, but he wasn't against it, neither. So I went and looked into it. Before we knowed it, the welfare department was callin' us up to see if we wanted to take care of a little boy. And that's how we got our Ralphie.

We was told Ralphie's mom had a problem with drinkin', and that she wasn't takin' care of him right. Ralphie's dad, he wasn't nowheres in the picture.

Ralphie was a cute little young'un, he was. Kinda

skinny, like he hadn't been fed good food. At first, it seemed like he hardly knowed how to eat at all. Four years old, and all he wanted to do was drink milk from a baby bottle. I never seen nothin' like it in a kid that age.

Edith, she useta sit with him at the table and try to coax him into eatin' somethin'. One day she says to me, all proud like, "Mama, Ralphie done ate six green beans for lunch!"

But after awhile, we got him to eat just fine. I useta laugh and tell Martin, "That boy, he eats more'n all three of our girls put together."

We all kinda took to Ralphie in our own way. Even though Martin wasn't real keen on havin' another kid in the house at first, he took to Ralphie right off the bat. I could tell he was tickled to have a little boy, after havin' three girls. Ralphie, he started followin' Martin around like a little puppy dog. Sometimes, he'd start a'bawlin' when Martin went off to work at the school of an evenin', and the girls and me would hafta sit down with 'im and love on 'im and tell 'im over and over that Martin was gonna come back home soon.

Coupla times, Martin tried takin' Ralphie along with 'im to the school, but he hadta put a stop to that. Ralphie kept on gettin' into stuff, and Martin couldn't get his work done.

I hafta say Katherine didn't pay a whole lot of attention to Ralphie. She had her mind on other things. She was always a'singin' and a'dancin' and puttin' on a show of some kind or 'nother. Rosalie, she played some with Ralphie. They was only five years apart in age. But I could tell she kinda resented the little guy, 'cause she was jealous of how much attention Martin was payin' him.

Before Ralphie come along, Rosalie was her daddy's favorite. She had a mind a lot like his. She was the one that likedta learn 'bout a lot of things, and she took to readin' books. She brung home good grades on her school papers and her report cards. Martin, he was so proud of that. Every now and then, I'd hafta to have a talk with 'im, tellin' 'im he shouldn't be so partial to her. Sometimes, I'd hafta make a point of favorin' the other two, so as to even things out.

Edith was the one that really took to Ralphie. I remember her holdin' that little fellow on her lap, cuddlin' 'im and lovin' on 'im like he was her own little baby. One mornin', she comes to me, her eyes a'shinin' like she done seen an angel or somethin'. She says to me, "Mama, I always knowed we had a little brother out there somewheres, waitin' for us to find 'im. And we did! We found our Ralphie!"

I never knowed how she come up with somethin' like that. Edith, she took after her daddy, in terms of her bein' a dreamer. All the time comin' up with things that ain't of this world. But what she said about findin' her little brother was just about the sweetest thing I ever heard tell of.

Yup, that Edith was just like a second mother to our Ralphie. She always been one that likes to take care of everybody.

When she was 'bout to leave the trailer after my bath this mornin', she says, "Mama, you'll be careful with Rosie this weekend, won't you? She's not gonna be here for supper. She's comin' in late. You'll see her tomorrow."

I says to her, "Why don't you have Rosalie run over here and say goodnight to me 'fore y'all go to bed?" I said that for Edith's sake, to prove to 'er that I'm tryin' to get along.

KATHERINE: Even though I visit Mom twice a year, coming back to Indiana is always a shock. When our plane landed in Indianapolis this afternoon, I started feeling uneasy. Like a dark cloud had come over me. Indianapolis is a big city, but compared to where Bryce and I live, it seems a little . . . . Well, I guess I shouldn't say that. I'm sure many people enjoy living there. Rosie seems to like it just fine.

Edie's husband was there at the airport to pick us up. Same old sour-puss Sam. Nothing about him ever changes, and he never has anything to say. On the drive down to Brown County, I tried to engage him in friendly conversation. I finally gave up, because it was pointless.

The most direct route from the Indianapolis International Airport to Brown County is to take the 465 bypass to State Road 135, which takes you all the way down to Bean Blossom. But I prefer taking 465 to Interstate 31 and going south toward Franklin. That route takes us through Greenwood.

Both Sam and Edie know I prefer taking the route through Greenwood. I don't even have to ask them to go that way anymore. They do it automatically.

Greenwood is just an ordinary small city, with a population of around 50,000. But it means something special to me. After I lived all those years in rural Brown County, Greenwood became my portal into the broader world. If I hadn't had that one year in Greenwood, I doubt that I ever would've made it to New York City.

Our little Lilly had been so good on the flight. But about the time we got into Sam's Jeep, she started fussing. It's no wonder. That Jeep rides so rough. I could tell the baby's crying was getting on Sam's nerves. Then, of all things, she had a messy diaper. Katrina discovered she was out of wipes, and she asked if we could stop somewhere to buy some.

Sam's face turned red, and he didn't say a word. But he did pull off at a pharmacy in Greenwood so Katrina could get what she needed. I was shocked by his ungracious behavior. You'd think he'd be more supportive of Edie's efforts to have her family visit. Bryce would never behave like that. He's always so kind and welcoming to our houseguests. If Sam and Edie would ever decide to fly out to visit us, he'd show them how company deserves to be treated.

As we drove down State Road 135 toward Bean Blossom, I couldn't help but notice how backward this part of the country is. Rundown houses. Unkempt yards. No decent places to eat. I could swear nothing has changed since I left here forty years ago. The farther south we drove, the more depressed I felt.

Don't get me wrong. The landscape is beautiful here, especially when the leaves are in color. This is gorgeous country.

By the time we hit Bean Blossom and turned east on Gatesville Road, I felt as if I was in a time-travel machine, going back a hundred years. The roads are so narrow and winding, and those blind curves scare me to death. I don't see how people down here can drive without having head-on collisions all the time.

And the climate! It's so humid here, like a sauna. Every time I visit Brown County, my hair frizzes up and looks a mess. And it's so buggy. The gnats and mosquitoes drive me crazy. People down here must get used to them.

By the time we reached Fox's Corner and turned north onto Bean Blossom Road, I felt as if I'd left the civilized world behind me. Then we turned east on Sprunica Road and went past my old elementary school. Does that ever bring back the old memories! Memories I'd just as soon forget.

When we turned north onto Sprunica Ridge Road, I thought, *I can't believe I ever lived here. It's way out in the middle of nowhere.* But I did feel a little better when we pulled into Sam and Edie's driveway. Sam pointed out where they'd done a little more work on their house. I was glad to see that.

I feel sorry for Edie. Her life never changes. It's the same thing, year after year. The only time she's lived away from this spot is when she was at Indiana University for two years. But that's only twenty-five or thirty miles from here. At least Rosie made it as far away as Indianapolis.

Thank God, Sam and Edie have made some upgrades to the house. This place was so rundown when we were kids. Mom and Dad didn't have the money to fix it up. It used to embarrass me terribly, and I hated bringing friends over here.

I'd like to say this feels like coming home, but I can't. Even as a little girl, this never felt like my home. I knew I didn't belong here. I was just biding my time until I could get out.

My mother and father raised us with a lot of love, and I'll always be grateful for that. But they lived such small lives. They didn't seem to want much of anything for themselves.

Dad was a wisp of a man, small and thin like my sister Edie. He had dark eyes and dark hair. Rosie was the only one of us who inherited those traits. Edie and I have Mom's coloring.

Even though Dad was a preacher, he was quiet and shy. Around home, he never talked much, and I never felt like I really knew him.

For the most part, his life was confined to this immediate area. He rarely traveled any farther than the seven or eight miles to Nashville. He might've driven to Bloomington or Columbus a couple of times a year. I don't think he left the state of Indiana in his entire life, and he probably never traveled any farther north than Indianapolis. I can't imagine living like that.

Mom was a beautiful woman in her day, with auburn hair and blue-green eyes. People have always said I'm the daughter who looks the most like her. I've seen pictures of her back in the 1940s, when she was a young woman. She was quite stunning. Before she put on weight, she had a knockout figure.

My father was a deep thinker, a dreamer. He had a lot of good ideas, but he was too timid to put them into action. Mom had a practical, simpleminded approach to living. She had a bolder personality than Dad did. I never thought they had much in common. Mom seemed to be constantly frustrated with him. I always felt sorry for her, being saddled with a man like him. She deserved someone who could give her a better life.

By the time my mother had three children, she looked like a ragged old hillbilly woman. She was constantly working, and she had no time to take care of herself. I remember how rough and dry her hands were. She always had them in dishwater or in the garden soil. Sometimes, when our junky old washing machine broke down, she'd wash our clothing by hand in the kitchen sink. Whatever needed to be done, she'd find a way to do it.

Back then, she didn't have any fancy lotions or moisturizers to keep her skin soft. I try to make it up to her now. When I bring her gifts, I bring her the best I can buy, so that she can have a taste of something special.

My mom never finished high school. She dropped out after the tenth grade. She always scoffed at higher education. "There ain't any amount of schoolin' that can give a person common sense," she'd say.

There's a lot of truth in that statement. Not that there's anything wrong with going to college. But I never went farther than high school, and I'm happy with the way my life has turned out. If I had to do it all over, I wouldn't do anything differently.

Mom may not have been educated, but she certainly was resourceful. She could put a delicious meal on the table when there was barely anything in our refrigerator. I remember her making a wonderful hash from a few shriveled potatoes, an onion, and a bit of leftover meat.

She never worried much. She never complained about her lot in life, and she didn't let her problems get her down.

I think I get those traits from her.

Mom made us girls work, too. We cleaned the house, did the dishes, mowed the lawn. We helped Mom plant her vegetable garden. We pulled the weeds. We picked the beans and peas and strawberries. We dug up the potatoes.

I never enjoyed that kind of work, and most of the time, I was bored out of my mind. But I didn't let the drudgery bog me down. I learned how to entertain myself while I worked. I'd be in the garden picking green beans, going down the row singing at the top of my lungs. Songs we sang in church, or in music class at school. Songs I heard on the radio. That's the only way I could get myself through a nasty job like that.

My mother always praised my cheerfulness. She loved to hear me sing. She never really understood that cheerfulness was something I cultivated to keep from getting depressed. My singing was a survival skill.

People who drove by our place would hear me singing while I worked in the garden. Sometimes, they'd slow down, or even stop, to listen for a while. I became known as "the little Rafferty girl with the beautiful voice."

When I'd dust the furniture or run the dust-mop over our old hardwood floors, I would dance. When I had to wash a mountain of dishes, I'd entertain myself by quoting lines from a play. Mostly, I made up the plays. I'd speak the different parts in different voices. If one of my sisters was drying the dishes, I'd assign speaking parts to her. I'd make my sisters laugh, and my mother would laugh, too. I think all my theatrics were too much for my dad. He'd make himself scarce when I was carrying on like that.

Edie never seemed to mind the hard work or the

boredom. She did her chores willingly, in her own quiet way. Rosie would pout if Mom assigned her chores she didn't like. Mom wouldn't tolerate a bad attitude, and Rosie got more than her share of swats on the bottom.

I love telling people the story about Mom's rag rugs. My friends can hardly believe something like that was part of my childhood. But the story shows how hard work and a little ingenuity can pay off.

Nowadays, people talk about recycling and re-purposing. Mom was the queen of re-purposing, way before that practice was in vogue. She never let anything go to waste.

When our curtains or sheets or towels would become threadbare, Mom would turn them into rags and crochet rugs out of them. Our school dresses were handed down from Edie to me to Rosie. When Rosie outgrew them, Mom would turn them into rags for her rugs. She would always turn the collar on Dad's flannel shirts to make them last as long as possible, but when both sides of the collar were frayed, she'd use the flannel from the shirts in her rugs. She'd sell these rugs as a way of bringing a little extra income into the household.

She had her technique down pat, and she worked very efficiently. She'd tear the old fabric into strips about two inches wide. She didn't measure the width, she just eyeballed it. She'd tear the strips down to about two inches from the edge of the fabric. She'd make a little snip with her scissors in the fabric two inches away from her stopping point. Then she'd start tearing in the opposite direction. She'd repeat that pattern over and over, and would get quite a long strip before she'd have to stop and sew the ends of two strips together. It seemed like she'd get a mile-long strip out of an old bed sheet.

She'd wind these long strips into a ball, like a ball of yarn. Then she'd take a giant crochet hook and start crocheting the rug. I remember her sitting in her old rocking chair, the rug on her lap, the ball of strips rolling around on the floor. The rug would get bigger and bigger, and after awhile, it took a lot of arm strength to keep maneuvering it around and around.

Her skill was amazing, as the rugs always came out in a perfect oval shape. She tried teaching Edie and me how to crochet rugs. I tried once, but I found the task incredibly boring, and my rug ended up curling up like a bowl. I decided that crocheting rugs wasn't my calling in life.

But Edie learned how to do it. She'd sit on the floor by Mom's rocking chair, crocheting along with her, perfectly contented. I wouldn't be surprised if she still crochets rag rugs. She always seems to have one inside her front door.

My father would set sawhorses out on the driveway and drape Mom's finished rugs across them, so that they would be in plain sight when people drove by. He took an old board and painted a sign that said, "Homemade rag rugs, $3 apiece."

The first time we put rugs out there for sale, Mom assigned Edie and me to sit by the road and wait for someone to stop by. She promised us that we would earn twenty-five cents for each rug that we sold.

It wasn't long before we had our first customer. The lady was clearly charmed, not only by the rugs, but by the children who were selling them. She wanted to talk to us and ask questions. Edie was tongue-tied, so I did all the talking.

After the lady left with two of the rugs, Edie ran into the house, crying. She told Mom she didn't want to sell any more rugs, because she didn't like talking to strangers.

Mom stood there with her hands on her hips, shaking her head, saying, "Edith, you scared little rabbit, what am I going to do with you?"

"It's okay, Mom," I said. "I'll do the selling." So Mom kept Edie inside to help her crochet the rugs, while I sat outside by the sawhorses.

When people stopped by to look at the rugs, I'd spin little stories about how they could be used for various purposes in their homes. I'd say, "If your legs get tired when you stand at the sink doing dishes, standing on one of these rugs will help." Or, "You should put one of these rugs by the side of your bed. When you get up in the morning, you won't have to put your feet on the cold floor." If the customers happened to have a dog in the car, I'd comment on how nice it was. Then I'd say, "One of these rugs would make a great bed for your dog."

People would chuckle at my sales pitch, and would end up buying two rugs instead of one.

When one customer asked me where my mom got all the rags for the rugs, I pointed out a strip of colorful fabric in a rug and told her that rag come from one of my old school dresses. She immediately bought that very rug. I realized using that kind of personal touch could increase my sales. So I started saying things like, "These rags came from our old living room curtains. This one came from my little sister's bed sheet."

One day when two women stopped by to look at the rugs, I gave them my usual sales pitch. As they walked back to their car carrying their purchases, I overheard one of them saying to the other, "Isn't she the cutest little hillbilly girl you've ever seen?"

Now, if Edie had heard someone saying something like that about her, she would've thought they were making fun of her, and she would've cried. But when I heard myself referred to as a cute little hillbilly girl, my mental wheels started turning. I thought about how I could use that image to my advantage. When I went into the house to hand the rug money over to Mom, I asked her, "What does a hillbilly look like?"

She shot me a funny look and asked, "Why do you want to know?"

"Those people that just left said I was the cutest little hillbilly girl they'd ever seen."

My mom smiled, and the twinkle in her eyes told me she'd caught the drift of what I was thinking. Both of us knew that my idea could increase rug sales.

"Well," she said, "I suppose a hillbilly wears overalls and a straw hat."

"Where can I get some overalls?" I asked.

"I'll check with your Aunt Della. Your cousin Wade might have some he's outgrown."

Within a week, Mom had a pair of overalls for me. They were pretty worn out, but she told me they would work just fine. She sorted through her bag of rags and pulled out the brightest prints to use for patching the holes. Then she had my dad pick up a cheap straw hat at one of the souvenir shops in Nashville.

I told my father we needed a different sign. "What do you want it to say?" he asked.

"Genuine Brown County Rag Rugs for Sale," I said. "And make the price $4.00 apiece."

My mom told me if I sold the rugs for $4.00 instead of $3.00, I would earn fifty cents commission on each rug.

So I sat out by the road wearing my hillbilly costume, and I sold those rugs so fast that Mom and Edie couldn't keep up with me. When Mom ran out of rags, neighbors and people at our church donated their rags to her.

My customers always smiled as they left with their purchases. Sometimes, they'd take pictures of me standing beside the display of rugs. Once, someone snapped a shot with a Polaroid camera and gave it to me.

I've kept that photo all these years. After Bryce and I got married, he had it enlarged, and then he framed it and set in on his desk at work. He thinks it's the cutest thing ever. He likes to tell people that the little girl in the patched overalls and straw hat is his wife.

It's amazing to think about where I started out in life, and where I am now. My world was so limited back then. Grades one through six, I attended Sprunica Elementary, the little school sitting out here in the middle of the woods. There were only four elementary schools in this county. That's how sparsely populated this backward place is.

All seventh through twelfth graders were bused to Brown County Junior and Senior High School in Nashville. When I started junior high, my tiny world opened up a little wider. Meeting kids who lived on the other side of the county was almost like meeting someone from a foreign country.

But the summer before my junior year, my life suddenly changed. My father accepted a pastoral assignment at a church in Greenwood, and our family moved up there. Everyone but Edie, that is. She was in college at the time.

Moving to Greenwood felt like a giant step up in the world. Compared to New York City, Greenwood is barely a speck on the map. But compared to the rural life I'd lived as a child, it seemed like a huge city. I can't tell you how excited I was about the prospects of living up there. It felt like my destiny was starting to unfold.

I loved my junior year of high school. I joined the choir and the drama club. I became a cheerleader. Being the new girl, I received lots of attention. I was popular with the boys, and I had a date every weekend. Sometimes, I had to turn down dates because I had so many offers. Life couldn't have been better.

The parsonage we lived in was a simple two-story home. But it was well-maintained, fully furnished, and nicely decorated. So much nicer than our shabby old house down in Brown County. Rosie and I each had a spacious upstairs bedroom. We had two bathrooms, one upstairs and one downstairs, which seemed like an undreamed of luxury. I wasn't ashamed to have any of my new friends come over to visit, even to spend the night. It felt like the Raffertys were a normal family, living in a normal house. I loved it.

Any wistful thoughts I have about my childhood are tied to that house in Greenwood. By today's standards, that parsonage wouldn't be anything special. But back then, it seemed like a mansion to me.

A few years ago when Sam was picking me up at the airport, I asked him to go a little out of his way and drive me past that house. He did it, even though he was grumpy about it. I feel the need to see the place again. Maybe on our way back to the airport on Monday morning, I'll ask Edie to take me there. The house doesn't mean anything to her, because she never really lived there. But it means the world to me.

Unfortunately, toward the end my junior year, things started falling apart for the Rafferty family. As it turned out, our stay in Greenwood was short-lived. We ended up moving back down to Brown County, back into the same old rundown house on Sprunica Ridge Road. And I had to go back to Brown County High School for my senior year.

I can honestly tell you I've never been so disheartened in my entire life. I felt like I'd gone backward in life. Like I was trapped in a place that was holding me captive.

But I was determined to find a way out. So I started making plans. A friend of mine, Sheila, shared my interest in singing and acting, and we started to fantasize about moving to New York City to start our careers.

Back then, we didn't have the internet for doing research, and we couldn't get our hands on much information about New York City at our high school. So we came up with the idea of having Sheila's father drive us to the Indiana University campus. We told him we needed to do some research for the English papers we had to write.

In the IU library, we had access to newspapers like the *New York Times*. We looked at ads and sent for information, brochures about housing and theatres and studios. All kinds of exciting things about New York City.

Whenever my mother noticed the packets that were coming in the mail, I'd tell her it was information I needed for a school assignment. At that point, she was so preoccupied with family problems that she didn't ask many questions. I ended up hiding a stash of information in a box in the back of my closet. Late at night, I'd pull out the box and look through the brochures, comforting myself with the idea that my life was about to change.

I wasn't as coldhearted about all this as I might sound. I told myself I'd stick around home as long as my mother needed me. I knew she couldn't manage everything on her own. Edie was in college at the time. Rosie wasn't living with us anymore. So I was all my mother had.

My mom and I became very close the year we spent in Greenwood, and the year after we came back to Brown County. We formed a bond that has lasted all these years, even though I now live hundreds of miles away from her. My mother trusts me, and I'll never let her down.

When Edie dropped out of college and moved back home, I knew it was my time to leave. I'd done my duty, and it was my sister's turn to help out. So I kissed my mother goodbye and hopped on a Greyhound bus bound for New York City.

For a long time, I hated my father for ruining our life in Greenwood. That's one of the reasons I left home. I couldn't stand to look at that pitiful man. I hated Rosie, too, because of the part she played in ruining things.

But I forgave both of them, a long time ago. It's never a good thing to hang onto anger and resentment. It poisons the soul. That's why I don't have any patience for Rosie's nonsense about not being able to get along with Mom.

FRIDAY EVENING

EDITH: Dinner went well. Thank goodness for that. One day down, two more to go. Kathy took us all out to eat, like I hoped she would. Isn't that awful of me?

Sam tried to pay for the meal, but Kathy insisted on picking up the check. Sam looked a little irritated. I think Kathy made him feel like less than a man. Like it was her way of telling him she knew he didn't make enough money to afford paying the bill. But secretly, I was relieved. When Sam finds out what I've done, he'll be glad he didn't incur the expense of taking the whole family out to eat.

Eating in a restaurant was a treat for Mom. She hardly ever gets out for something like that. I know I should be doing more of that kind of thing for her, instead of letting her sit in that little trailer day after day. But I just can't seem to find the time. I sound like a broken record with all my excuses, don't I?

Kathy let Mom choose where she wanted to go. Mom picked the Nashville House. I figured she would. That place has been around for a long time, and she actually worked there when she was a teenager. So being there tonight brought back fond memories for her.

When we girls were little, Mom used to tell us stories about working there as a waitress. She was young and beautiful, and she had to fight off the attention of the male customers. According to her, all of them wanted to take her out on dates. When she'd tell us that, her eyes would sparkle and she'd toss her hair like a coy young girl. I'd feel like such a loser, because I knew I'd never be beautiful or popular with the boys.

That's how my parents met, when my father came into the Nashville House to eat. "I could've had my pick of the men," my mother would tell us. And I'd always wonder whether she regretted her choice.

I was worried about how Kathy would deal with eating at the Nashville House. Don't get me wrong, the food there is delicious. They're known for their fried chicken and their fried biscuits. But it's not the health food Kathy likes to talk about. She ended up eating just a salad, while the rest of us ate all the fattening stuff.

Watching Kathy pick at her salad, acting so dainty, aggravated Sam. When we got home, he said to me, "As big as your sister is, she must be eating something besides salads."

I told him it wasn't nice to talk about her like that. But I wondered about that, too. Kathy's what you'd call a full-figured woman, and she's gained a lot of weight over the years. She looks like she's put on ten pounds since I last saw her. Well, I'm not going to talk about that any more. It's none of my business.

Mom was so pleased to be going out with Kathy. All through the meal, Kathy treated Mom like she was the guest of honor, making sure she had everything she needed. She told our waitress that Mom used to work at the Nashville house, and the waitress made a big deal over that. Mom loved the attention. It really perked her up.

I know I should be more like Kathy. She's so spontaneous and outgoing and friendly. She isn't scared of anybody or anything. She's fun, not a boring old person like me.

I've always felt so ordinary compared to my sisters.

Kathy is so glamorous and beautiful and talented. And Rosie's so smart. She's gone a long way with her career. I haven't done anything special with my life.

All my life, people have told me I should be more like Kathy. They don't say it directly. They just say things like, "Why are you so quiet, Edie? You shouldn't be so shy. You should open up and talk more. You shouldn't be so scared to try new things."

Even my mother criticizes me. She says, "For God's sake, Edith, why do you have that scared rabbit look on your face all the time? You don't have anything to be scared about. You need to stand up and let people know who you are."

Even Sam wants me to change. For years, he's said to me, "You should have more confidence in yourself, Edith. You sell yourself short. You let people walk all over you."

I wish everybody would leave me alone about all that. I am who I am. I'm sixty-one years old, and it's probably too late for me to change.

There's only one person who ever truly accepted me for who I am. Only one person loved the shy, scared little Edith Rafferty without telling her she needed to change. That was the man of my dreams.

I mean that in two ways. The man who was perfect for me in every way. And the man who's shown up in the dreams that have haunted me for the past forty years.

ROSALIE: I got here tonight even later than I thought I would. I tried to leave work on time, but that turned out to be impossible. Every time I thought I was about to wrap things up, something else popped up that needed my attention. Then, when I went to pick up Marty at his group home, the staff didn't have him ready to go. They'd forgotten he was leaving for the weekend.

So I had to rush around, packing his things and getting him cleaned up and properly dressed. Then, of course, it takes a little time getting him situated in my vehicle. Whenever I take Marty anywhere, I drive a van with a wheelchair lift.

We got to Edie's place around 9:00 PM. Her house isn't wheelchair accessible, so Sam had to help me get Marty up the porch steps and through the front door.

Edie had her bedroom set up for us. I put Marty in the bed. I'd brought along my own sleeping bag so that I could sleep on the floor. Edie said she and Sam would be sleeping upstairs. She looked dead tired, and I felt really bad, like Marty and I were an imposition. I should've waited to come down until tomorrow morning. I don't know why I didn't plan things that way. I guess Kathy had me all shook up with her lecture about neglecting family relationships.

Edie told me they'd all gone out for dinner, and that they'd just gotten back. When Marty heard that, he looked hurt. I knew what he was thinking. But just at that moment, Kathy came down the stairs. She went over to Marty and hugged him and kissed him on the cheek, gushing over him in her flamboyant way. "It's so wonderful to see you, Marty," she said.

His eyes lit up, and he stammered out, "It's wonderful to see you, too, Aunt Kathy."

"Why, thank you, sweetheart!" she said.

As much as Kathy irritates me, I love her for what she

did, making my son feel special. For making him feel like he counts.

As soon as I wheeled Marty into the bedroom, he started crying, saying, "Why couldn't we go out to eat with Aunt Kathy and Aunt Edie?"

"We got here too late," I told him.

"They should've waited for us," he pouted.

"You had your dinner at the group home before we came," I said. "Remember?"

"I could've had two dinners," he retorted.

Well, two dinners wouldn't have hurt him. The poor little guy has always been so thin. Right now, he's at his all-time high, one hundred and thirteen pounds.

"If you're hungry," I said, "you can have the snack I brought along for you."

It tears me up when my son doesn't feel like a part of things. "We're going to have the whole weekend with Aunt Kathy and Aunt Edie," I told him as I helped him eat his *Fig Newtons.* "You'll have lots of time to spend with them."

"Good," he said.

While I was putting Marty to bed, Edie knocked on the bedroom door. "I almost forgot to tell you, Rosie," she said. "Mom wants you to run over to the trailer to say goodnight."

"It's really late," I said. "Won't she be in bed by now? I'll go see her in the morning."

"She'll be upset," Edie said.

"Well, she'll just have to deal with it," I snapped.

Edie looked sad, and I felt bad. I know she feels stuck in the middle between Mom and me. She wants everyone to get along with each other. I don't mean to make this her problem.

After the last time I visited Mom, I decided I'd never again put myself in the position of being alone with her. It gives her the opportunity she's always looking for, to tear into me.

The last time I came down, I went over to the trailer to see Mom, trying to be cheerful. Just wanting to have a lighthearted visit. All was nice for about a minute. I asked her how she was doing, the way a good daughter should. She carried on for a while about her arthritis and how hard it is for her to get around. Then she talked about her high blood pressure and how she hates taking the new medication her doctor put her on. I tried to be sympathetic.

But she found a way to bring our conversation around to the subject of me divorcing Marty's dad. She started preaching to me, like she always does, about divorce being a terrible sin that could send me to hell. She told me that Richard and I should try to work out our problems and mend our relationship before it's too late.

"I pray every day that the two of you will get back together," she said, her face contorted in pain, tears leaking from her eyes. As if she was mortally wounded by the decision I made to leave Richard all those years ago. Apparently, she thinks that remarrying that abusive jerk is the only thing I can do to escape the wrath of God.

I reminded Mom that Richard has been married to another woman for the past fifteen years.

Thankfully, since he married Diane, Richard has stopped messing with me. No doubt, she's the one taking his abuse now. I feel sorry for her. She seems like a nice person. I met her several times when she and Richard came to visit Marty in the group home.

I think Diane is the only reason that Richard has anything to do with his son. I know she wants him to do the right thing. It's not that hard for them to come see Marty. They live in Fort Wayne, and that's only two hours from the group home. If Diane had her way, I'm sure they'd visit Marty more often.

I don't know how many times I've told Mom that I can't remarry Richard because he's married to someone else. She acts like she doesn't hear what I'm saying, and keeps right on preaching at me. She refuses to listen to anything that she doesn't want to be true.

When she started preaching at me the last time I visited, I reminded her that the Bible talks about God's love and forgiveness. She snorted at me. "People say things like that when they don't want to own up to their sins."

She was getting me riled up, and I did something I don't often do. I pulled out my big gun. "What about Kathy?" I asked her. "She's been divorced, too."

My mom didn't miss a beat. "Her case is different," she said. "There was unfaithfulness involved. Her husband committed adultery."

At that point, I sat back, amazed at how Mom can rearrange facts to support her point of view. Yes, there was infidelity involved in Kathy's divorce. She carried on an affair with Bryce for a year while she was still married to Rodney. She advanced her career by sleeping with her boss. Kathy was the cheater, not Rodney. Rod was a nice guy. His only fault was not being ambitious enough for Kathy.

Kathy's done all kinds of things that fly in the face of my mother's moral code. Far more than I've ever done. My mother turns a blind eye to all that, because Kathy is her favorite. My sister could commit armed robbery, and my mother wouldn't bat an eye. As long as Kathy keeps gushing over Mom and bringing her expensive gifts, all is forgiven.

I never cheated on my husband. All I did was divorce him. I had to, because he was ruining my life. And Marty's, too. I had to leave him before he destroyed both of us.

Richard Jacobson and I met when we were undergraduate students at Indiana University. We were both psychology majors. I don't think I ever was in love with Richard, although back then I didn't really know what being in love meant. I'd had no experience with dating in high school. I'd been quiet and introverted, invisible to the opposite sex, locked away in a cave of self-protection.

I often wonder why I pursued the relationship with Richard. I guess I thought he was the only man who would ever pay me any attention, and that if I didn't jump on the opportunity, I'd miss out on marriage and motherhood.

Richard seemed like a decent person back then. He was outgoing and charming, not to mention good-looking. In retrospect, I can see the warning signs that I missed. He always had to be right. Always had to be in charge. Always had to have things go his way. Because my self-esteem was so low, it was easy for me to cater to a man with an ego the size of the state of Texas.

A couple of Richard's ex-girlfriends came to me, warning me that he was a jerk. They told me stories about how badly he'd treated them. But I refused to believe them. I thought they were trying to ruin my relationship with Richard because they were jealous.

Richard and I got married the summer after we completed our undergraduate program. Our wedding was a lavish affair, far more ostentatious than what I wanted. But it was what Richard wanted.

God knows my parents had no money to pay for such a wedding. The bill was footed by Richard's parents, which, of course, gave them all the decision-making power. I had a whole string of bridesmaids, all wearing ridiculous puffy dresses. Everything was over the top. We had a live band and an open bar at the reception.

My sisters were bridesmaids, of course. Kathy made the trip from New York. Considering the fact that I'd been estranged from my mother for years, I was surprised when she and my father came to the wedding.

My dad was in poor health at that time. He'd never fully recovered from his mental breakdown. And then, he'd suffered a string of heart attacks. He was very weak, and looked like he was barely hanging on. At the wedding, he seemed dazed, as if he didn't know where he was or what was going on.

But my mother was on top of the world that day. Kathy had taken her shopping for her mother-of-the-bride dress. Then they got her hair and nails done. Mom was so happy to be dolled up like that. As if it was her day, not mine.

At the reception, while my father sat at the table looking like he was on the verge of collapsing, my mom was busy flirting with Richard's father. He was humoring her, turning on the Jacobson charm, and she was eating it up, every minute of it. The two of them got out on the dance floor for a slow dance. Mom didn't know a thing about dancing, and she was stepping all over Mr. Jacobson's feet. I was embarrassed for her. But she didn't care. She was enjoying herself.

I knew Mom thought I'd married into a high-class family. She acted like she was proud of me, which shocked me. At the reception, she gave me a hug and a kiss on the cheek, something she hadn't done since I was a small child. "Rosalie, you're a lucky girl," she told me. "You landed yourself a good man. I'm going to love your husband like he's my own son."

She didn't say what was undoubtedly on her mind, that in marrying Richard, I got more than I deserved.

Would you believe that the abusive side of my husband's personality showed itself the very day after our wedding? We'd flown to Aruba for our honeymoon. That first morning, Richard was getting ready to order room service for our breakfast, and when I told him I wasn't very hungry, he lost his temper.

He grabbed a full water glass from the table beside our bed. I was still in bed at the time, and he threw the water in my face. Then he hurled the glass across the room. It shattered when it hit the wall, glass flying everywhere.

Then he grabbed apples and oranges from our complementary fruit basket and started throwing them against the wall, right next to my side of the bed. As if he was letting me know that he could hit me if he wanted to.

I was so startled by my husband's behavior that I huddled under the covers, not fully comprehending what was going on. I couldn't figure out what had happened to make things take such an ugly turn.

Then Richard stood over the bed, ranting about how he'd brought me to one of the top honeymoon locations in the world, and how I was ruining everything for him. He screamed at me that I was ungrateful for everything he and his family had done for me.

"I'm sorry," I whimpered. "I'm sorry." But he kept going on and on. I was afraid that all the noise would alarm the other hotel patrons. I expected that at any minute, hotel staff would be knocking on our door. Or that someone would call the police.

When Richard finally stopped yelling, he hissed at me that that he wasn't going to order us any breakfast at all. I was afraid he wasn't going to let me eat all day. Then he turned and stalked out of the room, slamming the door behind him, leaving me alone in the mess.

I lay there, stunned, unable to move. My mind was so dazed by the violent episode that I couldn't think.

An hour later, Richard returned. When I heard his key rattling in the lock, I braced myself for another tirade. But he was in a euphoric mood, and spoke sweetly to me. He said he'd spotted a beautiful little cafe while he was out walking, and that he wanted to take me there for lunch.

He pulled the covers off of me and held out his hand to help me up. "Come on, sweetheart," he said. "It's a beautiful day, and we don't want to miss it."

As I showered and dressed, I told myself that Richard's outburst was the result of pent-up stress from wedding preparations. I convinced myself that it was a one-time occurrence.

While we were out for lunch, room service came in to clean. I wondered what they thought as they swept up broken glass and wiped splattered fruit off the wall. When we came back to our room, there was no sign of my husband's explosion. But then Richard found a single shard of glass on the floor, and he muttered about what a shoddy job room service had done.

Richard always expected others to clean up his messes. He was an only child, and he was used to getting what he wanted. He had an inflated view of his own importance. He couldn't seem to fathom a world that didn't cater to his whims. If he were one of my patients, I'd diagnose him with narcissistic personality disorder.

After our marriage, Richard and I rented an apartment in Bloomington. Both of us were planning to pursue advanced degrees in psychology at Indiana University. We'd talked about eventually going into practice together.

Unfortunately, Richard wasn't as good a student as I was. He was intelligent, but he didn't have self-discipline. He didn't like plodding through all of the hard work, and was always looking for the easy way out. While he'd managed to make it through the undergraduate program, he didn't have what it took to earn a masters degree. After one semester, he dropped out.

He never admitted to failure. He told everyone he quit the program because he realized psychology was a bunch of bull, and that he wasn't going to waste any more of his time on it. That was his way of saving face.

But I knew that, deep down, Richard was really angry with himself. His ego had taken a beating, and his way of dealing with that was to take his frustration out on someone else. And that someone was me. He demanded that I drop out of school, too, but I refused. Looking back, I'm so glad that I stood my ground. Where would I be now if I'd given in to him?

Richard's father was a big shot in the auto insurance industry. After Richard dropped out of graduate school, he started working with his dad. He eventually became an insurance agent, running his own office. Over the years, he worked his way up the corporate ladder, overseeing a number of offices. He's actually done quite well for himself. He's good in a position where he can manipulate and control people.

When I got pregnant with Marty, Richard started in on me again, telling me I needed to drop out of school. He said I should focus on the responsibilities of being a wife and mother. That was his way of trying to derail me from my career plan. He doesn't like having anyone show him up, especially a woman. Especially his wife.

But I kept right on going. I finished my masters program just days before I gave birth to Marty, who, unfortunately, came eight weeks early.

When Richard learned that his son had been born with cerebral palsy, he was furious. Having a disabled child didn't fit with his puffed-up image of himself. Right away, he started pinning the blame on me. He said if I hadn't pushed myself so hard to get through school, the baby wouldn't have been born early, and that he wouldn't have cerebral palsy.

That last part isn't necessarily true. Premature birth does raise the odds of a child being born with cerebral palsy, but that isn't the only cause.

I could've turned and pointed my finger at Richard. Shortly after our marriage, he'd started shoving me around, sometimes to the point where I'd lose my balance and fall down. He probably shoved me a dozen times during my pregnancy. I could've blamed the premature birth on that. But I knew better than to say such a thing. I'd learned to keep my mouth shut, so as not to pour fuel on the fire of my husband's temper.

After Marty was born, Richard and I stayed together for another six years. I was extremely busy, juggling the care of my special-needs child with working on my doctorate. Of course, Richard blamed me for not paying enough attention to him.

How could he expect any love or attention from me? He'd become an absolute tyrant. He'd yell, slam doors, throw things, shove me. It was impossible to make him happy. The best I could do was to stay out of his way.

One day, I said something Richard didn't like. I can't even remember what it was. He slapped me so hard that I fell and hit my head on the coffee table. Ignoring the fact that I was bleeding profusely from my head wound, he turned and stormed out of the room. Our six-year-old son happened to be sitting there in his wheelchair, in Richard's way. Richard grabbed the wheelchair and shoved it against the wall. As I watched Marty's frail little body flopping around like a ragdoll, I knew right then and there that I had to get out. I knew full well that things would only get worse for my son and me if I stayed married to Richard.

When Richard went to work the next morning, I packed up my things and Marty's things and went to stay in a battered women's shelter. Because of my training, I wasn't naïve about domestic violence and the challenges involved with leaving an abusive man. I knew full well that I was in for a rough ride. But I also knew that I had to put one foot in front of the other, until I got to a point where I could create a stable life for my son and me. And that's exactly what I did.

People often asked me why I kept Richard's last name after our divorce. Sometimes, I regret doing that. But at the time, I chose to keep the last name of Jacobson for Marty's sake. I wanted the two of us to share a last name.

Since then, there have been times when I've thought about changing it. But going back to the name of Rafferty doesn't seem like an improvement. Little Rosalie Rafferty was such an unfortunate character, and I don't want to be dragged back into that world. And professionally, I've been known as Dr. Jacobson for so many years. Changing my name would be awkward and inconvenient.

Richard did everything he could to obstruct our divorce. One of the tactics he used was to cozy up to my mother, getting her to side with him. While I was still trying to figure out a way to tell my family what had happened, he went to see my mother, crying and carrying on, telling her I'd left him.

I didn't even know he'd done this until I drove over to Brown County to talk to Mom and Edie. I'd no sooner set foot inside Mom's trailer than she tore me to pieces, telling me I'd made the biggest mistake of my life.

I remember her exact words, the degrading tone of her voice: "Rosalie, you done a lot of things to break your mama's heart, but this is worse than anything I could ever imagine you doin'. You know I didn't raise you to up and run out on your husband like that. For God's sake, what were you thinkin', girl? Have you plumb lost your mind?"

When I tried to tell her that Richard had been abusive to me, she said, "Your daddy give me more'n my share of problems. Did you see me runnin' out on 'im? No, you did not. I stuck by my husband 'til the day he died."

I could've confronted her on that point. The hateful way she treated my father after his mental breakdown wasn't exactly an example of loyalty to a spouse. But I kept my mouth shut. Mom's like Richard. If you try to stand up for yourself when she's tearing into you, she flares up all the more.

So I turned and headed out the door. When I was walking to my car, Edie came out of her house. I was crying too hard to talk, but she put her arms around me and held me for a minute or two. Then she said, "Mom told me you and Richard are splitting up. I'm sorry you're going through such a rough time. I love you, Rosie."

Bless her heart. I'll always remember that.

After that horrible encounter with Mom, I realized how foolish I'd been to ever trust Richard. When he and I started dating, I'd thought it would be safe to confide in someone who was planning a career in psychology. I thought he would be capable of understanding all that I'd been through. So I told him about the problems in our family, the things that happened when I was a teenager, those terrible events that broke my heart into a million pieces.

Now that I've been a psychologist for almost thirty years, I know there are just as many jerks in the field of psychology as there are in any other profession. I'm glad

Richard never followed that career. A lot of vulnerable clients have been spared from being harmed by him.

During the process of our divorce, Richard took all the information I'd ever entrusted him with and used it against me. He knew my mother had a different version of the stories I'd told him. He knew that if he agreed with her perspective on things, it would be easy to get her on his side. He drove over to talk with her four or five times.

The next time Edie saw Richard's car in the driveway, she called me. She said, "Did you know Richard is over at the trailer with Mom again?" She acted bewildered, as if she couldn't figure out his reason for being there.

I had to explain to her what he was doing. "Oh my!" she said. After that, she called me every time he came over. She was concerned about me.

Edie is such an innocent soul. I don't think she can conceive of how someone could be so duplicitous.

I don't know whether Richard thought Mom could persuade me to stay with him, or whether his intention was to punish me by turning her completely against me. By the end, he had her fully convinced that I was unreasonable and crazy and downright wicked. Every time she looked at me, I could see the contempt in her eyes.

Richard told my mom everything she wanted to hear. That she'd never done anything wrong to me. That I'd been an evil child who'd betrayed her. If she'd had any nagging guilt about what happened between us, he absolved her of it.

He convinced her that I was to blame for my son's premature birth, and for his disability. He made her believe that I'd been the abusive spouse. It was as if the two of them formed a club, those who'd been victimized by the terrible Rosalie.

Having the two of them against me like that, acting like I was a piece of trash—well, I can't even put into words how devastating that was. It felt as if I'd been put through a shredder and then dumped into the garbage.

I can't understand my mother's hatefulness toward her own child. A mother's natural instinct is to love and protect her offspring. I could never imagine not loving Marty. I'd take on anyone who threatened him. I could never wish bad things for him like my mother does for me. When someone who is supposed to love you condemns you instead, and seems to enjoy doing it, that cuts deeper than anything else in the world.

All this mess happened after my father passed away. I'd like to think that if he'd been living, I could've counted on him for support. But, no, that wouldn't have been possible. He'd been too weak, too debilitated. Too much under my mother's control to do anything to protect me.

So that is why, twenty-five years later, my mother can't even look in my direction without turning up her nose at me. The last time I visited her, I ended up crying all the way home. It took me a week before I felt like myself again. I don't have the stamina to go through that this weekend.

For that reason, I don't plan on being around her without one of my sisters there to act as a buffer. I'll wait until the next time Kathy goes to the trailer. If Kathy's there, all of Mom's attention will be on her. Kathy's presence fills up any room she enters, and it's easy for me to hide in her shadow.

SATURDAY MORNING

EDITH: Sam and I were dead tired when we went to bed last night. If you can call lying down on an air mattress going to bed. It wasn't very comfortable. Not like our own bed. We've been sleeping on a special mattress because of Sam's back problems. I guess I've gotten spoiled.

I felt so guilty about making my husband sleep on the floor like that. I kept going over the sleeping arrangements I'd made, wondering if I could've done something different. Finally, I told myself, "Edie, you did the best you could." I don't think I got to sleep until after midnight, because I was lying there worrying about everything.

And wouldn't you know it, another dream woke me up around three o'clock. Another dream visit from James. Oh, James! Why does he torment me like this? Why does he come and break my heart over and over again?

But I really don't want him to stop coming. His dream visits are all I have left of him. I'd be heartbroken if he never came again.

Sam doesn't know about James. None of my family knows about him. My mother and sisters never met him, although if circumstances had been different, they would have. He'd be part of their lives now.

I've never spoken of James to anybody, not even my closest friends. Only God knows my secret. Many times, I've asked Him to forgive me for what I did.

When I was eighteen, I started college at Indiana University in Bloomington. That was the time when everything was changing in our family. At the same time I was packing up to move into my dorm room at IU, my parents and sisters were packing up to move to Greenwood. That was because Dad was going to be the pastor of a church up there.

I don't take change very well, and this was too much for me to handle all at once. Starting college. Being separated from my family for the first time in my life. My family moving out of the house I'd always known as home. I was so young and so scared, and it felt as if I'd completely lost my bearings.

For the first month of school, I cried every day. Compared to my small high school, the college campus seemed so big and confusing. Sometimes, I'd get lost trying to get where I needed to go. I'd have to stop people on the sidewalk and ask them for directions. Most of the time when this happened, I'd be so upset that I was crying. People would look at me so strangely. I don't know how I managed to get to my classes every day, but I did.

The other students scared me to death. That was in the early 1970s. Everybody dressed wild and crazy back then, like hippies. But not me. I just looked like the same little mouse I'd always been. I had no idea how to fit in. How to be cool.

So when I wasn't in class, I was holed up in my dorm room. Hiding from the world, bawling my eyes out. There were many times when I wanted to call my dad and tell him to come and get me.

If my parents had still been living in Brown County, I never would've stuck it out. I would've dropped out and gone back home after the first week or two. But I had no home to go back to. Greenwood wasn't home to me. I knew I'd be just as lost there as I was at college.

My roommate Jenny was way more cool than I was. She had lots of friends. But she cared about me, too. She worried about me hiding in my room and crying all the time. She kept suggesting places where I could go to meet people and make friends. None of her ideas sounded good to me.

She knew that I came from a religious family, and that my dad was a preacher. One day, she told me I should try getting involved with the *Youth for Christ Campus Life* club.

"I'm not interested in the group myself," she told me. "But I think it might be good for you. I'll take you there the first time. After that, you can go on your own."

She kept bugging me about that *Youth for Christ* group, and I finally agreed to try it. So one Friday evening, she walked me across campus and showed me where the group met, in the lounge of one of the other dormitories. She made me promise to stay there at least an hour.

"I'll be back in the room waiting for you," she said. "When you come back, we'll talk about how it went."

Because I'd given Jenny my word, I walked into that room. I made myself stay, even though I desperately wanted to turn and run. I was having a panic attack. My heart was pounding like crazy, and my chest was so tight that I could hardly catch my breath.

The room was packed with students. They all looked cool, just like all the other students on campus. Long hair, bell-bottom blue jeans, tie-dyed shirts, sandals. I'd been hoping they'd be people more like me, more ordinary-looking. I felt stupid in the corduroy pants and pullover sweater I was wearing.

They were all talking and laughing with each other, as if they'd known each other forever. I knew I didn't belong there. But I'd promised Jenny that I would stay.

I remember exactly the way that room looked. I was staring at the furnishings so I wouldn't have to look at the people. Ratty-looking brown sofas. Enormous bean bag chairs in different colors: orange, red, yellow and blue. A print of Vincent Van Gogh's *Starry Night* hanging on one wall. A couple of posters advertising upcoming concerts. I remember staring at one of the posters and thinking how fun it would be to attend a concert like that. But I knew I'd never go, not in a million years, because I'd be too scared.

There was a table with refreshments on it: packages of *Oreos,* bags of pretzels, apples, and different kinds of Halloween candy. I watched people reaching into a cooler for cans of *Pepsi* and *Seven-Up.* I remember how dry my mouth was, and how much I wanted something to drink. But because I was so nervous, I was afraid that if I tried to eat or drink anything, I'd throw up.

I saw an empty beanbag in one corner. Without saying a word to anybody, I went over and sat down on it. I tried to sink as low as I could, hoping the beanbag would swallow me up so that no one could see me.

I reminded myself that I had to stay one hour, like I'd promised Jenny. I looked at my watch and saw that it was two minutes past seven. I told myself that at eight o'clock on the dot, I'd jump up and run out of there and never come back.

And that's exactly what would've happened if that nice young man wouldn't have crossed the room and sat down on the floor beside my beanbag.

One of the first things I noticed about the young man was how muscular he was. Like he lifted weights, or did a lot of hard work. He had on a short-sleeved polo shirt, and I could see how big his biceps were. His face and arms were deeply tanned, like he'd been out in the sun all summer. His hands looked rough and calloused.

In that room full of scruffy-looking hippie kids, this guy stood out as clean-cut. He had short brown hair, parted on one side. It made him look sort of old-fashioned, but I found that comforting. His blue jeans were clean and new. They were practical, like something a farmer would buy for working in the fields. Not like the raggedy bell-bottoms the other students were wearing. His sneakers looked clean and new, too, like he'd just bought them to wear at school that year.

When he sat down next to me, I was surprised when I didn't even cringe. He looked at me with kind, deep-set hazel eyes. His face was broad and clean-shaven. He wasn't exactly handsome, just pleasant and wholesome-looking. Like someone you could feel comfortable with. He didn't seem intimidating at all, and having him next to me helped me breathe a little easier.

He leaned in close so that I could hear him above the noise of the crowd. "Would you like something to drink?" he asked.

I shook my head, still afraid I'd vomit if I tried to swallow anything.

He smiled at me, and I could tell he sensed how nervous I was. "Are you sure?" he said. "I'll get it for you. Would you like *Pepsi* or *Seven-Up?*"

"I'll take *Seven-Up,*" I said.

He got up, then came back a moment later with two cans of soda. He sat down on the floor beside me again. It felt as if he was forming a protective barrier between me and the other people. I felt safe enough to manage swallowing a few sips of my drink.

"I'm James," he said. "James Miller."

"I'm Edith," I replied. "Edith Rafferty."

"That's an interesting name," he said. "I don't think I've ever met someone named Edith."

I felt myself blushing. "I know. Hardly anybody is named Edith anymore. It's really old-fashioned."

Then I completely surprised myself by blurting out personal things about my life. That's not the way I normally act. I'm usually a private person.

"I'm the oldest girl in my family," I told him. "So I was named after my two grandmothers, Edith and Mabel. I'm Edith Mabel Rafferty. How's that for a name?"

Right away, I felt embarrassed by what I'd said. I knew my face was bright red. I hoped James wouldn't notice.

James laughed. He had the nicest laugh. There was nothing ugly about it, and I knew he wasn't making fun of me. "That's a wonderful name," he said. "I love it."

He was quiet for a little bit, like he was thinking. Then he said, "Edie May. Short for Edith Mabel. Do people call you that?"

"No," I said. "A lot of people call me Edie. But nobody ever calls me Edie May."

"How about if I call you Edie May?"

"That would be okay." Would you believe I giggled right then? I hardly ever giggle.

"Where are you from, Edie May?" James asked.

"Brown County," I replied.

"Oh," he said. "Not that far from here. Do you live in Nashville?"

"No. I'm from way out in the country. East of Bean Blossom, on Sprunica Ridge Road. Way out there in the sticks." Then I surprised myself again, because I made a little joke about myself. I hardly ever do that. "I guess I'm just a hillbilly."

"I love hillbillies," James said. "Edie May is a perfect hillbilly name."

The way he said it was warm and kind. Again, I knew he wasn't making fun of me.

"Where are you from, James?" I asked him.

"Middlebury."

"I never heard of it."

"It's just a little town," he said. "Way up in the northern part of the state. In Elkhart County, close to the Michigan line."

"Oh," I said. "I've never been up that way. What's it like up there?"

"Lots of farmland. Lots of Amish and Mennonites. I'm a Mennonite."

That surprised me so much that I pulled myself up in the beanbag and looked him straight in the face. "Really? I went to high school with some Mennonite kids. There's a little Mennonite Church in Bean Blossom. When I was in high school, I was really shy. I was scared of everybody. Just like I am here at college. But I wasn't that scared of the Mennonite kids. I knew they wouldn't make fun of me or do anything to hurt me."

"I'm glad to hear that," James said. "Maybe you won't be afraid of me."

"Maybe I won't be," I said.

"I've been to the Bean Blossom Mennonite Church," he said. "Small world, huh?"

My eyes popped wide open. "Really? When?"

"I went to a Mennonite high school, and I sang in the choir. Sometimes, we went on tour. Once, we came down here to sing at the Bean Blossom Mennonite Church. Would you believe that's what made me decide to come down here to IU? I wanted to get away from home and branch out a little bit. I love this part of the state, with all the trees and the rolling hills. Up north, it's mostly flat."

He looked at me with those kind eyes again. "So that's how it came to be that James Miller the Mennonite is sitting here talking to Edie May Rafferty the hillbilly."

And I laughed. I hardly ever laugh. But James always had a way of making me laugh.

Just about then, the group was getting ready to start some kind of formal discussion. James stood up and held out his hand to me. "Let's get out of here, Edie May," he whispered. "Let's go some place where we can talk."

I didn't have to think twice. I knew right away that I wanted to go with James Miller. I was breaking my promise to Jenny, because I told her I'd stay at the meeting for an hour. But I didn't care, not one bit.

I took James's hand and he helped me out of the beanbag. At that moment, the strangest feeling came over me. Something sweet and warm and tingly. Something I'd never felt before. I wondered if I was falling in love.

James took me on a long walk across the campus and

into town, to an old store-front coffee shop. The evening was chilly, and my windbreaker wasn't heavy enough to keep me warm. When James saw me shivering, he took off his own jacket and put it over my shoulders. I couldn't remember anyone ever doing such a kind thing for me. I kept on shivering, but not because of the cold. It felt as if walking next to James charged me up with electricity. I didn't know how to handle it.

The night sky was clear, brilliant with a million stars. It seemed as if they were all looking down on me, watching this amazing event unfold in my life: my first date with a man. A wonderful man.

The coffee shop was a shabby little place, dark inside except for the candles burning in wine bottles on the tables. Every now and then, somebody would go up to the front of the room and read their poetry. I'd never been to a place like that. Actually, I hadn't even known any place like that existed. Normally, I never would've had the nerve to set foot in the door. But that night, I wasn't scared, because James was with me.

We found an empty table in the corner. I remember that the table was a little wobbly, and that we had to be careful not to spill our coffee. We sat there for hours. I'll never forget how James's face looked in the candlelight. Serene and glowing. It made him seem like more than an ordinary person. Like he was someone not of this world. That glowing face is the same face I see in my dreams.

He must have felt the same way about my face, because he said, "Edie May, you are so beautiful by candlelight." That almost knocked me off my chair. No one had ever called me beautiful before. People always talked about how beautiful Kathy was. They never said things like that about me. But I could tell James really meant what he said.

He talked about his family and his life in Middlebury. He told me he'd been raised on a farm. "Farming is a good life," he said. "But I don't know whether it's the life for me. I need to take some time to figure out what I really want. I figured going to college a few hundred miles away from home might help me get some new perspectives."

"Are you a freshman?" I asked him.

"No," he replied. "I'm a sophomore."

"What are you majoring in?"

"Biology. How about you?"

"I'm not sure yet," I told him. "But I've been thinking a little bit about elementary education. I like children. People tell me I'm good with them."

"I'm sure you are," he said. "You seem like such a loving and gentle person."

By the end of the night, I'd told James almost everything about my life. I told him about my father being a preacher, and about my family moving to Greenwood. I told him how sad I was about not being able to go back to my old home. I told him how lonely I felt there at college.

"Well, Edie May Rafferty," he said. "As of right now, you have at least one friend here at Indiana University. I want you to know that I'm here for you."

When we finally left the coffee house, James walked me back to my dorm. We stood out under the stars, and I wanted the moment to last forever. Then James said, "Can I give you a hug?"

"Sure," I said.

He wrapped his arms around me. His body felt warm and gentle, but strong. As he held me, it felt as if he was filling my scared little body with all the strength I needed. I snuggled into him. His arms felt like home to me.

He kissed me on the forehead. Then he lifted my chin and kissed my lips. "I'm sorry," he said. "I should've asked first."

"Don't be sorry," I said. "I liked it."

I'd never been kissed by a man before. Here I was, eighteen years old, almost nineteen, and that was my first time. The kiss was perfect. It was worth all those years of waiting. I wanted James to kiss me again and again, but that one kiss was all for the night.

When I walked into to my dorm room, it was two o'clock in the morning. Jenny was already asleep. That was different. It was usually me in bed, and her coming in during the early hours of the morning. She woke up and said, "Where've you been, Edie? I was worried about you."

"I met a guy," I told her.

She sat up and switched on the lamp beside her bed, staring at me like she couldn't believe what I'd just said. "Are you kidding me?"

"Nope," I said.

She got excited then, wanting to talk. "Tell me all about him."

But I didn't want to. I wanted to keep the memories of the evening all to myself for a little while. "Maybe later," I told her.

I lay in bed with my hands on my heart, holding onto the sweetness of my time with my new friend. I felt peaceful. My body felt warm and tingly. For the first time since I'd been there at school, I didn't cry myself to sleep.

I'm a married woman now. Whenever I think about James, I feel disloyal to Sam. And to my children, and even my grandchildren. Because whenever I daydream about a life with James, it's like I'm wishing that none of them had been born. That's not true, not at all. I'm happy with all of them. I really am.

I owe my loyalty to Sam, and to the family I've made with him. I shouldn't be dwelling on all this stuff that happened more than forty years ago. But I can't help it. I can't keep those dreams from coming.

Whenever Sam goes through one of his grumpy spells, I dream about James. Every time my stress level gets high, James visits me in a dream. It's kind of like he comes to take care of me, like he did when we were together.

After my dream early this morning, I went up to my chapel in the attic. I felt so overwhelmed by the dream and the stress of the weekend that I broke down and cried. I haven't done that in a long time. I must've cried myself to sleep, curled up in the armchair.

And, wouldn't you know it, I had another dream about James. This one was different than how they usually are. It was more vivid, more surreal. For a minute or two, James' presence was right there with me. I could feel his love wrapped around me, his strength flowing into me like a current of electricity. I can still feel it.

In real life, I have no idea where James is now. I have no idea what direction his life took after we parted ways. But this morning, his spirit was with me. He must have known I needed him.

When I woke up, the early morning sunlight was shining through my father's stained-glass window. I felt so safe and so peaceful that I fell back asleep.

I had no idea what time it was when I woke up again. It was fully light outside. All of a sudden, I realized that I hadn't made breakfast for my houseguests. I'd been planning on making waffles with blueberry syrup. I jumped up and rushed down the stairs.

When I got to the kitchen, I saw that my guests had fended for themselves. Somebody had made a pot of coffee. There was a cereal box on the table, and several bowls in the sink.

Then I saw Kathy sitting on the sofa in the living room with a cup of coffee. She was staring at her cell phone, looking kind of worried.

"I'm so sorry, Kathy," I told her. "I meant to get up and fix breakfast for everybody."

"It's okay," she said, not looking up from her phone. "Don't worry about it. We're all doing just fine."

"Where is everybody?" I asked.

"Katrina is lying down with the baby again," she said. "Lilly kept her up most of the night, and she's pretty tired. I think Rosie took Marty out for a walk. Sam came downstairs just a minute ago. He said to tell you he'd be out in the garage."

I feel so bad about letting everybody down with breakfast. I'll try to make up for it at lunch.

KATRINA DOUGLAS: This is the first time I've traveled with Lilly. She's a mess! She kept me up almost all night. I'm not doing this again until she's a lot older.

Just about the time everyone else in the house started getting up, Lilly finally decided she was ready to sleep. I could hear Aunt Rosie and her son moving around in the living room. It sounded like they were having a problem, so I went out to see what was happening.

Aunt Rosie said she wanted to take Marty out for a walk. She was hoping Sam would be around to help get him down the steps. I told her I didn't think Sam had come downstairs yet. I offered to help her, and she really appreciated that. We put Marty on the sofa while we moved his chair outside. Then Rosie picked him up and carried him out and put him back into his chair.

Rosie told me Marty is thirty-one. That's just six years younger than me. It's hard to believe he's that old, because he seems like a child. He's so small. But it's hard to lift him, because he's a dead weight.

Helping Aunt Rosie with her son made me feel so grateful that Lilly is healthy. I don't know what I'd do if I had a disabled child. I don't think I'd handle it as well as Aunt Rosie does. She's so good with Marty. I can tell how much she loves him.

I haven't been around Aunt Rosie very much. She's nicer than I thought she'd be. My mom's always aggravated with her. Every time she talks with Rosie on the phone, she's fuming by the time she hangs up.

Before my parents were divorced, my mom and dad and I used to come to Indiana to visit Grandpa and Grandma and Aunt Edie at least once a year. I barely remember Grandpa. He was always sick, and I never had much interaction with him. I remember playing with my cousins, Aunt Edie's kids. They're around my age.

Neither of my aunts ever comes to New York to visit us. I can understand about Aunt Edie. She's so timid and shy. New York City would probably give her heart failure. But Rosie could come if she wanted to. I don't know why she doesn't. It hurts my Mom's feelings that no one bothers to come and see her. She's the one that always has to do the traveling.

The last time I was here was the year before my parents' divorce. I was twelve. That was twenty-five years ago. Hard to believe.

I'm not sure why I stopped coming out here with my mom. Maybe it was because I didn't want to come without my dad. Before the divorce, traveling to Indiana was the only vacation my mom and dad and I ever took as a family. It meant a lot to me. But since my mom's been married to Bryce, they've gone almost everywhere in the world.

My dad loved it out here. He's lived his whole life in New York City. He loved Brown County's hills and woods. He thought being surrounded by nature was awesome. Once when we were here, he said to me, "If someone is lucky enough to be born in a place like this, why would she ever want to move away?" He made that comment when my mom wasn't around, because he knew she'd get mad if she heard him say something like that.

My dad thought Grandma was a little weird, but he was nice to her. He liked Aunt Edie and Uncle Sam and their kids. Every once in awhile, he mentions them and asks how they're doing.

The last time Mom and Dad and I were out here together, we were taking a hike on a little dirt road called Freeman Ridge. It's not that far from here. You have to drive up a really steep hill to get there.

It was Mom's idea to take the hike. I don't know why she wanted to, because she was constantly complaining about the heat and the humidity and the bugs.

She was walking along in a grumpy mood, not talking to my dad or me. Then we met some people coming the other way across the ridge. And just like that, she was all smiles, ready to stop and talk. My mom's never met a stranger. She can talk to anyone.

I remember those people so clearly. The image of them is burned into my brain, probably because of what happened right after we met them. It was a grandmother and a mother and a young girl around my age. The mother and girl didn't say much. The grandmother did most of the talking. She asked my mom where we were from, and Mom told her we were from New York City. She never mentioned the fact that she'd grown up here, and that we were visiting relatives. She acted like we were just regular tourists.

The grandmother got excited about the idea that people from New York City had come all the way out here to Brown County. She started telling Mom about the things we needed to stop and see in Nashville. Mom acted interested, as if she didn't know anything at all about Nashville.

"Tell all your friends in New York that this is a wonderful place to visit," the grandmother said.

And Mom said, "I sure will."

When we went on with our hike, my mom turned sour and grumpy again. "Why didn't you tell those ladies that you grew up here?" my dad asked her.

"That's nobody business," she snapped.

He was quiet for a few minutes, like he was scared to say anything more to her. Then he said, "Those women are lucky people."

"Why do you think they're lucky, Daddy?" I asked him.

"Because they get to live here in this beautiful place," he said.

My mom shot him an ugly look, and then shook her head like she thought he was nuts.

We kept walking along, and then my dad said to her, kind of tentative, "Honey, do you ever think about moving back here?"

My mom swung around and glared at him. "Why do you say stupid things like that, Rod?"

"Really, Kathy," he said, "what would you think about us getting a little house and living out here in the woods?"

"Are you crazy?" she yelled.

I remember my dad looking like he'd been crushed. He always looked crushed when my mom yelled at him.

I took hold of my dad's hand and said, "I'd like to live out here in the woods, Daddy. I think it would be fun."

"What on earth do you think your dad would do to make a living out here?" my mom hissed at me.

"I'd do anything," my dad said.

She shot him another dirty look. "Oh, sure," she said sarcastically.

My dad was never ambitious enough for my mom. I know she looked down on him, because he never made enough money for her.

That day on the ridge was the first time it hit me that

my parents weren't going to stay together. I always knew my dad aggravated my mom. It's like he got on her nerves just by virtue of being who he was. But that day, I realized that she despised him. I knew she wouldn't put up with him much longer.

I held my dad's hand, and we walked along behind my mom. It was like both of us knew she didn't think we were good enough to walk beside her. Nobody talked for the rest of the hike. I felt sadder than I'd ever felt in my entire life. I knew my dad was feeling the same way.

I love my mom to death. She can be so sweet and kind and generous. I don't know what I'd do without her. But she can be two-faced sometimes. She gives off the impression that she wants others to have of her, and it isn't always entirely honest.

It makes me so mad when I hear my mom telling people about why she divorced my father. She makes him out to be some kind of a bum. He wasn't a bum back then, and he certainly isn't now. He's sixty-seven years old, and he's still working.

My dad told me the story about how he met my mom. It's kind of sweet, really. He'd been working as a background musician in recording studios. You don't get rich from doing that kind of thing. But my dad wasn't ever driven to make a whole lot of money. He just wanted to earn a decent living doing something he enjoyed. Back when he met my mom, his work in the studios wasn't all that steady, and he worked as a custodian in a theatre to help support himself.

He told me that the morning he met my mom, he was in the theatre cleaning up after the previous night's performance. He was used to seeing people coming in for casting calls. He said he got a kick out of watching who came in, because he'd see some really weird people doing some really weird things.

Well, that morning, he was mopping the floor in the lobby, and he saw a girl coming out of an audition. He said she looked tired and discouraged. He knew right away that she was one of those kids who'd come to the big city to follow her dream, and that things weren't working out for her. He'd seen a lot of those girls.

He told me that this girl was exceptionally pretty. Even though she looked exhausted, he could tell that she was strong and determined. "How did your audition go?" he asked her.

She got tears in her eyes, and he felt sorry for her. He kept asking her questions. He found out she was staying at the Y, and that she was working the late shift as a waitress at an all-night restaurant so she could go to casting calls during the day.

He told me she looked skinny and hungry, and he figured she wasn't making enough money to feed herself properly. So he took her out for breakfast. The two of them started spending time together. He worried about her having to deal with the rough conditions at the Y, so he invited her to stay with him in his apartment.

My dad has always loved my mom. Their divorce devastated him. He's never remarried. Because my mom wasn't happy with him, he believes he doesn't have what it takes to make any woman happy. It's really too bad. He's such a nice guy.

A few years back, he ended up working the sound

system for one of her off-Broadway musical productions. He was glad to see her, and he tried to talk with her. But she wouldn't have anything to do with him.

My dad told me that once my mom didn't have to worry about keeping food in her stomach and a roof over her head, she started doing really well in New York City. Even though she wasn't able to land any acting jobs back then, she got a pretty decent secretarial job. She loved city life, and she loved being a career woman. When I was born, the two of them decided that my father would be the one to stay home and take care of me. That was because my mom had a fulltime job, and his work was sporadic.

That's probably the reason I've always been so close to my dad. He was far more involved in raising me than my mom was. When they got divorced, I wanted to live with him. But my mom wouldn't have it. Her boss Bryce, who later became her second husband, gave her money for a high-powered attorney, and she was able to get custody of me.

I talk with my father every day. He loves Lilly, and he's always asking to see her. He gets along well with my husband Roscoe, too.

Dad still lives in a small apartment, kind of like the one we lived in before my parents got divorced. He says that's all the space he needs. Even though he's got a little bit of money now, he says there's no point in spending it on something he doesn't need.

My mom looks down on him for that. His place is pretty dinky, compared to the mansion she lives in on Long Island. Every time she mentions what a bum my dad is, it gets to me, because he was the one who rescued her when she came to New York City. He was the one to help her get on her feet. But when things started going better for her, she was done with him.

I tried pointing that out to my mom once, but she wouldn't listen to me. She never listens to anything she doesn't want to hear. She prefers to live in the make-believe world she's built for herself.

Don't get me wrong. I love my mom. She and Bryce have been good to my husband and me. I've been married to Roscoe for fourteen years. The early years were rough for us financially, because both of us were trying to get through school. Roscoe was working on his degree in pharmacology, and I was in nursing school. Mom and Bryce were really good about helping us out when we were in a tight spot.

It's so nice to be able to make this trip with my mom again, to spend this time with her. Back home, she's so busy that I hardly ever get a chance to see her.

It's nice seeing my aunts, too. And Grandma, even though she's gotten pretty weird in her old age. I noticed that last night when we went out to dinner in Nashville. My mom was talking about health food, like she always does. She mentioned that she only drinks soy milk or almond milk. Grandma said she'd never drink anything but cow's milk. She said she wouldn't even drink skim milk, because they take all the vitamins out of it.

Aunt Edie jumped in and said, "No, Mama, the only thing they take out of skim milk is the fat. It still has vitamins and minerals in it."

But Grandma wouldn't believe a word of what Aunt Edie told her. She kept arguing the point until everybody else dropped the subject. My mom and grandmother are a lot alike. Both of them are stubborn. They get strange ideas in their heads that they won't let go of. You can talk until you're blue in the face, and you can't budge them. When it comes to arguing with Mom, I've learned to save my breath.

I'm a little worried about my mom. On the flight here, she mentioned that Bryce was upset about her traveling this weekend. I don't know what the problem is. I asked her about it, but she just changed the subject. She keeps checking her cell phone. He must be calling or texting her.

ROSALIE: I barely got any sleep last night. I never sleep well when I'm here. Even though I stay at Edie's house, I can sense my mother's presence across the yard in her mobile home. It makes me feel uneasy. Unsafe, actually. Like I need to sleep with one eye open.

To make matters worse, Katrina's baby cried half the night. I got up this morning feeling exhausted, wondering how I was going to make it through the day. I thought maybe if I took Marty out for a walk, it would energize me.

I'd promised Marty that I'd take him to visit his grandfather's grave this weekend. He's never been there before.

Marty loves hearing stories about his grandpa. He knows that he's named after him. Actually, Marty's first name is Richard, after his father. Richard's big ego would never tolerate his son being named after anyone but him. Martin is my son's middle name. Even though his dad refers to him as Richard, I've always called him Marty, and so does everyone at his group home.

When anyone asks Marty what his name is, he straightens up his twisted little body the best he can, and with all the dignity he can muster, he says, "Richard Martin Jacobson." That's quite a mouthful for him. Then he'll add, "But you can call me Marty."

"Your grandfather was a good man," I told Marty one day last week. "He was very smart and very kind."

"Like you and me," Marty responded. "We're smart and we're kind."

He melted my heart when he said that. He was drawing his grandfather into the circle of our little family.

I bent down and kissed the top of his head. "Yes, Marty," I said. "All three of us are smart and kind."

"Why didn't I know grandpa?" Marty asked.

"He died when you were a baby," I replied.

"Did he love me?"

"Absolutely!" I said that even though I wasn't sure I was telling the truth. By the time Marty was born, my dad's health was so far gone that he probably couldn't even register the fact that I had a child. But I like to think his spirit loved my son.

There was one incident, though, when I laid my infant son next to my father in his bed, and I saw a twinkle of recognition in my father's eyes. I decided to tell Marty about that.

"When you were a baby," I said, "I laid you beside your grandpa, and his eyes sparkled with love."

Marty looked up at me, his face shining with joy. "I loved Grandpa," he chortled, "and Grandpa loved me."

"Grandpa still loves you," I told him. "He's up in Heaven watching over you."

I'm not sure I believe that our departed loved-ones watch over us like guardian angels. But the idea works for Marty, and I use it to bring him comfort.

So going on a pilgrimage to visit his grandfather's grave for the first time was an important event for my son. I was hoping Sam would be around to help me get Marty out of the house and down the porch steps, but he was nowhere in sight. Just as I was trying to figure out how to accomplish that task on my own, Katrina came out of her bedroom and offered to help.

I really appreciated what she did. I've never known Katrina very well. I saw her only three or four times during her childhood. But the two of us working together to get Marty out of the house seemed to forge a little bond between us. Katrina is more down to earth than Kathy is. She must take after her dad.

Marty appreciated Katrina's help, too. He made a point of thanking her. Then he asked, "Do you want to come with us?"

Of course, Katrina couldn't understand what he said, and I had to interpret. She smiled at him and caressed his cheek. "I'd love to, Marty," she said, "but I have to stay here and take care of my baby."

A lovely interaction between the three of us. Like an unexpected gift. You never know when these special moments will happen. I try to make the most of them, to remember them at times when everything seems dark.

The cemetery is behind the church we attended when I was a kid, the church where my father preached. It's only a quarter of a mile down the road from Edie's house, but that's a fairly long trek when you're in a wheelchair.

We took our time. Marty gazed at his surroundings in awe. I realized that, for him, this was a luxury vacation, almost like visiting a foreign country. The breeze ruffled his hair. "I like feeling the wind on my face," he told me.

I pointed out things I remembered from my childhood. "See that tree over there? When I was a little girl, Grandpa made a tire swing for me. He hung a rope from that branch up there."

Marty's eyes traveled up to the branch. I knew he was trying to envision the swing.

I pointed to a neighbor's house with a spacious side yard. "When I was little, I had a friend who lived there. We ran around and played tag in that yard. Sometimes, her mom would give us some old jars, and we'd catch fireflies in them. Back then, we called the fireflies *lightning bugs.* We'd punch holes in the lids so the lightning bugs could get some air."

Suddenly, Marty looked sad. "I wish I could play tag," he said. "I wish I could catch lightning bugs."

I felt bad about being insensitive to his limitations. "I know you do, sweetie," I said. "I wish you could play tag and catch lightning bugs, too."

I was quiet for a little bit, not wanting to point out anything else that might hurt his feelings. But then he asked, "What else did you do?"

"I waded in the creek and caught tadpoles," I told him.

"What's a tadpole?" he asked.

"A baby frog," I said. "Before it gets legs."

Marty seemed to think catching legless baby frogs was the funniest thing in the world, and he giggled for a full minute.

"And you know what you do?" I said. "You operate that awesome chair. You've got one of the best wheelchairs in the world. You can do all sorts of cool things with it."

Marty grinned at me. Then, with his left hand on the controls, he showed off by wheeling his chair in a neat little circle.

"Excellent!" I exclaimed. I felt my spirits lifting, and I almost forgot about the dreaded task ahead of me that morning, the ordeal of going over to the trailer to see my mother.

When we reached the church, we turned to go down the long path toward the cemetery. There's not a lot of traffic that goes back there, and the dirt path was rough and overgrown. I had to take over pushing Marty's wheelchair, as the terrain was so uneven. I'd begun to rethink my decision to bring him out there. But he was enjoying the adventure, every bump in the road.

We passed the older section of the cemetery, with its ancient gravestones eroded by several hundred years of exposure to the elements. As we made our way to the newer section where my father was buried, it occurred to me that Marty had never been in a cemetery before. "This is where people's bodies are buried after their souls go to Heaven," I explained to him.

"I know," he said, sounding wise. "I know all about that."

When we came to my father's grave, I could tell by Marty's solemn expression that he was treating the occasion with reverence. I pointed to my dad's name on the headstone. "Can you read that?" I asked him.

"Martin Rafferty," he said slowly. Then he read off the numbers, one digit at a time. "One, nine, three, one, one, nine, eight, five."

"That's the date of his birth and the date of his death," I explained. "1931-1985. He died three weeks after you were born."

We were quiet for a few minutes. Then I said, "Hello, Dad. I've brought your grandson to visit you."

"Hello, Grandpa." Marty tilted his head and gazed up at the sky. Then he looked at me. "Did he hear us?"

"I'm sure he did," I said.

"I love you, Grandpa," Marty said, looking up at the sky again.

I suddenly wished I'd brought flowers to put on my father's grave. That would've meant a lot to Marty.

"Next time we come, we'll bring flowers," I told him.

Marty pointed to a patch of straggly black-eyed Susans growing at the edge of the woods near the cemetery. They were the last of the season, and were almost dead, but there were still a few bright yellow blooms in the middle of the blackened foliage. I walked over and picked a handful of the best ones. Then I laid them in front of my father's headstone.

"Next time," Marty said, "we'll bring some nicer flowers."

He'll remember that. Next time we come down, he'll expect to visit his grandfather's grave again. And he won't let me forget about the flowers. Knowing Marty, he'll be talking about those flowers days ahead of time.

As we were leaving the cemetery, a raggedy old black dog came bounding up to us, out of nowhere. He seemed happy to see us, and kept running in circles around Marty's wheelchair. Marty uttered a little yelp of fear, but I explained to him that the dog wouldn't hurt him. After a few moments, he started laughing, and reached out his left hand to try to pat the dog's head.

The dog followed us back to Edie's house, running alongside Marty's wheelchair. "Aunt Edie's going to be surprised," Marty giggled.

As we approached Edie's driveway, the dog took a notion to jump in the neighbor's pond for a swim. Then he jumped out and ran alongside us again, all wet and smelly. He followed us right up to Edie's front porch. Edie's cats looked offended and scurried away.

"You can't come inside," Marty announced to his dog friend. "Aunt Edie wouldn't like that."

I can't tell you how much I enjoyed that outing with Marty. He has the ability to appreciate every detail of an ordinary experience like that. He can make the mundane seem exquisite. Most people don't understand the gifts Marty has to offer.

A friend of mine once said to me, "Rosalie, God made you Marty's mother for a reason. You have both the heart and the intelligence for the job." Isn't that a lovely way to look at it? It's a whole different spin from the way my mother sees it. From the way Richard sees it. They view Marty as my punishment, a symbol of my wrongdoing.

FRANCES: This mornin' when I got up, I looked out my window to see what kind of a day it was gonna be. And you know what I seen? Rosalie walkin' down the road, pushin' her boy in his wheelchair.

I knowed right then and there where she was goin', and I felt my insides stirrin' up. She was headin' down to the graveyard behind the church, goin' to see her daddy that's dead 'fore she even come up to the trailer see her mama that's still livin'. But that's the kind of thing Rosalie does. Always refusin' to give me the respect I got comin' to me as her mother. She's a whole different kind of person than my other two girls.

Rosalie, she always favored her daddy over her mama. When things started gettin' bad, she sided with her daddy when he was fallin' apart, never givin' me any credit for holdin' things together.

Heaven knows if I'd a'thought Martin was gonna break down the way he did, I never woulda 'lowed us to make the move up there to Greenwood. But Martin had it in his mind that the Lord was givin' him a chance to do somethin' special. He thought he'd be doin' wrong if he didn't listen to what God was callin' him to do.

Things was goin' along just fine here with Martin preachin' at our little church. Everybody knowed him and respected him. Sure, there was problems. Anytime people get together, they always got problems. But it wasn't nothin' Martin couldn't handle. People would get to fussin' and arguin' with each other, and Martin would set 'em down and try to get 'em to talk things through. He was one that always wanted everything to be nice and peaceful. Time and again, I told 'im, "Martin, that just ain't the way people is."

Yup, we was gettin' along just fine. The girls was gettin' to be teenagers. Matter of fact, Edith was just about to finish up high school. She was sayin' she wanted to go to college, to be a teacher or somethin' along them lines. Martin was lookin' into havin' her go over there to Bloomington. Katherine was still in high school, and Rosalie was in seventh grade.

Then Martin got this call from a fellow who was some kinda big shot in the church. Lord, I wish he never woulda called. He told Martin there was some church up in Greenwood where the preacher had up and left. He said they was lookin' for somebody to fill that spot. He said the church was havin' a lot of problems, and that they was needin' some real good leadership to get things straightened out. He was wonderin' whether Martin was interested in takin' on the job.

Just about every day of my life, I think about that man callin', and in my mind, I try to do things over and make 'em turn out different. Lord, how I wish Martin had said, "Nope, that ain't nothin' I'm interested in." I wish he woulda hung up that phone and never said another word about that whole thing.

But the way that fellow talked, well, he got to pullin' on Martin's heartstrings. My husband was a tenderhearted man, and it was easy for people to get him worked up like that. He got to worryin' about the situation up there in Greenwood. He kept tellin' me he thought God was callin' him to help them people out.

I says to him, "Are you real sure about this, Martin?" He kept on a'tellin' me he had to follow the leadin' of the Holy Spirit. Said he didn't wanna be turnin' his back on God.

That man, he called Martin half a dozen times, and they kept on a'talkin' about the problems at that church.

After gettin' off the phone, Martin would be all stirred up. He'd go up there to that little room he made in the attic, and he'd be readin' the Bible and prayin' over the matter. Real serious about the whole thing, he was.

'Fore I knowed it, Martin told that man yes, that we was all gonna come up to Greenwood. So there wasn't nothin' I could do but start settin' out my plans and gettin' things in order.

Martin didn't feel too bad about leavin' our old church. There was this young fellow in the congregation by the name of Bill Donovan. He was startin' to get interested in preachin'. He was the father of the Reverend Donovan that's preachin' over there right now.

Martin, he kinda took Bill under his wing and taught him things he needed to know about preachin'. He let Bill have a turn behind the pulpit every now and then, and Bill was doin' real good. When Martin made up his mind that we was goin' up there to Greenwood, he said Bill was ready to take over the church. He said everything was workin' out accordin' to God's plan.

Edith, she didn't have much to say about the whole thing, 'cause she had her mind set on goin' off to college. But Katherine! She was so tickled about the idea of movin' up there to the city, and I couldn't help but get excited for her. I knowed she was thinkin' that goin' to a bigger school would be more fun for her. And I knowed she was thinkin' about all them new boys she was gonna be meetin'. While we was gettin' ready to move, my Katherine was right there beside me, helpin' me pack things up, just a'talkin' up a storm about how good everything was gonna be up there in Greenwood.

Rosalie, she didn't say much about movin', one way or the other. She just followed along with what her daddy wanted. That's the way she always was.

Of course, we had Ralphie to think about, too. By that time, he'd done been with us four years or so. He was a'comin' along real good, turnin' into a real nice little boy. We couldn't none of us imagine what it would be like not havin' Ralphie as part of the family. Every evenin' at supper we'd sit down at the table, me and Martin and the three girls and Ralphie, and that just seemed like the way things was s'pposed to be.

We never had no thought but to take Ralphie with us to Greenwood. We'd been a'talkin' to him about how we was gonna be movin', so he could get used to the idea. But a coupla weeks before we was set to go up there, this woman from the welfare department come to see how Ralphie was doin'. She'd been a'comin' about twice a year, and she never had no problem with how we was raisin' our little boy. She always said we was doin' right by 'im.

Well, when she come that time, we told her we was gonna be movin'. We never thought for a minute she'd have a problem with that. Well, I tell you, she just about hit the ceilin'. She blamed us for all kinds of stuff, sayin' we ain't been honest with her. She said we knowed we couldn't up and move Ralphie out of the county.

I'm tellin' ya the gospel truth. We never knowed they had a rule about that. We never knowed nothin' about that a'tall.

So that welfare woman, she said she was gonna hafta find another home for Ralphie. And then a week later, she come back and took him away. If you coulda seen that little boy's face. Every time I think about it, I cain't help but get tears in my eyes. His little face was white as a ghost. I could tell he was plumb scared to death, like he didn't know what was gonna happen to 'im. When he got in that car, we was all standin' there cryin' and sayin' we loved 'im. He looked at us like we was the only family he ever knowed. And I knowed in his heart, he was askin', "Why's they gettin' rid of me?"

After that car pulled away, I says to Martin, "Oh, Lord, what've we done?" Maybe I shoulda said that. Maybe I just laid more of a burden on my husband's heart. He was feelin' bad enough as it was.

Turns out that losin' Ralphie put a damper on everything. Every one of us lost heart about makin' the move, exceptin' maybe Katherine. Martin, he sat with his head in his hands that evenin', just a'bawlin'. He felt so bad about lettin' Ralphie go. He says to me, "Frances, I don't know nothin' about God's will no more. Surely, it ain't His idea to hurt an innocent child like this."

But it was too late to change our plans. We already give our word to that church that we was a'comin' up to Greenwood. Anyways, as mad as that welfare woman was, she wasn't never gonna give Ralphie back to us. In her mind, she made us out to be bad people.

Bein' so shook up about losin' our little boy . . . well, that got Martin off on the wrong foot with that new church. He needed a whole lotta strength to face what was comin' his way, and after losin' Ralphie, he just didn't have what it took.

Right off the bat, he walked into problems he didn't know how to handle. I tell ya, I never seen such a bunch of people fightin' with each other. Made the people down at our old church seem like a flock of little lambs.

See, just before we come up there, somebody'd up and died and left a whole bunch of money to the church. Sounded like a good thing, havin' all that extra money comin' in, but them people was a'fightin' like cats and dogs over how they was gonna use it.

Some of 'em wanted to put a new roof on the church, 'cause the old one was leakin' in spots. Others of 'em said they needed to build a fellowship hall where they could have their pitch-in dinners and such. Some of 'em wanted to buy a new piano for the church. Others of 'em said a musical instrument didn't even belong in the house of God, and they was tryin' to get rid of the one they already had.

Mind you, them people wasn't just fightin' about money. Nope, they was bringin' up all kind of problems. Some of 'em said the grounds wasn't bein' kept up like they oughta be, and they was tryin' to fire the fellow in charge of that. Some of 'em didn't like the way the Sunday-School program was bein' run, and they wanted to get rid of the woman doin' that. Some of 'em was gripin' about the songs they was singin' of a Sunday mornin', sayin' they was too old-fashioned. They was sayin' they needed to be singin' something more modern that would get more young people comin' to church. They even talked about havin' somebody play the guitar on a Sunday mornin'. Then some other people got up on their high horse and said, "We ain't havin' none of that nonsense goin' on in this church. If you start that stuff, we's up and leavin'."

Then things got real bad when some people started

accusin' one of the deacons of immoral behavior, sayin' he wasn't fit to be a leader of the church. They wanted Martin to get rid of 'im. Martin told 'em he couldn't do somethin' without knowin' every side of the story. Well, there was a whole lotta people that didn't like him sayin' that kinda thing. They said he was turnin' a blind eye to sin.

Seem like every evenin', Martin hadta go to some meetin', talkin' about one problem or 'nother. He always come back home lookin' all down in the mouth, sayin', "Frances, I just don't know what to do about all this mess."

I took to goin' to some of them meetin's with him, just to let my husband know I was standin' up for 'im. And I'd just sit there and watch them people runnin' all over the top of Martin, like they didn't even care what he had to say. I knowed right then and there that my husband was headin' into some big trouble. Somethin' in me knowed things was gonna fall apart quicker than you could shake a stick.

Martin, he was prayin' real hard. He tried preachin' sermons about people gittin' along with each other, but them people didn't like that. No, siree. They started in on him, criticizin' his sermons every which way you can think of. I always thought my husband preached real good sermons. He took his time writin' 'em up, studyin' on 'em real hard to get 'em just right. All of a sudden, they wasn't good 'nough for those people no more.

One Sunday after somebody tore into him real bad about his sermon, Martin plumb lost his nerve. That was 'bout eight, nine months after we moved up there. The next Sunday, I couldn't make him git outa bed in the mornin'. He says, "Frances, I just cain't do this no more."

So I had to think real quick 'bout what I was gonna do.

I called up one of the deacons and says to him, "My husband ain't feelin' good this mornin', and you're gonna hafta carry on without 'im."

Well, it turns out Martin wasn't up to preachin' the next Sunday, or the one after that. The church decided to put him on somethin' they called "sick leave." They had some substitute preachers come in and take his place behind the pulpit.

I started gittin' the feelin' that we was stayin' there in that nice parsonage on borrowed time. I knowed the church wasn't gonna put up with Martin not doin' his job, and that they was gonna be tellin' 'im he hadta leave. Then what was we gonna do? The thought of all that played on my mind, day and night.

I tried helpin' my husband. I tried to shore up his strength by speakin' encouragin' words to 'im. I tried every which way to git him up and movin' again. Nothin' worked. Nothin' worked a'tall. Seem like he was just done for.

After a month or so of Martin not doin' his job, the church put 'im on another leave. Only this time, they said they wouldn't pay 'im. I knowed they wasn't gonna pay him 'til he got up and dusted hisself off and got behind that pulpit again.

Well, since we wasn't gittin' no money from the church, somebody had to make sure there was food on the table. I hadta have a good talk with m'self. I says, "Frances, it's gotta be up to you to figure this out."

So I did what hadta be done. I started babysittin' for people's kids in my home. Katherine, she helped me work up a little notice for the newspaper, sayin' that I was in the business of babysittin'. I started runnin' next door to clean house for the old widow lady that lived there, and she paid me a little bitta money for that.

I tell ya, I was doin' everything I could to keep the family goin'. And, bless 'er little heart, my Katherine was workin' right alongside of me. She wasn't wantin' things to fall apart anymore than I was. Yup, my Katherine was my right-hand helper during them hard times. I'll never forget about that. To my dyin' day, I'll remember what she done for me.

Rosalie, she wasn't much help. She was too busy worryin' about her daddy. Martin would be sittin' on the couch in the livin' room, lookin' like death warmed over, and Rosalie would go over there and sit down beside 'im and lay her head on his shoulder. She'd get a look on her face like she was just about as bad off as he was. That aggravated me to no end. I wanted to tell the both of 'em to git up off that couch and do somethin'.

To tell ya the truth, I got to where I started feelin' resentful toward my husband. Here he was, sittin' around all day broodin' on his problems, while I was busy chasin' them babysittin' kids around and doin' all the cookin' and cleanin' and everything.

Things kept on a'goin' that way for a coupla months. Then one day, my husband up and went out in the garage, and I had no idea what he was fixin' to do.

I cain't talk about this no more. It's gettin' me too worked up, thinkin' back on it. My heart's a'poundin' like a jackhammer, and I cain't hardly catch my breath. Doctor says this kinda talkin' ain't good for me.

EDITH: I still feel bad about not fixing breakfast for everybody this morning. Soon after I went downstairs, Sam came in from the garage. He looked at me kind of funny and asked if I was okay. He knows it's not like me to fall down on the job like that. I told him I was fine, just tired.

I can't seem to bring myself into focus. This was what I was afraid of. Every time I have one of those dreams about James, it's like I'm living in another world for awhile, and I have trouble coming back into the here and now. I should be thinking about my husband and my houseful of company, but all I can think about is James.

That's the way it was when I was dating him. I was completely wrapped up in him. I didn't do very well those two years I was at IU. I was never a top-notch student. Not like Rosie. She's the brainy one in the family, and I don't think she's ever gotten anything less than an A. I was a B student in high school. But at IU, I barely got by, because all I could think about was being with James.

My roommate Jenny kept telling me, "Edie, you've completely lost yourself in that guy. You need to focus on yourself, too. Do you ever think about what you want out of life?"

Of course, I'd thought about what I wanted out of life. All I wanted was to be James's wife and the mother of his children. But I didn't tell Jenny that. She was into women's liberation. She would've lectured me about how I needed an identity of my own.

A couple of months after we started dating, James and I began having sex. That's when I really lost myself in him. I was raised to believe that I should wait to have sex until I was married. In my church, premarital sex was considered to be a sin. But making love with James didn't seem wrong to me. James didn't feel like it was wrong, either. We felt like we belonged to each other, just as much as if we were legally married.

This might sound strange to you, but all those months James and I were being intimate with each other, we were going to church together. Because he was a Mennonite, I wanted to be one, too. James had a car on campus, so every Sunday morning, we drove over to that little Mennonite Church in Bean Blossom.

The people in that church thought so highly of us. They never saw one of us without the other, and they were always telling us what a nice couple we were. It felt like in the eyes of the church and in the eyes of God, we were pretty much a married couple.

After the first time we made love, James wrote me a letter. The next morning, he slid it under the door of my room. I still have that letter. Of course, Sam doesn't know about it. I feel guilty about keeping it all these years, but I just can't bring myself to throw it away. Whenever I go through a rough time, I get it out and read it.

But I don't even have to get it out to remember what's in it, because I've memorized it. It says, *Dear Edie May, When you gave yourself to me last night, it was the most wonderful thing that ever happened to me. Our love amazes me. I wish you knew what a sweet and beautiful person you are. You're special, Edie May. I know you don't believe that now, but someday, I hope you'll come to know the truth about yourself. It would be a shame if you went through your whole life believing you are anything less than beautiful. I love you, love you, love you, and I can't wait to be with you again. Yours forever, James.*

I really can't start thinking about that letter now, or I'll never get my mind back to where it ought to be.

Sam knows nothing about James. Sam believes he's the first and only man I've ever slept with. He thought naive little Edith Rafferty was a virgin when he married her. I feel terrible about letting him believe that lie all these years.

KATHY: Bryce called me three times this morning. He keeps telling me that he's not feeling well. He wants me to come home so we can talk. I told him he needs to go out and do something to lift his spirits. Or at least start some work project that will focus his mind in a positive direction.

"You've got to listen to me, Kathy," he kept saying.

I finally got tired of hearing his whining. "Sweetie," I said, "you know I love you. But I'm not going to reinforce your negativity by listening to it. Please don't call me any more today." And then I shut my phone off.

I'm determined to have a good time this weekend. Who knows when I'll have the opportunity to be with my mother and sisters again?

Edie seems a little distracted, like she has something on her mind. She's more disorganized than she usually is. She wasn't able to get any breakfast around, and we all had to fend for ourselves. I know she felt bad about that. Maybe I should take charge of lunch.

Last night, my mom said she wanted to help with lunch today. She's not able to do much in the kitchen anymore, but I know it would do her good to be a part of things. I'm going to run over to her trailer in a couple of minutes. She used to make the most scrumptious biscuits. I'll help her whip up a batch right now. She'll love that. I'm sure Edie has some strawberries from the garden in her freezer. We'll make strawberry shortcake for dessert. Everybody will enjoy that.

ROSALIE: Well, I finally did it. When Kathy announced that she was going over to the trailer, I jumped up and said, "I'll go with you." I knew that could be my chance to get in my duty visit with Mom, without having to spend any time alone with her.

I gave Mom a hug, although I didn't like doing that. When I put my arms around her, I sensed all her brewing resentment, all her festering bitterness. She felt toxic to me. I wanted to step outside the trailer, to brush all that poison off of me and let the breeze carry it away.

But at least I didn't have to talk to her very much, as Kathy got her caught up in baking biscuits. The two of them were thick as thieves. It seemed as if neither one of them even remembered that I was there. So it turned out that I played my cards exactly right.

Kathy is larger than life. She's like a magnet, drawing everyone to her. She's been that way since she was a little girl, and will be that way until her dying day. Everywhere she goes, she lights up the room, and is instantly the center of attention.

Kathy takes charge of every situation. She dominates every conversation, and fills every awkward silence. She's always on stage. She can make up a dramatic story about any random five minutes of her life.

Even though I'm the one with advanced degrees and a professional career, I go unnoticed when Kathy is around. I do have a life, you know. I have one of the most interesting careers a person could have. If I ever had the chance to take center stage at a family gathering, I could entertain my mother and sisters with all kinds of stories about my work.

And I have hobbies. I've done oil painting. I've taken dance lessons. I've written poetry, and I even had one piece published in *The New Yorker*. But my mother and Kathy aren't interested in any of my accomplishments.

Sometimes, being around Kathy is an advantage, as I can hunker down and hide in her shadow. It's easy to be invisible around her, and that's a good way to avoid being dissected by my mother's laser gaze.

But the down side is that being around Kathy makes me feel like nothing.

It always amazes me how close my mother and Kathy are. They seem like they're from opposite worlds, the old hillbilly woman and the big city girl with her upscale lifestyle. But they truly love each other.

Kathy always likes to pretend she's something she's not. But as I watched the two of them working on the biscuits, I could tell she wasn't just pretending to love Mom. Her feelings for Mom are genuine.

And Mom is over the moon about Kathy. Edie waits on Mom hand and foot, and I know Mom appreciates that, but she never showers Edie with affection the way she does Kathy. More often than not, she's barking orders at her.

I wish I could love my mother. I wish I could be loved by her. I wish I knew how that felt.

SATURDAY AFTERNOON

ROSALIE: Well, my mother did it again! At lunch, she managed to ruin everybody's good time. When it comes to her speech, she has no filter, no edit button.

Poor Katrina is having such a rough time with her baby. Lilly is only four months old, and it seems as if the change in her routine has upset her. She's been crying nonstop. I can tell how exhausted Katrina is.

Right before lunch, she managed to get Lilly to sleep. But just as soon as we all sat down at the table, Lilly woke up and started crying again. Katrina jumped up to get her, and then brought her back to the table. She was trying to eat her lunch while holding Lilly in one arm, bouncing her to keep her quiet.

As if Katrina wasn't having a hard enough time, Mom started in on her. "Katrina, you're spoilin' that baby, runnin' to pick her up every time she starts a'bawlin'. You keep that up, and someday, you're gonna be real sorry. That's what parents do in this day and age, let their young'uns run the show. If these modern parents don't start teachin' their kids some manners, purty soon we're gonna have a world run by heathens."

I could tell Katrina was on the verge of tears. I felt so sorry for her. Kathy jumped in and said, "Mom, Katrina's a good mother to Lilly."

Mom didn't seem to hear her, and she kept on going, bragging about her own parenting, as if she did everything perfectly. "I made sure to keep a firm hand on my own girls. Just ask 'em. I never let 'em call the shots."

And I thought, *Not a firm hand. An abusive hand.*

What she called good parenting involved swatting us girls on our bottoms, yanking our ears, jerking us around by our arms, slapping our faces. And worse. I got more of that kind of treatment than my sisters did. I've never understood why.

Hearing her talk like that made me so angry that I couldn't stand to be at the table any longer. "Let me take Lilly," I said to Katrina, "so you can eat your lunch." So Katrina handed me the baby, and I went out to the living room and walked around with her until she quieted down.

You'd think that Mom would've learned by now to keep her mouth shut. But, no, she thinks the whole world needs to hear her opinions on everything.

You'd think she would've learned years ago that thoughtless speech can have dire consequences. Her damn mouth nearly caused my father's death. She doesn't seem to connect with that idea at all. As far as she's concerned, none of what happened had anything to do with her.

What I'm about to tell you isn't easy. Only a few people who are very close to me know about it. Years ago, I had to go through a lot of psychotherapy in order to deal with it. Nobody can work through such a life-altering event without some help.

Neither one of my sisters knows what happened. My mom doesn't want them to know. She made it clear to me that I was to tell no one. She said what happened was nobody else's business. Hearing about it would devastate Edie. There's no point in causing her that kind of pain. And if I tried telling Kathy, she wouldn't believe me.

It happened on a Saturday morning, about nine or ten months after we moved to Greenwood. Edie was away at college. Kathy wasn't home. She'd gone to the high school for cheerleading practice.

Emotionally, my father wasn't in good shape. The job with the new church in Greenwood wasn't going well for him. I didn't understand all the problems he was facing, as I was only in the eighth grade. But I could see how discouraged he was. Looking back, I understand that he was clinically depressed, and that his symptoms were becoming increasingly severe. He should've been in treatment, but I guess nobody recognized that fact.

I was worried about him, even if I didn't understand what was going on. He seemed so sad. Incurably sad. Nothing would cheer him up. I'd come home from school saying, "Guess what happened today, Dad." Then I'd launch into a funny story, hoping he would laugh. But he'd just stare at me with vacant eyes. I'd show him the "A" I'd gotten on a test, but that didn't make him smile the way it did when we'd lived in Brown County.

His sadness made me sad. I wanted to help, but I had no idea what to do. I know that one of the reasons I went into the field of psychology was to understand my father.

It seemed to me that the more depressed my father became, the more my mother hounded him. And the more she hounded him, the more depressed he became. That Saturday morning, she started in on him for the umpteenth time, berating him for not doing his job. For not being a man. For not taking care of his family.

She stood over him as he sat slumped on the sofa, her hands on her hips, her eyes blazing with anger. It seemed as if she was trying to get a rise out of him. As if she wanted him to yell back at her.

From time to time, she'd stop her tirade for a second or two, waiting for him to say something. When he didn't, she'd start in again, more viciously than before. The things she said got uglier and uglier. She pretty much let him know that he was a complete failure as a husband and as a human being.

I could see that what she was saying was devastating to him. I grabbed her arm and said, "Stop it, Mom. Leave him alone." She swatted me away and kept on going.

My dad sat there, his face slack and pale, his eyes vacant. It was the face of total despair. The father I'd always admired and looked up to was gone. What was left was an empty shell.

All of a sudden, he got up off the sofa and went out to the garage. My mom stood back and let him go. She had a smirk on her face, as if she'd gotten satisfaction out of finally getting him up and moving.

But an alarm went off inside of me. Something told me my father was heading for danger. I ran out into the garage after him, even though my mother was yelling, "Rosalie, you get back in here!"

And I saw my father standing there in the garage, holding a 12-gage shotgun. I watched him tilt the barrel of the gun toward his open mouth, and then close his eyes.

That shotgun had belonged to my grandfather. He'd done a lot of hunting in his day. When Grandpa passed it on to my dad, he stashed it away somewhere, and I never saw it again. He never used it himself, as he never went hunting. He was too softhearted to shoot anything. I'd had no idea that he'd even brought the gun to Greenwood.

When I saw my dad putting the gun to his mouth, my

adrenalin kicked in. I flew at him and knocked the gun out of his hand. It went off, and a pattern of birdshot hit the garage wall. I wonder if it's still visible there, a reminder to everyone that a former pastor living in that parsonage became so depressed that he tried to end his life.

When Mom heard the gunshot, she was out in that garage in a split second. "What on earth is goin' on out here?" she barked.

My dad had collapsed on the garage floor, and was sitting there slumped over. I said, "Dad tried to kill himself."

"What do you mean?" she asked.

"He had the gun," I told her, "and he tried to shoot himself. I stopped him."

Mom didn't say anything more. She pulled Dad to his feet and led him into the house and back to the sofa. He sat there with his eyes glazed over. It looked as if his mind was completely gone.

"Keep an eye on him," she snapped at me. "Don't let him move."

I stood in front of my dad, staring at him, frozen with shock and fear. I could not bring myself to sit down beside him and lay my head on his shoulder, the way I'd always done before. This strange, haunted man was no longer my father.

My mom got on the phone and called the police. Pretty soon, an officer came, and then an ambulance. Before I knew it, they'd taken my father away.

After everyone had gone, my mom gave me a withering look, as if I was the one who'd caused all the trouble. "Rosalie, don't you ever speak a word of this to anybody," she warned me. "This ain't nobody's business but ours. Do you hear me? Now you just put all of this nonsense out of your head."

I stood there trembling from head to toe. It felt as if every molecule of every cell in my body was quaking from the trauma I'd just been through. I was shaking so violently that my teeth were chattering. My legs felt like jelly. I leaned against the wall to hold myself up, but I didn't have the strength to stand. So I slid down the wall, collapsing on the floor.

My mom went out to the garage, muttering something under her breath. She came back into the house a moment later, carrying the shotgun and a box of shells, a disgusted look on her face. She took the gun and the shells into her bedroom. I could hear her moving things around as she stashed the gun in her closet. It seemed that when she put the gun away, she put the whole incident behind her. As if it was all over and done with.

When Kathy came home, Mom said to her, "Your daddy had a mental breakdown, and they took him off to the hospital."

Mom glanced over at me, still huddled on the floor. I'd been sitting there in a daze, unable to move, for more than an hour. She gave me a look that said, "You keep your mouth shut!"

Kathy looked shocked. "What do you mean?" she asked.

"Just what I said," my mom snapped. "We're on our own now. It's up to us to keep carryin' on."

So that's the expert parenting my mom was bragging about to Katrina. Your child has been through the biggest trauma of her entire life, and you do nothing to help. You tell her to shut up and not talk about it.

Even though I know Mom resents me, I still wonder why she never thanked me for my quick action. Ten seconds later, that birdshot would've lodged in my father's brain instead of in the garage wall. I saved her husband from committing suicide. I spared her the guilt of knowing that she played a role in her husband's death. Doesn't she owe me something for that?

Ever since the day of my father's suicide attempt, I've battled my own depression. Thankfully, it's never been as severe as his. I've had therapy, and I've taken antidepressant medication at times when I've needed it. So I manage. I'm capable of handling my responsibilities. I live a good life.

Still, there are times when I question my will to live. Sometimes, going through all the ups and downs of life just doesn't seem worth it. When I saw my father try to end his life, something broke inside of me. I'd been so close to him. I'd counted on him for guidance. When he decided his life wasn't worth living, it affected me profoundly.

Well, I stayed out in the living room, walking Lilly around until she stopped crying. I was so glad for the excuse to get a break from Mom. When Lilly finally fell asleep, I didn't put her down. Cuddling her warm little body helped me calm down a bit.

Then Mom called from the kitchen, "Rosalie, you better get in here and get some of this strawberry shortcake before it's all gone." She acted as if that strawberry shortcake was the only thing that mattered. As if all that ugly stuff she'd said to Katrina was of no consequence.

I almost said, "I don't want any." Then I remembered that Marty would want strawberry shortcake, and that I needed to get back in there to help him.

But when I walked back into the kitchen, I saw that Katrina was helping her cousin with his dessert. I could tell Marty was enjoying her attention. That touched me deeply. It looks as if Katrina and Marty are forming a friendship this weekend.

EDITH: I guess lunch went okay. Since Kathy doesn't eat meat, I made a vegetable soup with potatoes and carrots and peas from my garden. I hope that was enough for everybody. Of course, we had the strawberry shortcake that Mom and Kathy made.

Katrina was having such a hard time with her baby. Mom said some things to her that weren't very nice, and afterwards, conversation at the table seemed a little awkward. I try to talk to Mom about the way she speaks to people, but she doesn't pay any attention to what I say. Someone once told me that when people get older, they tend to say things they wouldn't have said when they were younger. Maybe that's what's been going on with Mom.

But really, she's always been one to give people a piece of her mind.

I was surprised that Kathy wasn't helping out with her grandchild. She was too busy helping Mom. I suppose that's understandable. Kathy has so little time with Mom. But Rosie jumped in and helped Katrina. That was nice of her.

I felt bad that I didn't offer to help. Katrina is a guest in my home, and it's my job to make her feel comfortable.

But today isn't one of those days when I can manage taking care of an infant. Sometimes, being around a baby triggers feelings that I can't handle. When my oldest child Brian was born, painful memories came flooding back to me. I loved my baby, and I took good care of him. But the memories were too difficult to deal with. I'd have spells when I couldn't stop crying.

My doctor told Sam I was suffering from post-partum depression. I went along with that idea, even though in my heart I knew it wasn't quite true. But I was scared to tell anybody what was really going on. Sam would've been devastated. He would've thought I'd been lying to him. And my mother would've blown up and said terrible things to me.

I wish now that I would've had the courage to confide in Rosie and Kathy. I should've trusted my sisters to be there for me, instead of carrying those memories all alone.

During the two years I was at college, Kathy tried to be there for me. She was the only one in the family who wrote me letters. At first, they were all about what she was doing at her new school. She'd go on and on about some cute boy she had a crush on. She was a cheerleader back then, really popular. Way more popular than I'd ever been.

I hardly ever wrote Kathy back. I should've taken the time to do that. I was just being selfish.

Greenwood isn't that far from Bloomington. You'd think I would've gone home a couple of times a month. Even thought I didn't have a car, I could've called one of my parents and said, "Come and get me."

But I didn't. That parsonage in Greenwood didn't feel like home to me. It would've been like spending the weekend at some stranger's house. I never felt comfortable there. Family life as I knew it ended when my parents and sisters moved away from our old home in Brown County.

But mostly, I didn't go home because I didn't want to be away from James. It wasn't easy for him to go home, because his family lived several hundred miles away. I wasn't about to go spend the weekend with my family and leave him alone on campus.

James did go home for Christmas that first year, and so did I. It was so hard to say goodbye to him.

While I was there in Greenwood, I sensed that things weren't going well. Mom and Dad both seemed to be under a lot of stress. Dad was worried about making sure the Christmas program at the church went okay. It was like he was afraid he'd be in trouble if he didn't do a good job. So we didn't have much family time together.

And all I could think about was James. I was sleeping in Rosie's room upstairs, and I spent most of my Christmas vacation up there, moping. I kept trying to imagine what my boyfriend was doing with his family up there in Middlebury. I kept thinking that I belonged there with him. Instead of enjoying time with my family, I was counting the days until James and I could be together again.

A few weeks after I went back to school, Kathy wrote me another letter. This time, it wasn't her usually happy-go-lucky type of thing. It was sad. She said, *I thought you should know that Dad has been put on a leave of absence from his job at the church. He says he can't preach anymore. Mom and I are both upset with him. We're afraid that if he doesn't hurry up and start doing his job, the church will fire him. Then what would happen to us?*

She ended that last sentence with three big question marks. That should've told me how scared she was. I should've gotten on the phone and called home right away, to see what was happening. To see if I could help.

But I didn't. I buried my head in the sand. I put Kathy's letter away and tried not to think about it. I didn't want anything to mess up the beautiful little world I lived in with James.

Two months later, Kathy sent me some devastating news. *Dad had a nervous breakdown,* she wrote. *He's in a mental hospital. But the rest of us are doing okay. Really, it's easier not to have him around.*

Well, that got my attention. I'd never known anyone who'd been put in a mental hospital. I didn't fully understand what a nervous breakdown was, but it sounded pretty scary. So I called home to see what was going on.

My mother answered the phone. When I asked her about Dad, she said, "It'll be okay, Edith. Don't worry about it. You just keep your mind on your studying."

She sounded kind of impatient, like I'd interrupted her in the middle of something and she didn't have time to talk. So I tried to do like she said and put everything out of my mind. I told myself that if they needed my help, Mom or Kathy would get in touch with me.

A few weeks after that, Kathy sent me another letter, telling me that Rosie had gone to stay with our Aunt Della in Brown County. *I don't know exactly what happened,* she wrote. *Rosie and Mom hadn't been getting along very well. Rosie went to school and told one of her teachers a bunch of garbage about Mom, and made trouble for her. I'm glad that she's gone. Mom doesn't have to put up with her crap anymore, so things are more peaceful around here. Now it's just Mom and me, and we're doing fine.*

I tried to do the right thing. I called home. Actually, I called two or three times. But no one answered the phone.

I've never known what happened between Mom and Rosie. No one wants to tell me. Once when I visited Rosie at Aunt Della's house, I asked her why she was living there. She started telling me something about Mom beating the crap out of her. Honestly, I didn't believe her. I'd never known Mom to do something like that. And I knew Rosie had a habit of exaggerating.

I didn't argue with her. I just didn't say anything back to her, and she stopped talking. I feel bad about that now. Maybe I should've taken her more seriously.

About a year ago, I asked Mom why Rosie went to live with Aunt Della. Mom looked away from me and refused to answer.

"Why won't anyone tell me about that?" I asked her.

Finally, she said, "Edith, that was a long time ago. There ain't no point in goin' back over that business again."

Once, I asked Kathy about it. She tossed her head and said, "I don't waste my time dwelling on the past. I've put all of that out of my mind."

I hate to ask Rosie about it again, because I know that was a painful time for her. So I've decided to let it go. I don't need to be sticking my nose into other people's business.

When all those problems were going on in my family, I talked to James about it. He was so kind. "Do you want me to drive you home to visit them?" he asked. He could've done that, because he had a car.

But I said no, even though something inside of me kept telling me I should go home for a visit. I was the oldest daughter. I should've been helping out. But my family wasn't asking me to, and I really didn't want to. All I wanted was to stay wrapped up inside that cozy little bubble I shared with James.

I know that's why I struggle with so much guilt now. Because I wasn't there for my family when they needed me. It seems like I'll never be able to do enough to make up for what I didn't do back then.

After school was out that year, Mom and Kathy moved back down to Brown County, back into our old house. Dad was still in the hospital, and Rosie was still with Aunt Della.

I went home for a few weeks that summer. I helped Mom and Kathy pack up the things in the parsonage and haul everything back down to our old house. My parents hadn't moved much furniture up to Greenwood, so it was mostly clothing and bedding and dishes that we had to move. We loaded everything into my parents' old car. It took three trips between Greenwood and Brown County to get everything moved.

That car was on the verge of breaking down. It kept stalling at intersections. Mom was at her wit's end. She started crying, and then Kathy started crying. I didn't know what to do for them. I felt so sorry for them.

Mom had told me she'd take me to see Dad in the hospital. But when it came down to it, she said, "I'm just too tuckered out, Edith. I don't have it in me to take you there right now." Secretly, I was relieved. I didn't know what state of mind Dad would be in, and I didn't really want to find out.

James and I had both signed up for summer classes at the university. That was a life-saver for me. I couldn't wait to get away from family problems and back to the campus to be with James again.

When I went home for Christmas during my sophomore year, it was to Brown County, not to Greenwood. Dad was out of the hospital by then. I'd called home to see if somebody could come and pick me up, but my mom said, "Sorry, Edith, I just can't make it. You'll have to find another way."

So James drove me home before he went up to Middlebury. He asked if he could come in and meet my family, but I said, "No, not right now." I didn't know how things would be. James seemed to understand that, and he didn't push the point.

And I ended up being so glad that I hadn't invited him in. My dad was like a pale, skinny ghost wandering around the house. He wasn't old. He was still in his forties. But he seemed like an old man who'd lost his mind and didn't know how to take care of himself anymore. It was shocking to see him like that. Horrible. He wasn't the father I'd known all my life. All I wanted to do was run away so that I didn't have to look at him in that condition.

My mom was constantly telling my dad what to do. She gave him orders all day long. Like, "Martin, get up and take a walk around the yard. You've been sittin' on that couch all mornin'. The hospital said you should be gettin' some exercise." When he started out the door, she said, "For heaven's sake, Martin, you've gotta put on your coat. It's cold outside."

Once, it was, "Martin, you spilled soup down the front of your shirt. Go put on a clean one."

And another time, "Martin, go to the bathroom and wash your face and comb your hair. You look a mess."

"Should I shave?" he mumbled.

"No," she snapped. "I'll help you with that later. Don't think you're gonna find your razor in that bathroom. I hid it. The hospital told me to."

One day, I heard her say, "Martin, go take this trash out to the burn barrel."

"Where are the matches?" he asked.

"I'm not lettin' you handle any matches," she scolded. "Just take it out. I'll burn it later."

I could tell how stressed my mom was. She was really cranky, and she barely talked to me. She didn't seem to care whether or not I was there. It wasn't like she was upset with me. She was just wrapped up in her problems. Both of my parents seemed shell-shocked. Sort of dazed, not really there.

And Kathy was depressed. I'd never seen her like that before. She wasn't singing or dancing around the house like she usually did. Most of the time, she was upstairs in her room. She didn't talk to me. She hadn't written me any letters since she and Mom had moved back down to Brown County. That should've told me things weren't going well.

I wondered about Rosie, but Kathy wouldn't tell me anything about her. All Mom said was, "It's best that she stays with her Aunt Della right now."

And of course, our little Ralphie wasn't there. The house didn't seem the same without him.

No, it wasn't the time to introduce my family to the young man I loved. So when James came to pick me up at the end of Christmas break, I was standing on the porch with my suitcase, waiting for him. "Get me out of here, James," I said when he drove up. "Everybody's falling apart. If I stay here, I'll fall apart, too."

All I could think to do was to run away from that house with all its problems. My future was with James. He was my family now.

James and I hadn't been stupid when we started having sex. We'd used protection. Almost every time. Well, at least ninety-five percent of the time. I guess that five percent is where we got caught. And it happened to us at the worst possible time.

In February, I realized that I'd missed two periods. I tried to convince myself that it was no big deal. I'd missed periods before. But when I told James about it, he went straight to the drugstore and bought me a pregnancy test. I didn't want to take it.

"We need to know the truth, Edie May," he kept saying. "We'll face it together."

So I took the test. When it came out positive, I screamed and almost fell to the floor. Never in my wildest dreams had I imagined being pregnant before getting married. James caught me and held me and told me everything was going to be okay.

The next month was really scary for me. I never would've been able to handle the stress, if it hadn't for James. He was wonderful. The day after we did the pregnancy test, he wrote me another letter. *I hope you know, Edie May*, it said, *that I'll stick with you all the way. We'll figure out what to do, and we'll do it together.*

He and I spent hours and hours talking, making plans for our future. Of course, it was James who took charge. "Both of us need to get focused and finish out this semester," he said. "That only makes sense. Then we'll get married over the summer."

"Are your parents going to be mad at you?" I asked.

"I'm not going to lie to you, Edie May," he said. "They'll be disappointed in me for getting a girl pregnant out of wedlock. Because of what our church teaches, it'll be really hard for them. But they'll get over it. They're good people, and they'll love you and accept you as part of our family. And they'll be wonderful grandparents to our child."

He talked about us moving up to Middlebury. He said he'd go back into farming with his father.

"What about finishing school?" I asked him. "You said you weren't sure about farming."

"If you remember," he said, "I told you that farming was a good life. The circumstances we're in right now have made up my mind for me. I'm okay with this decision."

The more we talked about our future, the more relaxed I felt. Actually, I started getting excited. Now, my life was linked with James's life forever. The deal was sealed.

James had shown me pictures of his family. He had eight brothers and sisters. The women in the family had long hair and wore plain clothing. "What will your mother and sisters think about how I look?" I asked. "Should I let my hair grow long? Should I start wearing dresses like theirs?"

"No," he said. "They won't expect you to do that. They'll accept you the way you are."

I was glad I didn't need to worry about how I was going to fit in. But if James would've asked me to, I would've completely changed my appearance to look like a Mennonite woman. I would've been more than happy to do that for him.

But whenever I'd start to get excited about our future, I'd remember that I was going to have to tell my parents about my pregnancy. The thought of that would make me shake all over, and I'd get sick to my stomach.

"I'll drive you over there so we can tell them together," James offered.

But I stalled for as long as I could. I was terrified about what my mother would say. I pictured her tearing into James, cussing him out, chasing him out of the house and telling him never to come back. She was already dealing with so many family problems, and I was pretty sure that hearing about my pregnancy would push her over the edge.

"Edie May, you're going to have to face this sooner or later," James would scold me. He finally got me to agree to a plan of going home the last weekend in March.

But that Friday morning, I woke up with terrible cramps. Then I realized that my pajamas were soaked with blood. I screamed, and woke up my roommate.

"What's wrong, Edie?" she asked. She jumped out of bed and came over to me. When she saw all the blood, she said, "Are you having your period?"

I shook my head. Then I choked out, "I'm pregnant."

"Oh my God!" she exclaimed. "You're having a miscarriage. Let me get James."

She ran down to the phone and called the dorm where James was staying. Ten minutes later, he was there at my side. He and Jenny took me to the campus health center.

No one has ever known about that miscarriage except for James and Jenny and the health center nurse.

I lay there in the bed at the health center, crying like I'd never cried before. James tried to comfort me and hold my hand, but I wouldn't let him touch me. He wanted to take me to the hospital. I refused to go, because I knew my parents would get a bill, and then the whole story would have to come out.

All of a sudden, I started looking at everything differently. I knew for certain that I'd been stricken down by God for having pre-marital sex with my boyfriend. And I felt wave after wave of unbearable guilt for running out on my family when they were having problems. While they'd all been struggling, I'd been caught up in doing sinful things with James, acting like I didn't care about my parents' rules. Acting like I didn't care anything about any of them.

Lying there in that bed, I felt like my family's problems were all my fault. I was one hundred percent to blame. I was the oldest daughter. I should've been paying attention when they were planning their move to Greenwood. But, no, my mind had been set on going to college. I should've been helping them make decisions. I should've told them to slow things down and think everything through.

When I saw how selfish I'd been, I could hardly stand it. It seemed like everything wrong in the entire world was my fault, and that I was the worst person who'd ever lived. I knew I deserved this terrible thing that had happened to me. I hated myself. I wanted to die.

And for the first time ever, I felt angry with James. I hated him, too. When I looked at him, he seemed like a stranger to me, and I wondered why I'd ever had anything to do with him.

I stayed in the health center for the rest of the day. Then I spent the rest of the weekend in bed in my dorm room. James was with me as much as he could be, even though I didn't want him there. I barely spoke to him.

I remember him sitting by my bed, tears running down his face. He'd reach for my hand, but I'd snatch it away from him. Then he'd get up and pace around my room, like he didn't know what to do. He never ran out on me. Any time he had to leave, he'd tell me he'd be back as soon as he could.

When I look back on that day, I feel so ashamed of myself. James had been sad, too. It was his baby that had died. But I never thought about his feelings. I never tried to comfort him.

On Sunday, James brought me another letter. He handed it to me, and then sat on the edge of my bed while I read it. *Edie May,* he'd written, *losing our baby tears me up inside, but it doesn't change how I feel about you. I still love you, and I still want to marry you. We can move on from here. Please don't pull away from me because of this.*

But I did pull away from James. I couldn't get past the guilt and the self-hatred. I started missing classes, even though James tried his best to get me to go. "I'm sad, too," he said, "but we both need to keep trying."

After my body got back to normal, James wanted to make love to bring us close together again. But I refused. I was cold and distant with him. I barely even let him kiss me.

"You don't love me anymore, do you, Edie May?" he'd say. And I wouldn't say anything back to him.

At the end of the term, I told James I wanted him to take me home. The way I said it sounded rude, and he looked worried. "Are you planning on coming back in the fall?" he asked.

"No," I said. "I'm never coming back here."

He tried to talk me out of that idea. "Don't throw everything away, Edie May," he said. "In a couple of months, you'll feel better."

But I was stubborn. When James tried to encourage me, I wouldn't listen. So he gave up and drove me to my parents' house. We barely talked on the way over, and when we got there, he didn't even ask to go inside to meet my family.

"I'm so worried about you, Edie May," he said. "I'm not sure being around your family is going to be a good thing for you. A few months ago, you begged me to take you away from here."

"You have no right to talk that way about my family," I snapped at him. I was aware of the fact that I was being unreasonable, but I couldn't stop myself.

He sighed, and I knew he was exasperated with me. "I can tell you don't want me around anymore," he said. "So I'm not going to bother you. I'll let you call me when you're ready to talk again." Then he gave me a piece of paper with his parents' phone number on it.

"Call me," he pleaded as I got out of the car. "Promise you'll call me, Edie May."

But I never did call him. I didn't realize for a long time that I'd turned my selfishness in a different direction, toward the man who'd been nothing but kind and loving to me. No one in my life has ever loved me the way James loved me. And I treated him terribly. I can't stop hating myself for that. I'd give anything for one more chance to speak to him, to tell him how sorry I am.

For the next year, I put all of my attention on helping my parents, trying to make up for how I'd neglected them. When Kathy left for New York City, I knew it was my job to stay home and look after Mom and Dad. I had no social life. I never went anywhere, even though my mom pushed me to get out of the house.

"For heaven's sake, Edith," she said to me. "You act like an old woman. You need to get out there and make a life for yourself."

I finally got a part-time job as a cashier at the IGA in Nashville. That's how I met Sam, when he came in to buy groceries. I knew who he was from high school. He'd graduated two years ahead of me.

He had to ask me out three times before I worked up the nerve to say yes. We started dating. I'm not sure I knew what I was doing when I agreed to marry him. I don't think I was in love with him. I guess I didn't know what else to do with my life.

But looking back, I'd say I made a pretty good decision. Things have worked out well between us. We've had a good life. We raised a good family. We have wonderful children.

Whenever people ask me how many children I have, I say, "Three." But in my mind, I have four. I always count the baby that James and I lost.

Sometimes, I daydream about the child I never got to know. I wonder whether it was a boy or a girl. What color of eyes it would've had. Whether it would've been small and thin like me, or stocky like James.

It's not just about the baby I lost. It's about the life I threw away, the life I could've shared with James. Hundreds of times, I've ask myself what would've happened if I'd picked up the phone and tried to work things out with him. I might be living on a farm in Middlebury right now.

I'm obsessed with that little town. I look Middlebury up on the internet and read about its history, its industry, the restaurants, the tourist attractions. Whenever I'm helping out in Margaret Brown's studio in Nashville, I imagine that I'm working in a little tourist shop in Middlebury. Someday, I hope I have a chance to visit that town.

After lunch, I felt so overwhelmed that I just wanted to be alone. Mom was tired, so Kathy took her over to the trailer. Lilly was finally sleeping, and Katrina lay down with her. Rosie said Marty needed a nap, and I think she took one, too.

So I got my time alone while I was cleaning up the lunch dishes. Thank goodness for that, because I just couldn't hold back the tears anymore.

SAMUEL CLEMENS: After lunch, I went out to the backyard to stack the wood I'd cut for the fireplace this winter. It was a good way to blow off steam. Conversation at the table had gotten me a little hot under the collar.

When I came back into the house, Edie was alone in the kitchen, doing the dishes. "Where is everybody?" I asked her.

"Kathy's at the trailer with Mom," she said. "Everyone else is sleeping."

Hearing that pissed me off. Everybody had run out on her, leaving her with all the mess to clean up. Edie's entire family takes advantage of her. Her sisters pile in on her, expecting her to take care of them all weekend. And every day of the week, she has her mother to take care of. My mother-in-law's a mean old witch. She runs my wife ragged. I tell Edie she doesn't have to jump every time her mom snaps her fingers, but she does it anyway.

Edie lets all of them run over her. I can't figure out why. She makes it way too easy for people to take advantage of her. I could run over her, too, if I wanted to. But I try not to be that kind of guy.

Edith Clemens is a wonderful woman. I'm a lucky man to have a wife like her. But I've never had Edie's full attention, and that bothers me. She's always running around doing something for somebody. Even when we do spend time together, it's like, mentally, she's not there. It's like she's holding something back. Sometimes, I think I've never really known the woman I've been married to for thirty-seven years.

I felt sorry for her, standing there at the kitchen sink looking so sad and lonely. So I picked up a dish towel and started drying the dishes she was washing. She looked at me and smiled. I could tell she'd been crying.

"What's wrong, honey?" I asked her.

"Nothing," she said. "I'm just tired."

Edie is always tired.

KATHERINE: After lunch, I took Mom back to the trailer so she could lie down. At her age, the commotion of a family gathering exhausts her.

While she slept, I browsed through her old family photo album. I always enjoy looking at the pictures of Mom when she was a young woman, and pictures of us three girls when we were little.

I thought about the rough life Mom's had, and how she's come through it all undefeated. At eighty-four, she still has a good mind and a strong spirit. I'm proud of her.

It wasn't an easy life for us girls, either. But I'm convinced that the challenges of my childhood have made me a stronger person. My mom didn't baby me, not at all. She expected a lot out of me.

One Saturday afternoon when I was twelve, Mom was busy canning green beans from the garden. All of a sudden, she said, "Katherine, I plumb forgot about something. There's going to be a pitch-in dinner at church tomorrow, and I don't have anything ready for it. I have my hands full with these green beans, so I'm going to have to count on you to come up with something to take. And don't you go making me ashamed by fixing some sorry mess that nobody will eat."

Then she turned her attention back to her canning, as if she was fully confident that I could do the job. I was scared, of course. But I've never been one to back down from a challenge. I sat down with Mom's cookbook and found a recipe for a chocolate sheet cake. When I checked the cupboards, I saw that we didn't have all the ingredients I needed, so I made a few substitutions. But when that cake came out of the oven, I thought it looked pretty good.

At the potluck dinner the next day, I kept my eye on the cake, wondering how people would like it. By the end of the meal, every last piece was gone. I was so proud of myself. That was the day I fully realized I could accomplish anything I set my mind on doing.

When Mom got up from her nap, I asked her what she wanted to do for the rest of the afternoon. She said, "Why don't we bring everybody over here for a game of Scrabble?"

Even though Mom isn't an educated woman, she's surprisingly good at Scrabble. That's the only game she ever plays. She's never played cards, because of her religious convictions.

So I went back to Edie's house. "Come on," I called to everyone. "Let's go over to the trailer. Mom wants to play Scrabble."

I don't know how willingly they all came, but they did. Rosie even wheeled Marty over here, and Sam helped her carry him up the steps.

But honestly, after that game, I'm starting to think that my plan for a happy weekend with my family is turning out to be a failure. No, I'm not going to indulge in that thought. I refuse to put that kind of negativity out into the universe. Let's just say the reunion isn't what I'd hoped it would be.

Edie seems so distracted. I don't know what's bothering her. Maybe it's just the stress of having houseguests. Sam is the same as he always is, sullen and taciturn.

And Rosie is so quiet and withdrawn. I don't understand it. Here she is, a professional woman who makes a living by communicating with others. She has to talk with the families of her patients at the hospital. She has to collaborate with the other professionals she works with. But she doesn't have two words to say to me. I try to start conversations with her. I share something from my life and wait for her to respond in kind. But she doesn't, and the conversation falls flat.

Really, the only people who talked during the game were Mom and me. Sometimes, this family exhausts me. I'd been looking forward to this weekend so much. But I can't make good times happen all on my own. I need some cooperation from somebody!

KATRINA: This afternoon I was up at my grandma's trailer, watching my mom and my aunts play Scrabble with Grandma. I would've enjoyed playing, but I had to take care of Lilly.

All of a sudden, my cell phone rang. I expected it to be my husband Roscoe, calling to check on Lilly and me. I stepped out of the trailer so I could talk to him in private.

Would you believe it was my stepdad Bryce? He never calls me.

"Your Mom won't talk to me," he said. "She turned her phone off."

"Why did she do that?" I asked.

"She doesn't want to hear what I have to say."

That sounded strange. I didn't know how to respond.

"How's she doing?" he asked me.

"She's fine," I said. "Just like she always is."

He was quiet for half a minute, and I was standing there trying to figure out why he called me. Finally, he said, "Katrina, there's trouble coming my way."

"What do you mean?" I asked. I was starting to get scared. Not for him. I really don't care what happens to Bryce. I was scared for my mom.

"Trouble with my business," he said.

"What do you mean?" I asked again.

"Katrina," he said, "you're an intelligent young woman. You know what I'm talking about."

Yes, I do know what he's talking about. My stepdad's a crook. I've known that for years. He's what you'd call a white-collar criminal.

He's a cheater, too. Roscoe's told me three or four times that he's seen Bryce out with other women. Other people have said things, too. Supposedly, my stepdad keeps his girlfriends in an apartment he pays for. It's a revolving door. He gets rid of a woman when he's tired of her, and then brings in another one. He's so high and mighty that he thinks he's entitled to any woman he wants.

My mom turns a blind eye to all that. She loves the lifestyle she shares with Bryce, and she isn't about to do anything to rock that boat. She allows Bryce his indiscretions. It's like some kind of unspoken agreement between the two of them.

At one point in time, my mom was one of Bryce's mistresses, one of his little playthings. He pretty much financed my parents' divorce, while supporting my mom in an apartment that she never could've afforded on her own. He lured her away from my dad, telling her everything she wanted to hear. Promising her everything she ever wanted.

My dad says men like Bryce Hudson get so much power that they start thinking they're God. They think they can do anything they want, inside or outside of the law. He's always predicted that Bryce would meet his downfall some day.

I'm not just mad at Bryce. I'm mad at my mom, too. She should've seen him for what he is. But she's never wanted to. My mom has a way of pretending everything's the way she wants it to be. That's the actress in her, I guess. The trouble is, she convinces herself that it's really true.

Still, I can't totally hate Bryce. He's given Mom the life she always thought she wanted. In his own way, he's treated her like a queen. With all of his connections in New York City, he helped my mom get involved in the theatre. She's not talented enough to be on Broadway, even though she'd like to think she is. But she's been in every off-Broadway production you can think of. That's been her life for the past twenty years. Bryce has also pulled some strings to get her on TV, doing commercials.

He's been good to me, too. I can't deny that. Some of his dirty money got me through nursing school.

"So what do you want me to do?" I asked Bryce.

"Talk to your mom," he said. "I want her to be prepared for what's coming."

"We're flying home Monday morning," I said. "Why can't you wait and talk with her then?"

He spoke slowly, sounding sad and defeated. "Katrina, it'll be all over the news by Monday morning."

I started feeling sick to my stomach, and for a minute, I thought I was going to throw up. I was still holding Lilly, and she was starting to fuss.

"Hang on just a minute," I told Bryce. Then I ran inside the trailer and handed Lilly to my mom.

She looked at me, bewildered. "What's going on?" she asked.

"I'll talk to you later," I said.

Then I ran outside again. "What's going to be on the news?" I asked Bryce.

"That Hudson Investments is being investigated by the SEC. The Securities and Exchange Commission."

When I heard that, the first thing I thought was that my dad's prediction was finally coming true. My stepdad's empire was about to fall.

Then Bryce started telling me about everything he and my mom stand to lose. Including that big house on Long Island they bought ten years ago.

"I'm so sorry, Katrina," he said.

"Don't apologize to me," I said. "My mom's the one you need to apologize to. This is going to be awful for her."

"I know," he sighed. "That's why I didn't want her to travel this weekend. I wanted to ease her into this, to prepare her for what's coming. I wish she'd talk to me. I'm going to have to count on you to start breaking the news to her. Maybe if you talk to her a little bit, she'll call me, and I can explain things to her."

"Why did you do it?" I blurted out. I wouldn't

normally have the nerve to speak up to Bryce like that. But now, he doesn't have the power to intimidate me anymore. He isn't the high and mighty guy he used to be. In my eyes, he's nothing but scum.

"Do what?" he asked.

"Why did you break the law? Why did you do the things that are getting you investigated?"

"Well, Katrina," he said, "when you're running a business, things aren't always black and white. Sometimes, the line between right and wrong gets a little fuzzy. You cross that line, and you justify it to yourself. Then you get used to crossing those lines. Before you know it, you've gone too far, and it all catches up with you."

I didn't know what to say to that. It sounded like he wanted my sympathy. I wasn't about to give it to him.

Then he said, "Talked to your mother, Katrina. Please. Explain everything to her. Tell her I love her. Ask her to call me. Please have her call me."

"I will," I promised. Not for his sake. I'd like to tell him to go to hell. I'll do it for my mom's sake.

"I love you, Katrina," he said. "I love you and Lilly like you're my own flesh and blood."

I didn't say anything back to him. I knew he was just trying to get on my good side. A minute ago, I said that I didn't totally hate him, but that's not true. I do hate him. Completely. With all that he's putting my mom through, I don't love him one bit. He gave her the world, and now he's taking it all away from her.

By the time we ended the call, I was shaking like a leaf. I've got a big job to do, and I'm not looking forward to it. My mom won't want to believe anything I have to tell her. She'll probably be mad at me for daring to say such things about her husband.

Well, this has really put a damper on my trip. So much for having a relaxing time out in the country. I'll be a nervous wreck for the rest of the weekend.

FRANCES: I enjoyed m'self so much this afternoon, playin' Scrabble with my girls. I tried to think when's the last time I had all three of my girls together. Been a long time, that's for sure.

After we got done playin', I told Sam to take a picture of all three of 'em so's I could have it for my photo album. They lined up and stood with their arms around each other. Katherine was in the middle, 'cause she's the tallest. Edith and Rosalie was on either side of 'er.

After Sam takes a coupla pictures, Katherine calls me to come up and take a picture with 'em. "Oh, no," I says to her. "Nobody wants to see this ol' face in a picture no more."

"You're beautiful, Mama," she says to me. "Now you come on up here."

Well, how do I say no to that? So I git up and go up there to stand next to Rosalie. When I go to put my arm around her waist, I could tell she didn't like it. She stiffened up, like she didn't want me touchin' 'er. She's always actin' like that around me, all cold and unfriendly.

And I couldn't help but think that if it hadna been for some of them things Rosalie done, we'd a'been a lot happier as a family. We'd a'been gettin' together more often, not just once in a blue moon like we do now.

While me and the girls was standin' there gettin' our

picture taken, I was prayin' in my mind, *Lord, don't let me be bitter toward my own child. Help me forgive 'er for what she's done.* But it's hard. You'd never know how hard it is unless you was in my shoes.

My Katherine, she was such a cheerful child. Always tryin' to keep everybody's spirits up. Edith was a quiet little mouse of a girl, but she was obedient. She never give me much cause to punish her. But Rosalie, she was another story altogether. She was my difficult child. She never liked it when I corrected her. She was one to sulk and pout, and I wasn't gonna stand for an attitude like that.

I s'ppose every mother goes through that kind of trial. My own mother went through somethin' like that with my sister Della. Hadta tan her rear end over and over again to make 'er listen.

Yup, I hafta say I spent more time on my knees in prayer over Rosalie than I did for my other two put together. Always askin' the Lord to lay it on her heart to turn away from her wrongdoin'.

After Martin got carted off to that mental hospital, Rosalie took to mopin' around the house all the time. The way she looked at me, I knowed she was blamin' me. I says to m'self, *Frances, this child ain't bein' fair to you. She's just feelin' sorry for her poor daddy. She ain't thinkin' about how you're workin' yourself to death keepin' body and soul together for this family.*

Like I told ya before, Katherine was always one to help. Always there by my side. Rosalie, I couldn't get that girl to move. There was one day when I told her she had to clean up her room. I says to her, "I'm comin' back in here in one hour, and this room better be spic and span."

But when I come back to check on her, she hadn't done one single thing. She was layin' there on her bed, buryin' her face in her arm, just like her daddy useta do when he was broodin' on his troubles.

And, I tell ya, I just had enough. I done had my fill of that kind of behavior in my house. Couldn't stand another minute of it. And I knowed it was time to knock some sense into her.

Maybe I got carried away a little bit. Maybe I took things a little too far. But there ain't no point in goin' over all that again. I think any mother in my situation woulda done the same thing.

Anyways, Rosalie knowed I meant business. That girl got up off her bed, and even though she was bawlin' her eyes out, she got that room cleaned up.

I thought the whole thing was over and done with. The next coupla days, Rosalie was actin' better. But the next thing I knowed, I was gettin' a call from the principal's office at school. And then some welfare people come a'knockin' on my door.

Here Rosalie had gone off to school and told everybody that I was abusin' her. Oh, she swore up and down to me that she didn't tell nobody. She said they seen it. But showin' somebody is the same thing as tellin' 'em.

That was her way of gettin' back at me. She couldna come up with any better way to break her mama's heart. Here I always been a decent person and a law-abidin' citizen. Never been in trouble my entire life. And my own child made it so I was hauled in and questioned like a common criminal.

That whole thing was somethin' that shoulda been kept

between me and her. I wasn't gonna tell nobody, and she shouldna done that, neither. The whole world didn't need to be knowin' all our family business.

Things was bad enough for us after Martin had his breakdown. Then Rosalie had to go and make things worse. Them welfare people told me that because of what I done to my own child, I wasn't allowed to be babysittin' other people's kids in my home no more.

"But that's how I been earnin' a livin' for my girls," I says to 'em. "Their daddy cain't work, and it's up to me to take care of 'em."

Well, them people didn't care none. They just told me I hadta find another way to support my kids.

They kept on askin' me questions, sayin' they needed to make sure Rosalie was gonna be safe in my home. I was hoppin' mad by then, and I told 'em that if Rosalie kept on disobeyin' me, I'd do the same thing all over again.

When my sister and me was growin' up, my parents wasn't afraid to tan our backsides if we was in the wrong. They put a few bruises on us, and nobody never thought nothin' of it.

The Bible says, "Spare the rod and spoil the child." From the git go, I told m'self I wasn't gonna be one to spoil my kids. I wasn't gonna be raisin' a houseful of whinin', snifflin' babies. If they needed correctin', then they was gonna git it.

But them welfare people don't look at things that way. They says to me, "Well, if that's the way it is, Mrs. Rafferty, we're gonna hafta remove your daughter from your home."

"You just go right ahead and do that," I says. Now

that mighta sounded kinda coldhearted to them people, like I didn't love my own flesh and blood. That wasn't the case, not at all. The truth was that I just couldn't take no more. I was plumb at the end of my rope. And I knowed that if Rosalie aggravated me to the point where I had to punish her again, I'd be in real trouble. They mighta hauled me off to jail, or somethin' like that. So it was best that I let 'er go.

Them welfare people worked it out for Rosalie to go stay with my sister Della. She was livin' down there in Brown County, out in the country south of Nashville. In my heart, I didn't feel too bad about that. I says to m'self, *Frances, that's the best place for Rosalie to be. Della will look after her just fine.*

Let me tell you what I'd been thinkin' before all that nonsense happened. When they took Martin to the mental hospital, I knowed that, sooner or later, me and the girls would hafta be movin' out of that parsonage. Them church people knowed Martin wasn't never gonna be able to get up and do his job again. They said they was bringin' in some other preacher to take his place. They said me and the girls could stay in the parsonage 'til they was done with their school year. "Then you's gonna hafta find your own place to live," they told me.

But I ain't one that gets taken down easy. I wasn't about to give up. In the back of my mind, I'd been a'thinkin' that maybe we could keep on livin' in Greenwood. We been rentin' out our old place in Brown County to my sister Della's oldest girl, Ginger. I figured between my babysittin' money and the money we was gettin' from rentin' out our old house, we could afford to move into another little place in Greenwood.

Tell ya the truth, Ginger wasn't real good about payin' what she owed us. Seem like every month, she was findin' some reason as to why she couldn't come up with the money. I been lettin' 'er slide some. But after Martin landed in the hospital, I knowed I couldn't let 'er get away with that no more.

So I up and called my sister and says, "Della, you gotta light a fire under that girl and make 'er pay up. It's gettin' to be a life or death situation up here."

See, I was tryin' to work this all out for the sake of the girls, so's they wouldn't hafta switch schools again. I was tellin' Katherine about my idea one day. "We can do this," I says to 'er.

She throwed her little arms around me and says, "I know we can do it, Mama. I'll help you any way I can."

But after Rosalie up and did what she did, I knowed we wasn't gonna have no more life there in Greenwood. I was ashamed to even set foot outa my front door, knowin' everybody was thinkin' so bad of me.

With me not bein' able to bring in babysittin' money, that last month me and Katherine stayed there in Greenwood was the hardest time of my entire life. I hafta say it was nice of them church people to let us keep on stayin' in the parsonage. But other'n that, they turned a blind eye to our problems. I stretched out the little bit of money we had for as long as I could. Then I hadta break down and go to a food bank, just so I could put some supper on the table. That hurt my pride somethin' awful. I felt like I wasn't no good for nothin' no more.

When it come down to it, there wasn't nothin' we

could do but move back down to our old place in Brown County. I hadta get on the phone and tell Ginger she hadta go someplace else, 'cause me and Katherine was gonna be needin' the house again.

Katherine, she was so upset when I made that call that she tried to grab the phone outa my hand. "No, Mama!" she was hollerin'.

"I'm awful sorry, sweetheart," I says to 'er. "If I could do things any other way, I would. But there ain't nothin' else left for us to do."

I knowed that just about broke Katherine's heart. Here she was gettin' along so good at her new school. She loved her cheerleadin' more'n anything, and she was all set to be the captain of the team her senior year. But now that was done ruined for her. Rosalie ruined it. For awhile, Katherine was talkin' real hateful about her sister. I didn't have the heart to correct her on that point, 'cause I knowed just how she felt.

When we drove down to the old house with our first load of stuff, Ginger handed me a coupla hundred dollars for her last month's rent. I was sure glad of that. But after we paid the electric bill and bought some groceries and some gas for the car, there wasn't nothin' left. And I says to m'self, *Frances, what're you gonna do now?*

The people from our old church down there did what they could to help us out. But they was all so poor theirselves, there wasn't much they could come up with.

Then the idea come to me to tell the welfare department in Nashville that we was back, and see if we could have Ralphie move in with us again. That woulda brung us in a little bit of money. And I was thinkin' that when Martin come back home, maybe havin' his little boy around again would do 'im some good.

But them welfare people said no. They said Ralphie was doin' fine where he was livin' with his new family, and that they wasn't gonna move 'im again. I asked 'em if there was any other kids I could take care of. And then they told me that because of what happened in Greenwood, I wasn't allowed to be a foster mother no more.

I didn't think they knowed about all that, but I guess they write reports on that kind of thing and pass 'em along from one place to 'nother. Makes me feel awful to think about it, my name on some kinda blacklist like that.

I told them people, "What am I supposed to do? I ain't got no money to support my m'self and my daughter." So they helped me get on food stamps, and they sent me places where I could get help with oil for heatin' the house and stuff like that. Katherine, bless her heart, she went to work up there in Bean Blossom at that little family restaurant, and every week, she brung home somethin' to help out.

Coupla months later, the mental hospital said Martin was ready to come home. But seems like they sent me home another child, instead of a husband. He needed a lotta lookin' after. I'd been hopin' that he could go back to preachin' at our little church down here, so's everything could be back the way it was before. But when he come home, I could tell he wasn't never gonna be fit for somethin' like that.

Nope, he never got behind that pulpit again. His mind was too far gone. After awhile, he was able to go back and do some cleanin' at the school, just a coupla hours of an evenin'. He brung us in a little money that way.

Just a few months after Martin come home, Edith dropped out of college and moved back in with us. That sure did take me by surprise. But I hafta say that I was glad. We needed her help around the house. I never did think my oldest girl was cut out for goin' to college. She's too nervous and bashful to do good in a place like that.

But wouldn't you know it, just as soon as Edith come home, Katherine up and left. I tell ya, I didn't think I was gonna git over that. My heart, it broke into a million pieces. Katherine had been the only one by my side, helpin' me out durin' all them hard times. Sometimes, the girl seemed like the only friend I had in the whole wide world, and I'd thank the Lord over and over that I still had her. I been thinkin' He give me that special child 'cause He knowed I was gonna be needin' her some day.

I hadta keep on a'tellin' m'self that Katherine done put in her time as my helper, and that it wasn't right for me to be selfish and keep 'er tied to me forever. The girl had a right to her own life. I knowed all along she was like the bud of a rose, just waitin' for her time to bloom. And to tell ya the truth, in my heart I knowed it was more important to see her bloom than to keep 'er by my side.

Martin's health, it started goin' downhill, and he didn't live but about ten years after he come home from that hospital. He wasn't but fifty-four years old when his heart give out. 'Bout a year after that, Edith and Sam was ready to move into the house, and they moved me into the trailer.

So the Lord worked it all out in the end. Every day, I thank Him that I don't hafta worry about a roof over my head or food on my table. Them hard times is over and done with.

Rosalie, she never did come back home. She stayed with her Aunt Della all the way through high school. I just let 'er be, 'cause I knowed she couldn't never face me after what she done to me. Oh, I kept on a'hopin' that she'd have it in her heart to come to me and ask for forgiveness. But she never did.

When Katherine was in her last year of high school, she seen her sister at school from time to time. Not much, 'cause Katherine was in twelfth grade and Rosalie was in ninth. Every now and then, I says to Katherine, "You seen Rosalie? How's she doin'?"

And Katherine would say somethin' like, "She's fine." I could tell she was still mad at her sister for ruinin' our life in Greenwood. I couldn't blame 'er.

When Edith come home, she acted like she was worried about Rosalie. Every coupla weeks, she took our old car and drove over to her Aunt Della's house to see her sister. Edith always was a softhearted girl. Too softhearted, I'd say. She always been one to pity people, whether they deserve it or not.

EDITH: I'm not very keen on playing Scrabble. But I did enjoy playing with Mom and my sisters this afternoon. It was relaxing. Well, it wasn't so much the game that relaxed me. It was not having to think about anything other than what word I was going to play next. For an hour, I got a break from the thoughts that had been tormenting me.

Rosie won the game, of course. She's so smart. I came in last, like I usually do. I didn't mind.

The game took up a big chunk of the afternoon. I'm so glad Kathy came up with the idea. I hadn't even thought about what we'd do all day. I'm such a dud when it comes to entertaining guests.

ROSALIE: When Kathy rounded us up to play Scrabble, she was all pumped up and excited, as if this game was going to be the big event of the weekend. Kathy is forever and always the cheerleader.

I didn't feel like playing Scrabble. But Kathy has a way of drawing everybody into her plans, and we all followed her over to the trailer.

Mom wanted to play with us three girls, so we sat around the table with her. She loved being the center of attention, sitting there like the queen bee surrounded by all of her subjects. She talked nonstop, pontificating about anything and everything. After watching her today, I know where Kathy gets her showoff tendencies.

Sam had brought a book with him. He sat on the couch and read, shutting out all the commotion around him. I would've preferred to do the same. Katrina was busy with her baby. There was hardly any space to park Marty's wheelchair, and he ended up sitting in the middle of the room. We were all crowded into that tiny trailer when we could've been more comfortable at Edie's house. It seemed pointless. But Mom and Kathy wanted all of us there, and they always get their way.

By the way, I was the one who bought that Scrabble game for Mom, ten or twelve years ago. The board has a base that swivels, and ridges around each square to keep the tiles from sliding out of place. It's good for an elderly person.

When I gave the game to her, it made her smile for a

few seconds. But it didn't earn me any points with her. It wasn't enough to wipe any of my so-called sins off the ledger.

Now, Mom doesn't remember where the gift came from. Before we all sat down to play, I heard her bragging to Edie that Kathy had brought the game for her all the way from New York City. That fits her perception of reality. Kathy provides her with everything. I offer her nothing.

I bet Mom has played a thousand games on that Scrabble board. She's not a very good player, but she's extremely competitive, and she gets a kick out of showing up her opponents. I hate seeing her self-satisfied grin every time she makes a score over ten points. I hate watching her big hand with the thick, arthritic fingers laying down those little tiles. I recall all too clearly that same hand coming toward me to slap my face or yank my hair or twist my ear.

I hate being touched by those hands, even though I do go through my dutiful hugging routine with Mom every time I see her. When someone beats you to within an inch of insanity and then leaves you collapsed in a puddle of terror and shame, no touch by that person is ever welcomed.

After the day when I knocked the gun out of my father's hands, I stopped sleeping at night. Every time I closed my eyes, I saw his haunted eyes, his tortured face, the gun pointed toward his open mouth. Whenever I'd manage to drift off to sleep, I'd hear a gunshot going off inside my head, and the sound would jerk me wide awake again.

I was awash with grief that I didn't understand, sorrow that I couldn't begin to deal with. My mother had told me never to tell anyone about what my father had done, and I knew I didn't dare expose my family's shame to the outside world.

Later, I realized the grief was about more than just the fact that my father had tried to take his own life. He and I were a lot alike, and I'd counted on him to be an example for me. I'd counted on his love and his guidance. But in the end, he'd abandoned me. He hadn't cared enough to stay strong for me, to keep going for my sake. The father I'd trusted had given up, leaving me with no example other than to break down when the going got tough.

I was just a child at the time, and I felt completely lost and adrift. I was so exhausted from the emotional strain and the lack of sleep that I could barely put one foot in front of the other. I tried not to fall asleep during my classes, but sometimes I couldn't keep from putting my head down on my desk and taking a two-minute nap.

My mother was becoming increasingly irritated with me. I don't know what she expected of me. I was trying my best to keep up with what I was supposed to do. After all, I'd just stopped my dad from shooting himself. I'd think she'd know to cut me a little slack.

One Saturday morning, she told me to clean my bedroom. In my state of exhaustion, the task seemed overwhelming to me. I fully intended to do what she asked of me. But I was so tired that I decided to stretch out on my bed for just a few minutes.

Lying there on my stomach, I drifted off into some much-needed sleep. I was actually sleeping more soundly than I had in several weeks. But I was abruptly awakened by a rain of blows coming down on me, on my bottom and my back and my legs. Heavy blows that hurt like crazy. I couldn't figure out what was happening to me. I thought someone was trying to kill me.

Then I heard my mother's voice screaming at me to get up off that bed and get to work. And I realized it was her that was beating me.

Instinctively, I curled up, trying to protect myself from the blows, but she kept beating me, harder and harder. Then she grabbed me by the arm and yanked me off the bed, and I fell down on the floor. As I fell, I caught a glimpse of her. Her face was hideous, contorted with rage. In her upraised hand, she was wielding my father's belt, ready to strike again.

While I lay there on the floor, I suddenly understood why my father had wanted to take his own life. Because at that moment, I wanted to die. I wished I could just stop breathing and end it all. I actually believed my mother's intention was to kill me, and I wished she'd hurry up and get it over with.

Those thoughts of wanting to die have never completely left me. They flared up really bad during my marriage to Marty's dad. That's one of the reasons I knew I had to get away from Richard. And I have a resurgence of those feelings every time I see my mother. Whenever I'm in her presence, I feel the life force draining out of me.

My mom hit me a few more times while I was lying there on the floor. "You better have this room cleaned up by the time I come back in here, or you're gonna get another whippin'," she bellowed. Then she stomped out of my room. She slammed the door behind her, hard, as if she was reminding me of what she was capable of doing to me.

Well, I got up off that floor, and I got the room cleaned up. Even though I was in a state of shock. Even though I was hurting so bad that I could hardly move.

For the next two days, I tried to stay out of my mother's line of vision as much as possible. I tried my best not to cross her in any way.

At night, I couldn't lie on my back. It hurt too bad. I was afraid of lying on my stomach, as that was the position I was in when the attack came. Lying on my right side hurt too much, as I had several big welts on my right hip. So I curled up on my left side, not sleeping, just lying there all night long, unbearable thoughts churning in my mind.

When I went to school Monday morning, I was overwhelmed with feelings of shame and humiliation. I walked down the hallways of the school in a daze, not speaking to anyone, keeping my head down, hoping no one would notice me.

That afternoon, I had my physical education class, which required changing my clothes in the girls' locker room. As I was putting on my gym suit, I faced away from everyone else, trying to stay unnoticed.

My gym teacher came walking through the locker room, telling all of the rowdy girls they needed to quiet down. All of a sudden, she gasped, "Rosalie!"

I swung around to face her, startled. She looked aghast. Then she walked over to me and spoke in a low voice. "Put your clothes back on and come to my office. I need to talk with you."

A few minutes later, I walked into my gym teacher's office, assuming that I was in trouble, preparing myself to accept whatever punishment was about to come my way.

After I'd been beaten by my mother, it felt as if the whole world was ready to attack me. But my teacher spoke to me in a gentle tone. "Rosalie, what happened to your back?"

Now here's where my mom gets the story all twisted out of shape. She claims that I showed the gym teacher my back. As if I walked up to her and pulled up my shirt and said, "Look at what my mother did to me." She thinks I did this deliberately, to get revenge. To ruin her life.

That's not the way it was. Not at all. I knew my back hurt like crazy. Before I went to school that morning, I'd cried in the shower, because the water hitting the welts hurt so bad. But I hadn't thought about how those welts looked. I hadn't checked them in the mirror.

I never intended for my gym teacher to see my back. I was too mortified to let anyone know what had happened to me. Back then, I blamed myself for the beating, and all the events that followed. But I refuse to blame myself any more. Over the years, I've seen a few therapists, and every one of them has told me that none of what happened was my fault. That's what I'd tell a patient of mine if something like that happened to them.

When my gym teacher asked what happened to my back, I tried to feign ignorance. "What do you mean?"

Then she had me take off my clothing so she could inspect the rest of my body, and she saw the marks on my bottom and my thighs. "Who did this to you?" she asked

"I can't tell you," I said.

"You need to tell," she insisted.

I just sat there, refusing to talk. So she took me to the principal's office, and the two of them kept asking me questions until I finally confessed that my mother had beaten me. And because I broke down under interrogation and told the truth, my mother has blamed me and hated me ever since that day. For more than forty years.

Well, the principal called my mom and talked to her, and then she was investigated by child protective services. I wasn't privy to those talks, and I can't tell you exactly what happened. But I wasn't allowed to go home from school that afternoon. I was placed in an emergency foster home in Greenwood for a few days, and the next thing I knew, I was being carted off to my Aunt Della's house in Brown County.

Everything happened so fast. I was in a daze, and the memory of that time is a blur.

There was only a month of school left. My former teachers and classmates in Brown County were surprised to see me. Early on, I realized I needed a story to tell in order to handle all the questions that came my way. So I told everyone that my father was sick, and that I had to stay with my aunt for awhile. That story was true, even though it wasn't the whole truth.

I've never spoken with my sisters about the beating incident. I know Kathy completely buys into our mother's version of the story. Trying to convince her of the truth would be a waste of my breath. Once, I tried to tell Edie what happened. But she looked so distraught that I realize she couldn't handle hearing anything more. So I stopped talking.

And I never told my dad. His state of mind was such that I couldn't confide anything in him anymore. He was working as hard as he could just to keep a grip on his own reality. Hearing such a shocking story would've been too much for him to handle.

When I first moved to Aunt Della's, I thought it was my mother's decision to send me there. I didn't realize until later that the state had made the decision, that they had officially removed me from my mother's care because they didn't believe I was safe in her home. I was Aunt Della's foster child. She got paid for taking care of me, just like my parents had been paid for taking care of Ralphie Dixon. I ended up staying at Aunt Della's until I graduated from high school.

After those two horrible events—Dad's suicide attempt and the beating incident—I had to grow up fast. I could no longer look at the world through the eyes of a child. Even though Aunt Della was legally required to provide food and shelter for me, emotionally, I was on my own. I knew it was up to me to find my way in life, because there was no one else to lean on.

Aunt Della was a hot-headed woman, a lot like my mother. She'd been divorced for as long as I could remember, and she pretty much raised her five children singlehandedly. All of her kids were older than me. Her three daughters, Ginger, Barbara, and Audrey were out of the house when I moved in. Her two boys, Curtis and Wade, were still living with her.

As far as I could tell, Aunt Della's sons were juvenile delinquents, and she was constantly fighting with them. Curtis and Wade were supposedly in high school. But they were truant more often than not, and were always in some kind of trouble with the law. Aunt Della would rage at them, but she had no control over them. I did my best to steer clear of those boys. Thankfully, they didn't even seem to notice that I was in the house.

And my female cousins were the craziest girls I'd ever met. All of their lives were fraught with drama. When Mom and Kathy moved back into our old house, Ginger and her two children moved back in with Aunt Della, because they had nowhere else to go. Ginger's kids were completely undisciplined, and Aunt Della yelled at them just like she did her own children. Every now and then, Ginger's ex-husband would come around, demanding to see his kids. Ginger would refuse, and the two of them would have a terrible row.

Both Barbara and Audrey had the habit of dating nasty and uncouth men. Evidently, the girls couldn't stand the thought of peace and quiet, because if they weren't fighting with the men in their lives, they were fighting with each other.

So my foster home was in constant uproar. The only way I could cope with the turmoil was to remove myself from the fray and try to be as invisible as possible. I had a tiny upstairs bedroom, and that's where I isolated myself from the rest of the household. Over and over, I'd tell myself that as long as nobody bothered me, I'd be fine.

Meals in that household were an irregular affair. Every few days, Aunt Della brought in a load of groceries. Everyone fended for themselves, and the groceries would disappear within several hours.

I've heard foster parents complain about their foster children hoarding food in their bedrooms. Certainly, it's annoying, but I understand why the children do it. I formed a habit of grabbing cans of soup or boxes of macaroni and cheese, stashing them away in my room so that I could be sure of having something to eat. Then, when no one else was around, I'd go down to the kitchen to prepare my food. The only balanced meals I got were my school lunches.

Aunt Della barely paid attention to me. I was just there. I didn't cause her any problems, and I didn't ask for much. I'm pretty sure the only reason she was willing to have me there was that my presence in the household ensured her a monthly check from the welfare department.

If I was around when Aunt Della was frustrated with one of her children, I'd end up being a captive audience for one of her rants about their incorrigible behavior. I can't recall her ever asking me how I was doing. As long as I was quiet and didn't bother anyone, she took it for granted that I was okay.

I was glad she left me alone. Even though she didn't hassle me, I felt uncomfortable around Aunt Della. Her short temper with her children and grandchildren reminded me of the way my mother treated me. But while I never wanted to get close to my aunt, I do owe her a measure of gratitude. She provided me shelter at a time when my own mother couldn't—or wouldn't—take care of me. And that was all I needed from her.

My adolescence wasn't anywhere near normal. The few friends I hung around with at school knew nothing about my home life. There was no way I was going to invite anyone over to witness the craziness of Aunt Della's household.

I joined several clubs at school and served on the student council. These activities kept me after school and away from Aunt Della's house. But I did all those things in a behind-the-scenes kind of way. I wanted to keep from being noticed. After what I'd been through, I decided that being invisible was the best way to ensure my safety.

Aunt Della's checks from the welfare department were supposed to cover all my basic needs. But I quickly learned that asking her for what I needed was an ordeal I didn't want to go through on a daily basis. If I told her I needed a notebook, a bottle of shampoo, or socks for my gym class, she'd grumble about how tight her finances were. She'd promise to get them, but would put it off for as long as possible.

One day when I was having my period, I told Aunt Della that I was running out of sanitary napkins. She mumbled something about picking some up the next time she went to the store. I told her I couldn't wait that long, but she ignored me and walked away.

By the next morning, I was down to my last pad, and I knew I couldn't go to school that day without taking a supply with me. I could hear the school bus rumbling at the end of our road. In my panic, I did the only thing I could think to do. I ran into my cousin Ginger's room, rifled through her drawers, and grabbed a handful of her pads. I stuffed them into my purse and rushed out the door, just in time to meet the bus.

On the ride to school, I stared out the bus window, tears running down my face. I'd never wanted to be a thief. I hated the fact that circumstances had driven me to stealing.

So I knew I had to take matters into my own hands. I got a part-time job at a drugstore in Nashville, stocking shelves and sweeping the floor. I went there directly from school, as the store was within walking distance.

Unfortunately, Aunt Della forgot to pick me up after my first evening of work, and my boss Mr. Smith had to take me home. After he realized that Aunt Della couldn't be counted on, Mr. Smith took it upon himself to make sure that I got home every evening. I ended up working in Mr. Smith's store through all four years of high school. He always praised me for being a good worker. I owe him a great deal of gratitude for helping a struggling teenager develop a measure of self-confidence.

I was able to earn enough spending money to pay for some of what I needed, sparing myself the worry about having to depend on Aunt Della for everything. Besides, I knew I had to practice being independent. I was well aware of the fact that, in a few years, I'd have to be entirely self-reliant.

My guidance counselor Mrs. Meyer was a godsend to me. Because she knew I didn't have family support, she took it upon herself to meet with me once a week during my study hall hour. After months of meeting with her, I was finally convinced that she was a person I could trust, and I started talking with her about the trauma I'd been through.

Her wonderful, caring responses amazed me. She was so unlike my mother, who blamed me for everything she could think of. Mrs. Meyer helped me understand that I wasn't bad or stupid or crazy. She told me that I had to be a very strong person to survive what I'd been through.

I admired her, and I wanted to be like her. She's one of the reasons that I chose a career in psychology.

Mrs. Meyer suspected that I had thoughts about suicide, and I finally admitted that to her. She kept saying to me, "Rosalie, you are not your father. You have the power to make different choices."

She also talked with me about college. She helped me with the application process, and with applying for financial aid. Since I was a foster child, there were extra options available to me, and my good grades qualified me for several scholarships. I can't imagine how I would've gotten myself prepared for college if Mrs. Meyer hadn't been there to help me.

About ten years after I graduated from high school, I looked up Mrs. Meyer and thanked her for what she did for me. She was surprised. She wasn't aware of how much her help had meant to me. She didn't realize she'd actually served as my surrogate mother. If I ever do for anyone else what Mrs. Meyer did for me, then I could say I'd lived a worthwhile life.

During the years I was staying with Aunt Della, I was supposed to be going home on the weekends to visit my parents. That was part of the Welfare Department's case plan. We were supposed to work out our family problems so that I could eventually move back home. But things didn't go that way.

I did have one official visit. But my mom gave me the cold shoulder and barely spoke to me all weekend. That was the first time I fully understood that she considered herself to be the victim of her vengeful child. She wasn't going to warm up to me unless I bowed down and begged for her forgiveness.

Well, I wasn't about to do that. I preferred hiding out in Aunt Della's dysfunctional household over going home and having my mother treat me like a piece of garbage.

That first visit home was the first time I'd seen my father since the day of his suicide attempt. That was hard. He wasn't himself at all, and looking at him made me want to cry. It seemed as if he hardly knew who I was or why I was there. But I didn't take that personally.

From time to time, I'd wonder whether he blamed me for the problems that happened after he was hospitalized. I really didn't think so. I figured his mind wasn't even running along those lines, as it took all of his mental strength to deal with the basics of daily living.

At one point, my mother pulled me aside and told me, in no uncertain terms, that I was not to bring up the issue of my father's suicide attempt. "He don't remember that whole affair with the gun," she growled at me. "And he's too weak-minded to handle anyone tellin' him about it. So you just keep your mouth shut."

I wanted to come back at her and say, "I wasn't planning on doing anything like that. How stupid do you think I am?" But I didn't. I could tell Mom was braced for combat, primed and ready to take me on if I caused her any more trouble. So I kept my thoughts to myself and spent most of that weekend alone in my room.

After that, I never again went home for an entire weekend. However, every couple of months, Aunt Della would decide to visit Mom, and as an afterthought, she'd demand that I go with her.

"You and your mom are startin' to act like strangers," she'd tell me. "You gotta keep rememberin' that you're family."

So I'd ride along with her and sit in the living room while she and my mom talked at the kitchen table. I could tell that Mom wasn't any happier to see me than I was to see her.

Aunt Della never pushed the point of me going back home to stay. I knew she wasn't interested in losing her monthly check. It was easy money, because she got paid for doing next to nothing.

During my freshman year, I'd see Kathy at school from time to time. Our paths didn't cross much, but when we did run into each other, she'd act like she didn't know me. At best, she'd acknowledge me with a dirty look.

That's one reason why I can barely tolerate her sermons about me needing to be a better sister and daughter. At the most difficult time of my life, she wasn't a sister to me. She wasn't sticking up for me at all. I know she was just a kid back then, and I suppose I should let all of that go. But I don't think her attitude toward me has ever changed.

Edie was different, though. She acted like a sister to me. After she dropped out of college and moved back home, she came to see me at Aunt Della's house two or three times a month. Edie wasn't much of a talker, but we'd sit together in my tiny bedroom and hang out for awhile. Sometimes we'd take a walk together. Sometimes she'd drive me into Nashville and buy me an ice cream cone at the Dairy Queen.

Edie made the effort to stay connected with me, when no one else in the family did. That meant the world to me. I love my big sister for that. Whenever I see her, those memories warm my heart. I'd like to find a way to spend more time with her. But seeing her always means that I have to contend with Mom.

SATURDAY EVENING

EDITH: I was planning on having a cookout for dinner this evening. I'd invited my kids and grandkids over so they could spend time with their relatives. I thought everyone would enjoy that.

Originally, I'd thought about having barbecued chicken. Then I realized I wasn't going to be able to get around to doing that, and I suggested to Sam that we just grill some hotdogs and hamburgers.

But just about the time I was ready to ask him to fire up the grill, I realized I'd forgotten to buy veggie burgers for Kathy. And then I looked in the refrigerator and saw that we were almost out of ketchup. I was so upset with myself. It seems like I can't do anything right this weekend.

"Can we just order pizza?" I asked Sam. "We can order one with cheese and veggies for Kathy."

Sam looked aggravated. "I suppose so," he grunted. "I guess I'll run down to Big Woods Pizza in Nashville." Then he jumped in his Jeep and took off.

This whole weekend has really gotten on his nerves. I don't know how I'm going to make it up to him. I sure hope he doesn't forget the veggie pizza for Kathy.

KATHERINE: I'm so happy to be here this weekend! Oh, I know, I was a little worried this afternoon when everything fell flat. But this evening was wonderful. Mom had such a good time. She had her three daughters, her five grandchildren, and her nine great-grandchildren all together at one time. Who knows when that will ever happen again?

In all likelihood, never. This weekend, I noticed how much Mom's health has declined since I last saw her. She probably has only two or three years to live. So I'm especially grateful for this time with everyone.

Edie's children are wonderful. I hadn't seen them since they were teenagers. I spent time talking with each one of them, getting to know something about their lives. Brian and David are both professional people. I loved hearing them tell stories about their work.

Megan is such a sweet girl. She's a busy stay-at-home mother. She has three of the cutest little girls you've ever seen. I told Edie they reminded me of us three girls when we were little. All of Edie's grandkids are just adorable. My mother lights up when they're around. I'm so glad they can bring her joy in her old age.

I was snapping pictures all over the place. I can't wait to show them to Bryce. He'll wish he could've been here. He'll be upset with himself for not taking the opportunity to come along with me.

Speaking of Bryce, Katrina told me he called her this afternoon, while we were playing Scrabble with Mom. "He wants you to call him," she said. Then she gave me a strange look. "Mom, you and I need to talk."

"Not tonight, sweetie," I said. "I'm really tired. We'll talk tomorrow afternoon."

"Why not tomorrow morning?" she asked.

"Because we're going to church with your grandmother," I told her.

I'm surprised at what Bryce did. Actually, I'm shocked. It's not like him to go behind my back and manipulate Katrina into making me do something.

Honestly, I don't know what's made him go off track like this. When I get back home, I'll sit him down and have a long talk with him. Both partners in a marriage have a right to some personal privacy. I've always tried to respect his boundaries, and he needs to respect mine.

Maybe he's been under more stress at work than I know about. Maybe we've both been so busy that we've lost touch with each other. We'll have to work on that.

EDITH: Well, we sure had a houseful this evening! My kids and their spouses and Katrina started playing charades in the living room, and things got pretty rowdy. Toward the end of the evening, Kathy took Mom over to the trailer and put her to bed. Then my sisters and I sat around the kitchen table, talking and drinking the wine Kathy had brought with her. Of course, we wouldn't have done that in front of Mom. She doesn't believe in drinking, and she would've had plenty to say to us about that.

Out of the blue, Rosie asked, "Has anyone ever heard anything about Ralphie Dixon?"

"Ralphie Dixon," Kathy said. "He was that little boy who lived with us for a few years, wasn't he?"

My son Brian overheard us talking. "I have one of Ralph Dixon's kids in my geometry class," he said. "He's got a bunch of them, by three or four different women."

Then Sam chimed in. "Ralph Dixon worked on the assembly line at Cummins a few years back. He didn't last long. He was let go because of his poor attendance. Probably because of his drinking. I saw his name in _The Brown County Democrat_ a couple of weeks ago. He'd been arrested for drunk driving."

"That figures," Kathy said. "His mother was a drunk. That's why he was in foster care."

I just kept quiet. I couldn't tell everyone what I knew about Ralph Dixon. They'd all think I was crazy for what I did.

Because last week, Ralph Dixon came to my house.

Sam was at work. I'd been over at the trailer helping Mom with her bath. I was walking back to the house when a junky old car pulled into our driveway. A man got out. I didn't recognize him. He was tall and thin, kind of rough-looking. But handsome, in a way. He was staring at the house with a funny look on his face. That made me feel a little nervous.

"Can I help you?" I asked.

"I used to live here," he said. "This place sure has changed a lot."

I was totally thrown off. I couldn't imagine who he could be, because since the house was built ninety years ago, it's only been family living here.

"Does the Rafferty family still live here?" he asked.

"My husband and I live here," I said. "I'm Edith Clemens. My name was Rafferty before I got married."

Then he broke into a big smile and held out his arms like he wanted to hug me. "My big sister Edie!" he exclaimed. "I'm Ralph Dixon."

Wow! I just about fell over from shock. I walked over to him and let him hug me. All the while, my mind was racing back to almost fifty years ago, to the time when little Ralphie came to live with us.

Ralphie Dixon was such a sweet little guy, four years old when he became part of our family. I loved him the minute I saw him. I knew he belonged to us. I knew he belonged to me.

He was kind of backward at first, like he hadn't been raised right. He barely talked, and he didn't know very much. He didn't know the names of ordinary things around the house.

I used to sit with him on my lap, pointing at different things in the room. I'd tell him the name of something and have him repeat it. "That's a window," I'd say.

He'd point with his little finger and say, "Window."

"This is a cup," I'd say.

He'd point and repeat, "Cup."

Then I'd point to myself and say, "Edie."

He'd laugh and throw his arms around me. "Eee-dee."

He was a good little student. He learned fast, and he caught up in no time. By the time he went to school, he was as smart as any of the other kids.

I was fourteen when Ralphie came. In my mind, he was my baby. I looked after him more than my mother did.

But when my parents moved to Greenwood, the Welfare Department took Ralphie away from us. That broke my heart. Back then, I couldn't let myself feel all that pain. If I would've let myself feel how sad I was over losing Ralphie, I would've fallen to pieces. I was getting ready to go to college, and I had to focus on that.

It was after I dropped out of school and moved back home that I really started missing Ralphie. I kept telling myself that I should've talked with my parents before they made the decision to move. Everything happened so quickly, and the plans were all made in a rush. I should've said, "Think this over carefully." I should've realized that the welfare department would never have allowed them to take Ralphie up to Greenwood.

If my parents had known that, maybe they would've decided not to move. My father probably would've thought keeping Ralphie was more important than helping out that church in Greenwood. Ralphie could've stayed with us until he was grown. If we had given him a stable home, I'm pretty sure his name wouldn't have shown up in the paper for drunk driving.

Well, after I got over the shock of seeing the grownup Ralph Dixon standing there in my driveway, I invited him into the house to talk. It would've been rude not to do that.

We sat in the living room. At first, we just talked about memories from his childhood. He pointed to the staircase and said, "I remember sliding down those stairs on my belly."

I laughed when I pictured him doing that. "Yes, I remember. It seemed to me like it would hurt, but you thought it was fun. You'd do it over and over again. Mom would finally make you stop. She'd say, 'Ralphie, you're gonna wear the skin plumb off that little belly of yours.'"

Then we reminisced about other fun times, like playing on the tire swing my dad hung on the branch of the wild cherry tree. "You always wanted me to push you high," I told him. "But I was always afraid you'd fall and get hurt."

He remembered catching grasshoppers and lightning bugs in the neighbor's field. He said he kept the insects in mason jars in his room, until Mom would make him throw them out.

"You always did like to catch things," I said. "Remember how you'd go to the creek and poke a crawdad with a stick, to get it to hang on with its pincers? Then you'd bring it up to the house and chase Rosie around with it. She'd end up crying."

Ralph laughed. "Yeah, I remember doing that. I used to dig holes, too. I dug holes all over your backyard. I used to bury my little cars and trucks. Then the next day, I'd go dig them up again. Stupid little kid, huh?"

"No, you weren't stupid," I told him. "You were actually very capable. When we'd all go down to play in the creek, we girls would just splash around because we didn't know how to swim. But you taught yourself to dog paddle. That amazed me."

He smiled and said, "Yeah, I forgot all about that."

"Do you remember the ice skating?" I asked him. "We had one pair of ice skates that my cousin had given me after she'd outgrown them. As each of us girls grew into them, we tried to learn to skate on the creek when it froze over. None of us ever learned how. But when you grew into the skates, you went zipping around that frozen creek like nobody's business. I could never figure out how you learned on your own."

We talked about playing hide-and-seek in the woods, and sliding down the hill in the winter on an old inner-tube. "We sure had some good times," Ralph said. "It didn't take a lot to keep us entertained, did it?"

Then, out of the blue, he asked, "Why did you guys get rid of me?"

"Oh, Ralphie!" I said. I couldn't help using his childhood name. "Is that what it felt like to you?"

"Pretty much," he said. "I wondered what I'd done to make you guys not want me anymore."

"You know about my parents' move, don't you?" I said. "They were all set to take you with them, but the Welfare Department wouldn't allow it."

"I know," he said. "My caseworker explained all that to me. Still, it was a bummer. I thought I'd be staying with your family forever. I didn't remember anything about my life before I came to live with you."

Then I asked, "How've you been doing, Ralphie? I always wondered how things worked out for you."

Maybe I shouldn't have asked him that, because I opened up a floodgate. He started telling me about all the problems in his life. He and his girlfriend had just broken up. She kicked him out of the house, and he had to sleep in his car. She wouldn't let him see his kids. He got laid off his job, and was way behind on child support. He told me that if he didn't come up with some money real quick, he was going to be facing jail time.

He'd been so upset about the breakup that he'd gone out drinking. "That was really stupid of me," he said. "And wouldn't you know it, I got pulled over by a cop. Now I've got a bunch of fines and court fees to pay off."

I felt so sorry for him. "Oh, Ralphie," I kept saying.

"I don't know what to do, Edie," he fretted. "Life won't stop crapping on me." He sat there with his head in his hands, crying. And all I could think was that my little Ralphie was in trouble and needed my help.

He didn't outright ask me for money. But I knew he needed it, and that he'd be really grateful if I gave him some. So I got up and went to the desk to get the checkbook, and before I knew it, I was writing out a check for five hundred dollars.

When I handed it to him, he cried all the harder. Then he stood up and hugged me. "You have no idea what this means to me," he said. "Edie, you're a wonderful woman. You were more than a big sister to me. You were like a mother."

As he was leaving, he said, "I'll see you later."

And I called back, "See you later."

After he'd gone, I got to wondering whether he'd be coming around again, and whether he'd be wanting more money. And I told myself that maybe I'd opened a door I shouldn't have opened. I wondered whether my little Ralphie had turned out to be a bit of a con artist. I hated thinking that. But when I looked back over what had happened between us, something seemed a little off.

I'm really scared about telling Sam. He'll be furious. He always tells me I'm too naïve and gullible. He's tried to teach me to be careful about things like this.

I hope I was wrong about Ralphie. Maybe he just came over because he wanted to see his old family again. I'd love to have my little brother back in my life.

This evening after the kids and grandkids left, I went to my bedroom to get the clothes Sam and I will need for church tomorrow morning. I wanted to do that before Rosie and Marty got settled in for the night. Our computer is in the bedroom, and I decided to check my email.

When I came out with our clothing, Sam asked, "What took you so long in there?"

"I was checking my email," I said. He frowned at me.

I've been on the computer way too much recently, especially on Facebook. Sam doesn't like that. It's almost as if he suspects I'm up to something. And he's right. I'm ashamed to say it, but he's right.

He never liked the idea of me going on Facebook in the first place. He asked me why I felt the need to do that. I told him it was a way of staying in touch with my friends.

"Why don't you just pick up the phone and call them?" he asked.

I didn't have an answer for that. But here's the truth: there is only one reason why I signed up for Facebook. I've been trying to find James.

Every time I can steal a few minutes when Sam isn't around, I'm on Facebook trying to look up James. I feel guilty about it, like I'm being unfaithful to Sam. But I can't seem to stop myself.

It seems like there are a million James Millers on Facebook. You couldn't find a more common name than that. But there was nothing common about my James Miller. He was one of a kind.

I've spent hours looking through all the James Miller profiles, trying to see if the information matches my James. I haven't found any James Miller from Middlebury, Indiana. Maybe he isn't on Facebook. Or maybe he moved away from Middlebury. Maybe he isn't even alive anymore. I have no idea. Not knowing drives me crazy.

The other day when I was working at Margaret's gallery, a man who looked almost exactly like James came into the store. For a split second, I thought it was James. I thought maybe he'd been looking for me, too, and that he'd finally found me. But when he stepped closer, I realized the man was young, not more than thirty-five. James would be in his sixties by now.

The young man had James's muscular build, his broad

face and sandy hair. For a second, I wondered whether he might be James' son. I wanted to ask him his name, on the chance that his last name might be Miller. Then I told myself I was getting carried away.

Later, I felt silly about my little fantasy. But the whole thing shook me up.

I've promised myself that if I ever find James on Facebook, I won't bother him. I don't want to disrupt his life. I just want to know how he's doing.

ROSALIE: Well, that was quite an evening. Edie's house was teeming with her children and grandchildren. She's the quintessential mother hen, constantly tending to her brood.

Sometime, I'd like to spend a weekend with Edie alone, having her nurture me like she does her family. Having her wait on me hand and foot like she does our mother. Isn't that a selfish thought? But I've never had that kind of nurturing. I have no idea what it would feel like.

I didn't get that type of treatment from my mother when I was little. She'd sooner give one of her babies a swat on the butt than a pat on the head. She doesn't deserve how well she's being treated by Edie now. Somehow, in her case, karma has gone awry.

When I was a teenager living at Aunt Della's house, I'd go for months without having anyone touch me. I developed some odd habits during that time. I'd sit cross-legged on my bed, wrap my arms around myself, and rock. Sometimes, I'd thump my arms and legs with my fist. I'd smack my own cheeks and tug at my hair. Looking back, I realize that was my way of providing myself with some much-needed skin stimulation.

It isn't fair to expect any special attention from Edie. I've hardly ever done anything for her, so why should she knock herself out for me now?

While Marty's cousins were talking and laughing in the living room this evening, I wheeled him over to a spot where he could feel like a part of things. He enjoys socializing, even though he can't converse much.

When Katrina saw him coming, she said, "Come over here and sit by me, Marty." He got the biggest grin on his face. Katrina is such a sweetheart.

But as I was getting him ready for bed tonight, I could tell how exhausted he was. Completely spent from all the noise and commotion going on around him.

Because Marty isn't able to interject anything in rapid-paced conversations, he often needs to process his thoughts and feelings about an event when the two of us are alone. Knowing this, I sat down on the bed, waiting to hear what he had to tell me.

"Aunt Edie has a pretty house," he said.

"Yes, sweetie," I agreed. "She has it fixed up really nice, doesn't she?"

"Uncle Sam doesn't smile."

"No, he doesn't smile very much. He's a serious kind of guy."

"Katrina's nice. I like her."

I'm pretty sure Marty has a crush on his cousin. After we get home, he'll be talking about her for days. "I think she's nice, too," I told him. "She's a lovely young woman."

"Aunt Edie's grandchildren run all over the place." He waved his left hand in circles.

"Yes, little kids can be active. But they're cute, aren't they?"

"They're loud. They give me a headache."

"I know," I said. "This evening was pretty noisy."

"Aunt Kathy is pretty. She's sp-sp-sparkly." Marty has difficulty with the s-p sound, and there's often a bit of spitting until he gets it out.

I smiled at him. "Yes, Aunt Kathy is sparkly. She wears beautiful clothing, doesn't she?"

Every time I see Kathy, she's wearing a flashy outfit. Colorful blouses, bright scarves, showy jewelry—anything to add bling to her appearance. I've never seen her look less than dazzling.

Then Marty said, "Aunt Kathy has a big butt."

I couldn't believe my ears. "What did you just say?"

"Aunt Kathy has a big butt."

I tousled his hair. "Why, you little nut!"

Marty started laughing, so hard that his frail little body flopped around in his chair. I was afraid he was going to have a seizure.

"Okay, buddy," I said. "Time to settle down now." But I couldn't help laughing along with him. After the emotional heaviness of the weekend, I was more than glad for the comic relief.

Kathy and I both take after our mother, in that we struggle with our weight. Edie's the lucky one. She's like our father, thin as a rake. If I slack off at the gym for even a few weeks, I find myself packing on the pounds. And Kathy seems to grow steadily heavier, in spite of the healthy lifestyle she brags about.

This evening, she was wearing a pair of form-fitting designer jeans that made her butt look a mile wide. It's the most amazing rear-end you've ever seen. You could pin a blue ribbon on that butt, like a prize-winning pumpkin.

But in spite of her weight, Kathy looks spectacular in everything she wears. She could weigh four hundred pounds and still manage to look gorgeous. I've always envied Kathy's looks and sense of style. No one can deny the fact that even at fifty-nine, she's a beautiful woman.

There have been times when I've tried to emulate Kathy's style. I can't pull it off. She's one of a kind.

This evening, I noticed something a bit disturbing. When my sisters and I were sitting around the table drinking wine, Edie and I each had one glass. Kathy had at least three. Maybe four. She's always talkative, but the more she drank, the more talkative she became. To put it nicely, she was getting rather ebullient.

Lilly had been sleeping, and when she woke up crying, Kathy called out to Katrina, "I'll get her, sweetheart."

Katrina shot her a dirty look and said, "I don't think so!" And she went to get Lilly herself.

I wondered what that was all about. Is Katrina concerned about her mother's drinking? Well, that's not my business. I've got enough to worry about.

Marty is completely exhausted. When I put him to bed, he was crying a little bit. I should've known three days away from home would be too much for him.

Truthfully, I'm exhausted, too. I shouldn't have planned to come for an entire weekend. I'll need time to leave the world of Rosie Rafferty and get back into the role of Dr. Jacobson before I go to work on Monday. That's not an easy transition.

"We'll go home tomorrow morning," I told Marty.

"Good," he said.

KATRINA: Tonight after everybody went to bed, I called my husband. "Roscoe," I said, "Bryce is in trouble. He's being investigated. He's probably going to prison."

Roscoe was surprised, but not totally. "So they finally caught up with that son-of-a-bitch," he said.

"We're going to have to help Mom," I told him. "They're going to lose almost everything they have."

He was quiet for a few seconds. I knew what he was thinking. He was imagining Mom piling in on our lives. Don't get me wrong. He loves her. But he sometimes finds her a little hard to take.

"What's she saying about all this?" he asked.

"Well, she doesn't exactly know about it," I said. "Bryce has been trying to call her, but she won't answer her phone. This afternoon, he called me. He wants me to talk to her. But you know how Mom can be. She believes what she wants to believe, and shuts everything else out. Every time I try to talk to her about it, she puts me off."

Roscoe and I talked for awhile. He finally agreed that Mom can come live with us until she gets something else worked out. He's not thrilled about the idea. "She's going to have to show me more respect," he said. "I'm not letting her run me down in my own home."

Mom hates the idea that Roscoe is a pharmacist. She doesn't believe in taking medication. She only takes natural supplements. She tells my husband he's working for an industry that poisons people's bodies, and that he needs to get out of that profession. When she gets going on her health ideas, she doesn't care whose toes she steps on.

She can be such a hypocrite. Talk about poisoning the body, every time I go over to their place, Bryce has a cocktail in his hand. And Mom's drinking right along with him. She drinks more than she'll ever admit to.

But Mom and Bryce have helped us out so much. They gave us a big chunk of money to go toward the down payment on the house we bought a few years ago. The only decent thing to do is to return the favor.

Mom is the eternal optimist. She raised me to believe that when something goes wrong, there's always a silver lining. The way I see it, the positive side of having Mom stay with us is that we'll have a live-in babysitter. Ross and I won't have to take Lilly to daycare when we go to work. That will save us a bunch of money, and we'll be able to pay off a lot of bills. Of course, Mom will have to cut down on drinking if she's going to be watching Lilly.

This afternoon when I tried getting Mom alone so we could talk, she scolded me like I was a little kid. She said we came out here to be with family, and that we should make the best of the time we have with them. She said we'll have plenty of time to talk on our flight home.

I was at a point where I was getting mad at her. But I knew what was really going on with her. She was afraid to hear what I had to say. Somewhere inside herself, she knows trouble is coming.

I don't want to spring everything on her at the last minute. She needs time to adjust to what she'll be facing when we get home.

SUNDAY MORNING

EDITH: Here I am, running behind schedule again. I wanted to make a vegetarian lasagna for lunch and get it in the oven before we leave for church. But I got a late start, and ended up throwing the lasagna together in a hurry. I hope it turns out okay.

I need to run over to the trailer to make sure Mom is up, and to see if she needs help getting dressed. Then I'll come back home, finish my hair and makeup, and put the lasagna in the oven.

I didn't dream about James last night. I expected him to make another dream visit, because he's been in my thoughts constantly the past few days. Honestly, I was relieved that he didn't. I needed a break from those overwhelming emotions.

But I did wake up in the early hours of the morning. It felt like something woke me up for a reason. I had no idea why. I just had a strong feeling that I needed to go up to the chapel in the attic again.

No, I told myself. *Not this morning. I need to rest.* I rolled over on that uncomfortable air mattress and tried to get back to sleep, but that feeling wouldn't stop nagging at me. So I slipped out from under the covers and tiptoed up the stairs to the attic.

I lit the candle on the altar and sat there gazing at it, trying to relax my mind. "I want to hear you speak," I whispered to God. "My father used to sit in this room listening for your voice. I'm listening, too."

And then a thought floated into my mind. It was a quiet thought, a gentle thought, but it spoke to me with conviction. *Edith, you've been carrying a load of guilt. Unnecessary guilt. It has held you back.*

In my mind's eye, I pictured the guilt as a big burlap sack strapped to my back, filled with heavy rocks that weighed me down. I saw myself plodding along with that load of guilt, so tired that I hardly had the strength to draw a breath. But I'd keep on going, trying to take care of everybody. Trying to make sure everyone was happy. Trying to make amends for all the wrong things I've ever done in my life. I knew it was time to throw that load off my back, to stand up straight, to breathe, to be free.

"Why do you feel so guilty, Edith?" I whispered to myself.

I sat there in the silence and allowed everything to come to me, washing over me in a wave of darkness. I've never experienced such darkness before. It was unbearable.

I can't do this, I thought. *It's too much.* But I made myself sit there and take it all in. One by one, the problems rose up and stared me in the face. The guilt about not being there for my family when they were struggling. The guilt about Ralphie having to leave our home. The guilt about his life not turning out well. The guilt about having sex with James. The guilt about treating James so badly after my miscarriage. The guilt about my obsession with James. The guilt about keeping secrets from my husband. The guilt about not taking better care of my mother. The guilt about never doing enough for my husband, my sisters, my children, my grandchildren.

That heavy, stifling guilt felt as if it was going to suffocate me. I felt like such a wretched person. I wanted to die right then and there.

"Help me, God," I pleaded. "Please help me through this."

The darkness was so heavy that I could hardly breathe. Tears started pouring from my eyes. It felt as if I was weeping from the depths of my soul. But strangely, I started to feel lighter. I knew God was lifting the burden off my heart. And then another thought came to me: *Edith, you're not a bad person. You don't deserve to feel like this. You need to forgive yourself for your mistakes. You need to let go of all this baggage so that you can move forward with your life.*

"How do I do that?" I said aloud. But even before the words left my mouth, I knew where I needed to start. I had to let go of James. I had to stop hanging onto my fantasies about him. I saw the pattern I'd been stuck in for almost forty years. Whenever my life had become stressful, I had turned my thoughts to the dream of a perfect life with James. An unreal life.

As I sat there in the attic, I had a grownup talk with myself. *Life wouldn't have been perfect with James. We would've had problems, because that's the way life is. James and I were hardly more than children when we met. We were still teenagers. Maybe over time, we would've discovered that we really weren't suited for each other. In the end, we might've decided not to get married.*

I knew the obsession had to stop. I had to put the memories of James to rest. I knew there was a certain thing I had to do, and I knew it would be very difficult.

I got up, went to my father's old desk, opened the bottom drawer, and pulled out the three letters James had written me. I had kept them all these years, hiding them in a place I knew Sam would never look.

I wanted to read those letters one last time, but I didn't allow myself to do that. I'd already read them too many times, and they'd always pulled me down into sadness and longing. My change had to start right now.

I knelt down in front of the altar and tore the letters into tiny pieces. I didn't do it in an angry way. James hadn't done anything to deserve my anger. It was in a loving way. I made a ceremony of it, as if God and I were doing this thing together. And while I shredded those letters, I whispered, "Goodbye, James. Thank you for the time you shared with me. Thank you for loving me. I'm letting you go now. I wish you the best." I left the torn scraps of paper in a little pile on the altar, like something I was turning over to God.

Then I sat there thinking about Sam, the sweet, grumpy husband who's been with me for almost forty years. The man who's been at my side through all the ups and downs of our life. The man who's provided for me and looked out for me. All of a sudden, I felt silly about clinging to the memory of a teenage boy I'd known for only a year and a half. I knew that hanging onto James had kept me from loving my husband with my whole heart.

I thought about the fact that my life with Sam is quickly slipping by. I told myself that I didn't want to waste another minute of it by living in a fantasy world.

When I got done with all this thinking, daylight was streaming through the little stained glass window, and I realized I had to get downstairs and get started with my day. I sure hope the lasagna turns out okay. But if it doesn't . . . well, starting today, I am resolving not to waste any more of my time feeling guilty about things like that.

Sometime in the next couple of days, when I'm alone, I'll take the scraps of those letters out to the barrel and burn them. No, I have a better idea. I'll bury them in one of my flower gardens. It'll be like burying a seed in the ground and seeing what grows from it.

FRANCES: Edith was over here just a minute ago, wantin' to make sure I was gittin' ready for church. I hardly never go to church no more. It's just too much for me. But today, we was all plannin' on goin' together as a family. Somethin' we ain't done in a long time. I cain't tell you how much I was lookin' forward to it.

Then Edith come over here tellin' me that Rosalie and her boy was already goin' home. Rosalie was sayin' the boy was too tired. I don't know what could tire that kid out. He just sits in that chair all day long. Seems to me Rosalie's comin' up with an excuse. She always finds a way to spoil somethin' for me. That girl! She sure does know how to stick a knife in my heart and twist it.

Truth be told, I think Rosalie's afraid to step foot in the house of God, for fear the Lord will prick her conscience. I bet you anything she don't never go to church up there where she lives in Indianapolis.

But at least Katherine will be there with me this mornin'. I'll enjoy sittin' beside her while we sing them old hymns. Yup, I'm lookin' forward to that. Katherine's got such a beautiful singin' voice. She useta sing solos in church when she was a little girl, and I was so proud of 'er. Sung like an angel, she did. Everybody said so.

EDITH: I feel bad that Rosie is leaving early. It's probably hard to take care of Marty in someone else's home. Maybe I should've helped her out more. But I've done the best I can this weekend, and I'm going to leave it at that. No more guilt.

Because she lived away from home when she was a teenager, I've missed out on a lot of time with my little sister. That makes me sad. I hope a day will come when she and I can be closer.

KATHERINE: Even though I'm a spiritual person, I haven't followed my parents' religion in forty years. Bryce and I have found a path that works for us. But my mother's religion works for her, and I respect that. So I plan on going with her to the service at our old church this morning. Edith and Sam are coming, too.

Rosie is getting ready to leave for home. I wish she'd stick around long enough to go to church with us. It would mean so much to Mom to have all of us together in church one last time.

There's a lot of unfinished business between Rosie and Mom. If Rosie would find it in her heart to do something like this for Mom, it might go a long way in resolving the problems between them.

I keep telling Rosie that she needs to take the high road and be the one to bridge the gap between the two of them. I don't believe Mom is capable of taking that step. She's been hurt so bad by Rosie that she doesn't have it in her to reach out to her any more.

I've talked with Rosie about the detrimental effects of harboring negativity. I've told her she'll never be able to move forward into happiness and prosperity until she releases her anger toward Mom. She didn't seem to like that idea, but I hope it gave her something to think about.

I'm so glad I don't have the problems Rosie has.

ROSALIE: I feel guilty about taking off so abruptly. I'm acting like a terrible daughter. I'm ashamed to say this, but I didn't even go over to the trailer to say goodbye to my mother. I knew if I did, I'd get a lecture about not going to church this morning. And I just couldn't face that.

I'm exhausted. I haven't been feeling well, and it's going to take all my strength to get Marty back to Indianapolis and situated in his group home. Then I have to get myself home and ready for work tomorrow.

I do feel bad about not going to church with Mom and my sisters. I know my mother was looking forward to having us together for old times' sake. But I can't bear the thought of sitting with her in church, knowing that she's worshiping a God who loves her and condemns me. I don't have the stamina to go through that. Not this weekend, anyway.

I think that somewhere inside of her, my mother would like to be on better terms with me. But it would have to be entirely on her terms. She would accept me if I'd grovel and apologize for everything she imagines that I've done to her.

There would be no reciprocation from her. I'd have to be the one to do all the changing. Doing all that would entail complete self-rejection on my part. I'd end up having a mental breakdown like my father did. And I refuse to do that to myself.

I know my mother wants my attention, in the same way she craves attention from Edie and Kathy. I'd like to offer her loving attention and have her accept it. I've tried, I really have. But she invariably ruins my overtures by hurling back some venomous barb that makes the moment crumble.

I can't deny my resentment toward my mother. She's self-centered. She makes impossible demands on others. She can be downright nasty. She never holds herself accountable for anything she does.

But sometimes, I catch a glimpse of her vulnerability. I remember times from that year in Greenwood, when my father's breakdown dumped a load of responsibility on her shoulders. My mother had never been one to cry. But there were times when I saw her standing at the kitchen sink washing an endless pile of dishes, tears streaming down her face.

That memory touches my heart. It makes me want to throw my arms around her and tell her I know what she went through.

She was a strong, determined woman, I'll give her that. Nothing daunted her. Nothing broke her spirit. She made it through some incredibly tough times, and is still going strong.

I dread the day when I hear the news that my mother has entered the terminal stage of her life. I'll want to be at her deathbed. I couldn't live with myself if I wasn't by her side at the end.

But I'm afraid her last look at me will be judgmental, her last words condemning. I don't want to be left with memories like that.

I hope her final illness is such that I can come to her when she's unconscious and unable to speak. Then I'll hold her hand and whisper loving words in her ear. I'm determined to make this conflict between us end on a peaceful note.

I know everybody thinks I ran out on them this weekend. But I really am tired. I'm not just making excuses. I've been chronically exhausted for the past few months. It takes everything I have to get through my work day. In the evenings, I collapse and can hardly do anything. For the past couple of weeks, I haven't even been able to get myself out of the house to get groceries.

I've also had episodes of feeling nauseous and dizzy and a little lightheaded. A couple of times, I had a weird pain in my left shoulder. I finally took a day off work and went to see my doctor.

I was stunned when he said he thought I'd had several small heart attacks. He told me that heart attack symptoms in women are different than those in men, and often go undetected. I told him I haven't had any significant chest pain, but he said I could've had a heart attack without chest pain. He handed me a brochure about heart attacks in women. When I read it, I realized I've had every symptom.

Hearing this news triggered my old feelings of wanting to die. Heart disease is the same illness that took my father's life. It seems as if I'm following in his footsteps. As if I'm headed for the same unfortunate end.

For a few moments, I fantasized about having a massive heart attack that would end it all. It would be a quick and easy exit from this troublesome life. Then I gave myself a mental kick in the backside. *You have Marty to think of,* I told myself. *Who would look out for him if you weren't around?*

So I made the choice to seek treatment. My doctor referred me to a cardiologist, and I have an appointment this upcoming week. He'll be running a number of tests.

I'm not giving up. I'll do whatever my cardiologist recommends. I'll make the necessary changes in my lifestyle. I'll do this for Marty's sake.

And for my own sake. I'll stay alive, just for me.

Something nice happened as we were leaving Edie's house. Sam was helping me get Marty down the porch steps. He was in a surprisingly good mood. He said to Marty, "I'm going to build a portable ramp for your wheelchair, so the next time you visit, it'll be easier for you to get in and out of the house."

That surprised me. But it also touched me. It made me feel as if Marty and I are something more than just an inconvenience for him and Edie. Like we're actually welcome in their home. We'll have to come for another visit. Soon.

But right now, I just need to get home and get myself straightened out. I'm way off kilter—I can feel it. I'll try to stay lighthearted on the drive home. In spite of being exhausted, Marty had a wonderful time this weekend, and I don't want to put a damper on that.

KATHERINE: Sitting with my mother in church this morning felt like traveling back four decades. Those people have stayed the same all these years. Nothing about the church service has changed. We listened to the same dreary sermon. We sang the same droning hymns. When we sang "The Old Rugged Cross," one of my childhood friends, Marlene Johnson, started caterwauling in her terrible soprano voice. She sounded just like her mother did forty years ago.

I can't imagine how anyone could be content with this. If it weren't for my mom, I'd never give my old life a backward glance. It isn't healthy for a person to stay stuck in the past.

I've enjoyed being with my family this weekend, but I can't wait to get back home. My life with Bryce feels dynamic. He and I welcome change. We venture out and try new things. We never allow ourselves to become stagnant.

By the way, that dress Mom wore to church today was absolutely dreadful. I think it's the one she wore to my father's funeral, and that's been more than thirty years ago. I can't believe Edie hasn't taken her shopping to get something new. When I get home, I'll go out and buy her a nice outfit and send it to her.

FRANCES: I'm so tuckered out from goin' to church. I'm gonna hafta lay down for a spell. I don't know what come over me durin' that service.

A lot of people was glad to see me there. They was all sayin', "Howya doin', Frances?" They was glad to see my girls, too. They all knowed Edith, but not Katherine. I was introducin' Katherine all around, proud as can be, tellin' everybody she was my daughter from New York City.

Well, I was sittin' there durin' the sermon, Katherine on one side of me, Edith on the other. I was tellin' m'self that I'm a blessed woman, havin' two girls that care so much for me. But I couldn't make m'self be as happy as I shoulda been. It felt like somethin' was missin'.

I knowed what it was, of course. I was missin' havin' Rosalie there with us. A long time ago, I come to terms with the fact that my youngest girl wasn't gonna be who I wanted her to be. No matter how hard I prayed, no matter how much talkin' I did, she seemed to have her mind set on goin' down the wrong road. I learnt that a mother can do all she can do, and that still ain't no guarantee that her child is gonna turn out right.

I was sittin' there thinkin' about all that, to the point where I was hardly payin' attention to what Pastor Donovan was sayin'.

Then all of a sudden, it seemed like the Lord put somethin' else in my mind. Somethin' like a vision, maybe. Somethin' only I could see. I don't hardly know how to explain it. All's I can say is that it was real as real can be.

In my mind, I seen a picture of me and Rosalie when she was just a little thing, maybe four, five years old. We was walkin' along the road leadin' to the graveyard, the same way I seen her walkin' with her boy yesterday mornin'. Rosalie was always one that liked to take walks, and when she was little, she was always askin' me to go with 'er. She liked spendin' time alone with me that way.

Anyways, in my mind, I seen Rosalie holdin' onto my hand and turnin' her little face up to me. She was a chubby little thing back then, with fat little cheeks. And big brown eyes like her daddy's. So precious, she was.

Well, she was turnin' them big brown eyes up to me, lookin' kinda scared. Like she was lookin' to me to keep her safe. Like she was trustin' me. She had no thought but to trust me.

And it was all I could do to keep from bustin' out and bawlin', right there in church. I was thinkin', *Oh, Lord, I failed my baby girl. I ain't taken care of her the way I was s'pposed to. All this time, she been out there all alone, and I ain't done nothin' to help 'er. I ain't done nothin' but turn my back on 'er.* The thought of that brung so much sorrow to this ol' heart of mine that I could hardly stand it.

I sat there callin' to mind all the harsh things I ever said about Rosalie. All them things I said behind her back, and the things I said to her face. Made that girl cry a few times, I did.

I felt so ashamed of m'self. And I knowed right then and there that was somethin' I hadta stop. If my girl needs any judgin' or correctin', then I'm gonna let the Lord do that. That's gonna be His job from now on, not mine.

How's we gonna fix all these hurt feelin's between us? I was askin' the Lord. I ain't wantin' to die with this on my conscience. But I'm afraid it might be too late for me and Rosalie to get things straightened out between us. I wouldn't even know how to go about tryin' to fix things with 'er. But if we cain't get it done here on earth, I trust the Lord's gonna give us a chance to set things right in Heaven. I trust Him to lead us both down the right path so's we can see each other again after we leave this earth. I cain't bear the thought of not meetin' up with my little girl in Heaven.

I told Edith to go ahead and have dinner without me. I need to rest. I think maybe I need to lay down and have m'self a good cry.

SUNDAY AFTERNOON

KATRINA: This afternoon, I finally came up with a way to get some time alone with my mother. I told her I wanted to go on a nature walk across Freeman Ridge, like we did when I was a kid.

She thought it was a good idea. But before I knew it, she was trying to get everybody else to come along. Of course, Aunt Rosie and Marty were already gone. Grandma was over at her trailer because she wasn't feeling well. Sam said he had too much to do. Aunt Edie said, "Let me stay here and take care of Lilly while the two of you go."

Mom agreed, a little grudgingly. I know she didn't want to be alone with me. We borrowed Aunt Edie's car to drive to the ridge. All the way there, Mom complained about the car, and then about how hard it was to drive up the steep hill to the ridge. I kept my mouth shut, because I knew things were only going to get worse.

I had to work up the nerve before I could bring up the subject of Bryce's investigation. As we hiked along the ridge, Mom carried on about the humidity, the weeds, and the bugs. We saw a snake slither off the dirt road into the brush, and Mom had a fit. She said she couldn't wait to get out of this nasty place and back to New York City.

"Mom," I blurted out, "things aren't going to be that great when you get home."

She looked at me like I was crazy. "Why not?"

"Because Bryce is in trouble."

"What on earth are you talking about, Katrina?" she asked.

"He's in legal trouble," I said. "He's being investigated. He's probably going to be arrested."

She shot me a dirty look, then shook her head like she thought I was talking nonsense. "I don't know how you came up with a story like that."

"Bryce told me," I said, "when he called me yesterday. He's been trying to tell you himself. That's why he didn't want you to travel this weekend. That's why he keeps calling you. When you wouldn't listen to him, he asked me to talk to you."

Mom started walking so fast that I could hardly keep up with her. "It can't be as bad as all that, Katrina," she snapped. "Bryce has his attorneys. Things have come up in the past, and they've worked it out for him."

I was starting to get angry. I was ready to say, "The heck with it. You can think whatever you want to think." But just then, we met a man and woman coming across the ridge toward us. So I stopped talking.

The woman and I looked at each other, and all of a sudden, we recognized each other. "I remember you!" we said at almost the same time.

It was the same girl that my mom and dad and I had met all those years ago, the last time we hiked across the ridge as a family. She'd been with her mother and grandmother. She and I were both amazed at the coincidence of meeting again.

Then Mom jumped in and took over, like she always does. "It's a beautiful day, isn't it?" she said, which was the complete opposite of what she'd been saying to me a few minutes earlier.

She talked so cheerfully to that woman and the man

she was with. I couldn't believe it. It was like she'd completely tuned out what I'd been telling her. She asked the woman how her mother and grandmother were doing.

"My mother's doing great," the woman said. "But my grandmother passed away two years ago."

Mom acted sympathetic, as if she really cared about this woman losing her grandmother. She said, "I'm sure this has been a hard time for you." She was doing like she always does, acting like her own life is perfect and feeling sorry for everybody else. I wanted to grab her by the shoulders and shake her.

The woman mentioned that she and the man had just gotten married. Mom congratulated them and gushed all over them.

Of course, she ended up telling them about her life in New York City, never mentioning that she grew up here in Brown County. She talked about her off-Broadway shows and her TV commercials, and she got those people believing they were talking to a celebrity.

Then Mom said, "Well, it was nice talking with you. My daughter and I need to finish our walk. Then we have to get our things packed. We're flying back to New York City tomorrow morning." Just as if she was going home to her wonderful life, instead of to the nightmare she's about to face.

After we passed the couple, I blurted out everything else I had to say. "Mom, Bryce has been doing illegal things in his business for years. He's going to prison. You're going to lose the house. I've already talked to Roscoe. You can live with us until you get back on your feet."

Mom strolled along like she wasn't hearing a word I was saying. "Do you understand what I'm telling you?" I asked her.

"I've lived with Bryce for more than twenty years," she said sharply. "I know my husband, and I know how he operates his business. I don't think you have your story straight. I'll talk things over with him when we get home."

"Mom!" I protested.

"Just drop it, Katrina," she demanded, raising her voice at me. Like I was a misbehaving kid.

So I shut up and didn't say another word to her. I did my part. I'll let her deal with this problem in her own way.

I wouldn't want my mom's lifestyle for anything in the world. All the showing off and pretending. All the lies. Roscoe and I live a down-to-earth lifestyle. We're just ordinary people, like my dad.

Speaking of my father, he's going to find this news interesting. He'll be glad Bryce is finally getting what he's had coming all these years. But he'll feel sorry for my mom. He's never been truly angry at her, because he thinks the divorce was Bryce's fault, not hers. He's never loved anyone but her.

You know what went through my mind while my mom and I were walking along the ridge? I was hoping that Mom would divorce her crook of a husband. Then maybe she and my dad could get back together. Wouldn't that be awesome? Lilly could grow up with only two sets of grandparents, Roscoe's parents and my own. Things would be less confusing that way.

But that's just a little girl's dream. It's never going to happen. And I don't want it to, really. If my dad thought my mom needed help, he'd jump right up and do everything he could for her. He'd probably take her in all over again. But I wouldn't let him do that. Because she'd stick around just long enough to find herself a better deal, then off she'd go. I don't want to see him heartbroken all over again.

In the end, it'll be okay. Bryce will go to one of those country club prisons. And my mom will land on her feet. That's the kind of woman she is. She might have her faults, but she's the strongest person I know.

EDITH: I had so much fun taking care of Lilly this afternoon. It wasn't hard on me at all. I'd like to think that shows I'm making progress in letting go of the past. I'm trying.

When Kathy and Katrina came back from their walk, Kathy went upstairs to her bedroom and stayed there for two hours. That's not like her. I was getting worried, and was just about to go up and check on her.

But then she came downstairs to use the bathroom. Her eyes were red and puffy. Her makeup was smeared, and her hair was a mess. I'd never seen her in such a state.

I knew she'd been crying. Kathy's never been one to cry, not even as a child. She wasn't sensitive like me. She took everything in stride.

"Are you okay, Kathy?" I asked.

She turned her head to avoid looking me in the eye. "I'm fine," she muttered.

She didn't sound very convincing. I wanted to do something to help, like give her a hug. But her mood seemed so cold and prickly, and I sensed she wasn't open to that. So I just reached out and touched her arm. "Are you sure you're okay?"

She jerked away from my touch. "There's nothing for you to worry about, Edie." She sounded grouchy.

"I'm sorry," I said.

I wondered whether she and Katrina had argued when they were on their walk. But I can't imagine Kathy would cry over that.

Anyway, I've never heard Katrina speak up to Kathy. Kathy demands respect as a mother. My children used to argue with me all the time, and more often than not, they'd get their way. Sam would say I let the kids run all over me. But Kathy's never tolerated that kind of behavior from Katrina. Katrina is mild-mannered, and I've never heard her challenge Kathy's authority.

For a minute, I got stuck on the idea that I'd done something to offend my sister. But then I said to myself, *Edie, don't start feeling guilty about this. You haven't done anything wrong.*

When Kathy came out of the bathroom ten minutes later, I saw that she'd fixed herself up again. She had a smile on her face. "I've got to get my things packed," she called as she headed back up the stairs. "We need to get an early start tomorrow morning."

I told myself that Kathy's problem isn't my business. She seems to be handling things just fine.

ROSALIE: I just got Marty back to his group home. I let the staff know that he's had a busy weekend, and that he'll need a long nap this afternoon. Even though he's all worn out now, I'm glad I took him with me this weekend.

Afterwards, I came out here to Holcomb Gardens. I'd love to create beautiful flowerbeds like Edie does, but I've never had the time or the space to do that kind of planting. Coming here is the next best thing.

For the past ten years, Holcomb Gardens has been my special place for grounding myself when I'm feeling anxious. I let the sights and the smells and the sounds flood my senses. Soon, my mind stops racing and I feel more peaceful.

The fall flowers are in bloom now, the mums and the asters. I can't begin to describe how gorgeous it is. I believe the universe is built on love, beauty, and goodness, and spending time in settings like this is my favorite way of connecting with those divine attributes.

If I think of myself only as the child of Martin and Frances Rafferty, I feel so limited. And incredibly depressed. The father I loved and admired had a mental breakdown and tried to take his own life. My mother abused me, blamed me for things I've never done, and hates me to this day. Where is the hope in that?

In order to stay sane, I have to broaden my perspective. I tell myself that I'm a child of God, a child of the universe. The fact that I arrived on earth through Frances Rafferty's birth canal does not define me. My reason for being here has nothing to do with her.

I'm going to confess something that sounds a little crazy. I developed a habit when I was a young teenager in foster care, and I've never let go of it. Because I found the real story about how I came to earth to be unpalatable, I spun whimsical tales about my origin. I'd tell myself that I was a mermaid in the ocean, brought to land in a fisherman's net. Or that I was the child of the sun and the moon, carried to earth in the arms of an angel. Or that I was raised by gnomes and fairies in an enchanted forest. Sometimes, I entertain Marty with tales like that. I tell him make-believe stories about how he came to be my child. He enjoys the fantasies as much as I do. They carry him into a realm where the limitations of his body are no longer real.

It's silly, isn't it? Here I am, a doctor of psychology, grounded in the world of science. But sometimes, I need a way to soothe myself, and those stories do the trick.

When I get back to my condominium, I'll call Clem and tell him I'm home. He'll be glad to hear from me. He was worried about me traveling this weekend, because he knows I haven't been feeling well.

No, I haven't told you about Clem. I haven't told anyone, except for a few close friends. I'm keeping him under wraps, waiting to see what direction our relationship will take. My family doesn't know about him. They're not ready for him yet.

Clem is short for Clement. Clement Cooper. An old-fashioned name that fits an old-fashioned man. I mean old-fashioned in a good way: sweet, thoughtful, well-mannered, protective.

Kathy would look down her nose at Clem. He's not flashy enough for her. My mother wouldn't like him just by virtue of the fact that he isn't Richard. She'd be rude to him, and he's too nice of a guy to be subjected to that kind of treatment.

Maybe when Mom's gone, I'll take Clem down to Brown County to meet Edie and Sam. He's a down-to-earth kind of guy. He'd fit right in with them.

If I'd met Clem twenty or thirty years ago, I wouldn't have given him a second glance. I regret having to say that, but it's true. He isn't what you'd call a good-looking man, although his kind eyes and warm smile make him attractive. He's stocky, a bit overweight. He's bald. He's an inch shorter than me, and I'm not a tall woman. He's not a professional man. He's a retired truck driver.

But I met Clem only six months ago. At this point in my life, those old standards about how a guy looks and what he does for a living no longer matter. What I want now is love and kindness and loyalty and integrity, and Clem possesses those traits in abundance. And even though he's not highly educated, he's naturally insightful. He has a wealth of practical knowledge, and a whole lot of common sense. He has a way of balancing me out when I get worried and frantic.

"How on earth did you meet this guy?" one of my friends asked me. It's an interesting story. For a number of years, I'd occasionally attended weekend dances for single people. Most people go to those dances hoping to find someone to date. But not me. I was going only for the sake of dancing. I'd long ago given up on dating, and I certainly couldn't imagine myself being interested in any of the men there.

One evening, a short, stocky man a few years older than me asked me to dance. I accepted, as I never turn down an opportunity to dance unless the guy is utterly reprehensible. I wasn't expecting much. But when I started dancing with this man, I was surprised at what a delightful experience it was.

He looked like such an average fellow, a blue-collar guy. But one of the first things that stood out about him was his impeccable manners. He graciously asked my name, and then introduced himself as Clem Cooper. He was well-spoken, and a very good dancer. He knew steps in the waltz, the foxtrot, the swing, and even the Latin dances. I could tell that he'd taken lessons, and that he'd practiced the steps diligently.

I also had the sense that he wanted to provide his dance partner with the best experience he could give her. He led me so well that I ended up executing steps I'd never done before. I was amazed and enthralled. He was such a joy to dance with, and from the start, he had me smiling from ear to ear. We kept on going, one dance after another. I couldn't break away from him.

During a waltz, he looked into my eyes and said, "Miss Jacobson, your ravishing beauty takes my breath away." I knew it wasn't a line. He was speaking from his heart.

Never in my life had anyone referred to me as a ravishing beauty. That's Kathy's thing. She's been told she's beautiful every day of her life. The most I've ever aspired to be is attractive.

But in that moment, I knew Clement Cooper truly saw me as beautiful. I had a few seconds of feeling weak in the knees. I wanted to break down and cry at the tenderness of it. I wanted to stop dancing and fall into his arms and have him hold me like a small child.

I could tell that Clem didn't expect women to find him attractive, and that he wouldn't make any overtures unless he thought a woman would be receptive to them. When we finally decided to take a break from dancing, I told myself,

That was nice, Rosalie, but Clem Cooper isn't your type of guy. Don't lead him on. Thank him and walk away.

But that's not what happened. I thanked Clem profusely for all the wonderful dances we'd enjoyed, but I didn't walk away. We stood there talking at the edge of the dance floor, barely able to hear each other over the loud music. After a few minutes, Clem suggested that we go some place for a cup of coffee.

And I've never been able to walk away from that darling man. On paper, it looks all wrong, a woman with advanced degrees dating a man who never went past high school. But in real life, it works. Clem's warmth and kindness have drawn me in, and I couldn't extricate myself from him even if I wanted to.

And I don't want to. Having his strong, protective arms around me is a comfort that I've never known before. I never want him to let go.

Clem is a widower. His wife died six years ago. They never had children, so he's made my son his son. Marty's disabilities mean nothing to him. He never resents my obligations toward him. Whenever I visit Marty, Clem is right there by my side. He keeps both Marty and me wrapped up in that big heart of his.

My son enjoys watching baseball on TV. He's a loyal fan of the Cincinnati Reds. The day Clem found this out, he announced that he was a Reds fan, too, which made Marty's eyes light up. Then Clem sat down next to Marty and started chatting with him about the different players. And the two of them became the best of friends.

The next time we visited, Clem brought along a bag and laid it in Marty's lap. "It's for you," he said.

I held the bag while Marty used his left hand to pull out a bright red tee shirt with *Reds* emblazoned across the front of it. He was so thrilled with his gift. He wants to wear that shirt every day.

When Clem did that for my son, I fell completely in love with him. It scared me. Terrified me, actually. I didn't want to lose my heart like that, but I couldn't help it.

I've told Clem about my past. He's not put off by it. He just tells me that I need love, and that he has all the love in the world to give me.

Clem has been hinting about the possibility of us having a future together. I know he won't outright propose to me until he senses that I'm ready. Up to this point, I've held back a little. But getting away for the weekend has given me a new perspective on our relationship.

The trauma I experienced when I was thirteen made me feel as if all the love I'd ever known had been ripped away from me. I built a protective wall around me to shield myself against any more pain. I never let anyone close to me after that, other than Marty.

I've always prided myself on being an independent, self-reliant woman. That woman was born when I was removed from my home and placed in foster care. She was born out of necessity, out of pain.

But now it's time for me to be more than that. Especially now that my health is in question, now that I'm faced with the fact that I won't be here forever. It's time to let my guard down, to experience true intimacy with another person.

You know what? I'm not going to wait until I get home to call Clem. I'm going over to sit on the bench by the fountain, and I'm going to call him right now. He'll ask how my weekend went, and I'll tell him all about it.

But first, I'm going to tell him that I love him. He's been saying that to me the past few months. I haven't said it back to him yet. He's been waiting patiently. Today, I'm ready.

I now know something with certainty, something I'd been unsure about. If Clem asks me to marry him, I will accept his proposal. No hesitations. I'm ready to plunge into this.

If I marry Clem, I'll take his last name. I no longer want to be reminded that I was once Richard Jacobson's wife. And I don't want to carry the last name of Rafferty. I'll start a new identity by becoming Rosalie Cooper, a woman who can relax and enjoy the small pleasures in life, confident in the knowledge that she has a loving, loyal partner.

At my cardiology appointment next week, I expect to be told that I need to cut back on my work hours. Maybe I'll do more than that. Maybe I'll decide to retire early, so that Clem and I can spend more time together. At our age, we don't have a whole lifetime ahead of us. I want to make the most of every moment we have to share.

And I don't want to continue to hide my relationship with Clem. I'm proud of him. I'm proud of us.

Maybe I'm ready to take a risk. Maybe I'll take Clem down to Brown County to meet my family. Soon, not years from now when my mother is gone. I'll try one last time with Mom. Oh, I know it might backfire on me. But I'm going to throw caution to the wind and introduce her to the man I love. I'll give her the chance to love him, too.

SUNDAY EVENING

KATHERINE: I went to bed early tonight, but I couldn't fall asleep. Every time I closed my eyes and tried to relax my mind, I started thinking about what Katrina told me this afternoon. She dropped quite a bomb on me.

I tried to convince myself there was nothing to worry about, that she was making more out of the situation than is actually there. I told myself that Katrina has never given her stepfather the respect he deserves from her. That she's always sided with her dad, and that affects how she looks at Bryce.

As I tossed and turned, my uneasiness grew. I felt trapped in that tiny room. It seemed as if I'd been traveling back in time all weekend, and being in that upstairs bedroom made me feel like ten-year-old Kathy Rafferty, living out in the middle of nowhere with her backward and impoverished family.

I couldn't stand to stay in that room another minute, so I decided to get out of bed and slip out of the house for some fresh air. I pulled my robe on over my nightgown. It's an expensive set of silk lingerie, a gift from Bryce.

As I walked down the stairs, I could hear Sam and Edie talking in their bedroom. Sam's voice was raised, and he sounded angry. Just as I stepped into the living room, he came out of the bedroom. It was an awkward moment, coming face-to-face with my brother-in-law in the darkness like that.

"I'm going outside for a minute," I told him. "If you don't mind, I'd like you to leave the door unlocked."

"Fine," he grunted, plopping himself down on the sofa.

It was cooler outside than I expected it to be. It had been so warm and humid all weekend. But the temperature was dropping, and when I stepped off the porch, I could feel a few sprinkles. At first, I didn't know whether the wetness on my cheeks was from the raindrops or my tears.

Damn it, Kathy, I scolded myself. *Don't you start crying again. It's not going to help anything.* But the tears came of their own volition, cascading down my face like a waterfall.

I desperately needed a tissue, and I put my hand in the pocket of my robe, hoping to find one there. But what I found was something hard and rectangular. My cell phone. When I'd left the bedroom, I'd picked it up out of habit. I never go anywhere without my phone.

As I ran my fingers over the phone's cool surface, I knew finding it in my pocket at just that moment wasn't an accident. There was a reason that I'd carried it out of the house unthinkingly.

This is a sign, I told myself. *A sign that you need to call Bryce. It's time to hear what he has to say to you.* Fumbling in the darkness, I turned on the phone that I'd shut off two days ago.

"Katherine!" my husband exclaimed when he answered the phone. "Thank you for calling me. I've been waiting to hear from you all weekend."

At first, I tried to be my normal upbeat self. "How are you, sweetie?" I asked. "Are you feeling any better?"

There was a long pause before he said, "Has Katrina talked to you?"

Then my composure gave way to fear, and my anxious thoughts came tumbling out. I moved away from the house so no one could hear me. "Bryce, Katrina said you're in trouble. She said you're going to be arrested, and that we're going to lose everything. Tell me that's not true, Bryce. She got the story wrong, didn't she? She's blown the whole thing out of proportion."

The silence on the other end of the line seemed to go on forever. "For God's sake, Bryce," I screamed, "tell me it's not true!"

"Calm down, Katherine," he commanded. "Calm down and listen to me."

I squeezed my eyes shut, trying to ward off the disastrous news I knew I was about to hear. My hand shook so hard that I could barely hold the phone to my ear.

Then the dreaded words came, slow and sonorous, echoing in my head. "Katherine, what your daughter told you is the truth."

Suddenly, the world started spinning around me. The ground under my feet heaved and tilted, threatening to topple me over. I thought I was going to fall, so I sat down on a landscape boulder in one of Edie's flowerbeds. The cold rain drizzled down on me, plastering my robe and gown to my skin.

"Katherine," Bryce said. "Katherine, my love. How can I possibly tell you how sorry I am? I've turned your life upside down. I regret this more than I've ever regretted anything."

"Why, Bryce?" I whispered into the phone. "Why did you do this?"

His voice hardened, sounding defensive. "Running a company is complicated, Katherine. You know that, even though I've tried to protect you from all the problems that come up in my business. To make a profit, a businessman has to take risks. And sometimes, those risks don't pay off. Things get out of hand."

"You knew better," I said, my voice rising again. "You knew you could get caught. You put both of us in jeopardy."

"Go ahead, Katherine," he said. "Let me have it. Call me every name in the book, if that makes you feel better. Get it all out of your system. I deserve it."

A wave of dizziness, accompanied by nausea, washed over me. I jumped up off the rock and ran across the road, where I vomited into the brush at the edge of the woods. Once again, I fumbled in the pocket of my robe for a tissue, and when I found none, I was left with no choice but to wipe my mouth on my silk sleeve.

"I trusted you, Bryce!" I screamed into the phone. "I trusted you with everything! I trusted you with my life!"

"Calm down, Katherine!" he shouted back at me. "Pull yourself together and listen to me!"

I stopped ranting, waiting for his next words. "Trust me one last time, Katherine," he said, his voice soft and pleading. "I've got things worked out for you. I moved some funds around so that you'll have plenty to live on while I'm . . . while I'm gone. We'll go over all that when you get home."

Anger welled up in me, a hideous, murderous rage I'd never known before. In that moment, I saw my husband for who he really was. I knew everything about him, everything I'd never wanted to let myself know. "Bryce Hudson," I hissed, "you lying, cheating son-of-a-bitch. I don't want any more of your filthy money. I don't want another penny from you." Then, using all of my strength, I hurled my phone into the woods.

In the darkness, I stumbled blindly down Sprunica Ridge Road, lost and alone in the middle of nowhere. I had no idea where I was going. There was nowhere to go.

After what seemed like hours instead of minutes, I reached our old church. Without thinking, I turned down the weedy dirt path toward the cemetery, feeling like a phantom in my long, pale robe. As I approached the gravestones at the edge of the cemetery, I knew this was the place for me to be. The place of death. Because Katherine Hudson, the glamorous wife of worldly millionaire Bryce Hudson, had died.

Even though I hadn't visited my father's grave in decades, I knew exactly where it was located. I made my way there and sat down on his headstone, and as the cold rain poured down on me, I began to sob. Deep sobs that wrenched and tore at my insides. I'd never known it was possible to cry that way.

I knew I was grieving for more than the loss of the life I'd shared with Bryce. I was crying for everything I'd ever refused to cry about before. For young Kathy Rafferty who'd set her jaw and braved the big world, blinking back tears of disappointment. For the grownup Katherine who was worn out from posturing and pretending, who'd kept a smile plastered on her face, a band-aid covering the ever-widening crack in her polished veneer. Who'd drowned all her fears and misgivings in glasses of expensive wine.

The sobbing emptied me out, leaving me limp and spineless. I could no longer hold myself upright on my father's headstone, and I collapsed and fell into the soggy, un-mowed grass around his grave. The cold wetness seeped through my thin clothing, ruining the lingerie I no longer cared about.

As I lay there gazing up at the overcast sky, I realized the rain had stopped. A crisp, refreshing breeze swept through the cemetery, promising that the downpour was over. And then I saw the most breathtaking thing I'd ever seen in my life, more breathtaking than all the grandeurs I'd witnessed on my travels with Bryce. More splendid than a Hawaiian sunset. More magnificent than the snow-covered Swiss alps. More dazzling than the crystal blue waters surrounding the Greek islands.

The clouds parted ever so slightly, and a single star shone down on me. A single ray of light.

There would be new life. There would always be new life.

SAM: Thank goodness, Edie and I got to sleep in our own room tonight. When we went to bed, Edie told me she needed to talk. "I'm too tired," I said. "I have to go to work tomorrow, and I need to get a good night's sleep."

"Please, Sam," she said. "I need to get something off my chest. It'll take just a few minutes."

Then she proceeded to tell me that Ralph Dixon had showed up at the house last week. I sure hadn't expected to hear anything like that. It really ticked me off. I don't know Ralph Dixon personally, but I've heard plenty of things about him. He's got a reputation in this county.

"That son-of-a-bitch had no business coming over here," I growled at her. "He didn't try to put the moves on you, did he? I've heard he's quite the tomcat."

Edie laughed. "No, Sam, he didn't try anything with me. I'm a sixty-one-year-old woman. He wouldn't be interested in me in that way. Anyway, he's family. He's my little brother. I helped raise him."

Edie had told me before about Ralph being a foster kid in their home. She's sentimental about things like that.

"Well, I hope he's not coming back," I said.

"I don't know whether he will or not," she replied. "When he left, he said, 'See you later.'"

By then, I was so riled up that I knew I wasn't going to get any sleep. "Edie, I don't want him hanging around here. If he shows up again, you need to tell me right away. Call me at work if you need to. I don't care. I need to know what's going on around this place. Okay?"

I thought we were done talking, and I was trying to calm myself down. But Edie said, "There's more." And then she told me that Ralph was having financial problems, and that she'd written him a check for five hundred dollars.

When I heard that, I just about hit the ceiling. "What the hell were you thinking, Edith?" I exploded at her. "Our property taxes are due this week, and now we don't have enough money in our account to pay that bill. I'll have to take money out of our IRA. Or put the taxes on my credit card. You know I don't like running up a credit card debt. We can't afford to do that at our age."

I was so mad that I jumped out of bed and went out to the living room to sit on the couch. I was already at the end of my rope, dealing with Edie's family all weekend. Being hit with the bullshit about Ralph Dixon was more than I could take. Then, finding Edie's sister wandering around the house in her nightgown didn't help matters.

I sat out there fuming, thinking that if I ever laid eyes on Ralph Dixon, I was going to get in his face and tell him that he'd better never set foot on my property again. And that if he bothered my wife in the future, he'd have me to answer to. But after I cooled down, it hit me that this was as much my fault as it was Edie's.

Sam Clemens, you've turned into an old curmudgeon, I told myself. *Your wife's a good-hearted woman. That's why you love her. And sometimes, you treat her like crap. If you wouldn't be such a bear to live with, your wife wouldn't be so scared to talk to you. She'd let you in on everything that's going on in her life. And she wouldn't be doing things like this behind your back.*

So I got up and went back to the bedroom. "We'll work it out, Edie," I said. "But you've got to promise me something. If Ralph Dixon comes over here again, don't let him in the house if I'm not around. If he starts pressuring you for more money, tell him you need to talk to your husband first. And don't let him wear you down."

"I promise," she said. "I know where you're coming from, and I agree with you." But she seemed sad. I knew she was still thinking about Ralph Dixon being her brother, and I softened up a little bit.

"I don't mind if he comes over sometime when I'm here," I told her. "Let me size him up. If I think he's genuine about wanting family relationships, then okay. But if I get the feeling he's only out to use you, then he'd better stay the hell away from here. You understand what I'm saying?"

"Yes, Sam," she said. "I trust you on this. You're better at reading people than I am."

"Edith," I said. "You need to let me in on everything. We need to communicate more."

She just busted out laughing. "Sam Clemens, I never thought I'd live to see the day when you'd say a thing like that!"

EDITH: I worked up the nerve to tell Sam about Ralphie this evening. He was upset. I knew he would be. He got out of bed and went to sit in the living room.

While he was out there, I did my own thinking. *You've got a good husband, Edie,* I told myself. *Even if he is an old grouch, he's always done right by you. He's never turned his back on his responsibility toward you and the children. Not for one minute. He's got a right to be mad about this. You need to give him time to cool down.*

He came back to bed sooner than I thought he would. And then we had a good talk. We talked more than we have in years.

"Edie," Sam said, "I know your heart was in the right place when you gave Ralph Dixon that money, even if it wasn't a good idea. You're the most unselfish person I know."

Wow, that threw me for a loop! All my life, I've beaten myself up for being selfish. Every time I felt that way, I tried harder to do things for other people, just to prove to myself that I'm not a selfish person. And here, my husband doesn't think I'm selfish at all.

Then Sam said, "You're working yourself to death, Edie. There's no reason for you to do that. You need to slow down and take care of yourself. I'm interested in having my wife around for a good long time. I want you and me to enjoy our retirement years together."

I think he's said things like that before, but I'd never paid any attention. This time, I tried to take in what he was telling me. And I realized how much Sam really cares for me. Not many women are lucky enough to have a husband like mine.

The image of James is fading from my mind. After having dominated my thoughts for so long, I'm surprised at how quickly he's drifting away.

This morning, I had the idea that I needed to tell my husband all about James and me. Come clean about the pregnancy, and everything. But the more I thought about it, the more I realized dumping all that on Sam would only hurt him. It would be a long time before he got over it.

So I'll put the memories of James to rest on my own. Then I can turn my attention to the here and now. To the real love of my life, Samuel Clemens.

Or to Edith Clemens.

I can't believe I just said that. It sounds terrible, doesn't it? But I've got to learn to love me. Before it's too late, I've got to learn what it's like to put myself first sometimes.

My friend Margaret Brown is offering sculpting classes in her studio. Because I work for her on weekends, she said she'd put me first on the list to take her class, if I wanted to. I automatically said no. I told her I was too busy. The truth of the matter is that I've never seen myself as someone who would do something that interesting.

I'm going to tell Margaret that I've changed my mind. I'm going to take that class. It's like something my father would've done. I think I may have inherited some of his artistic tendencies, and I want to find out something about Edith Clemens the artist.

So here's what I plan to do tomorrow. First thing in the morning, I'll run Kathy and Katrina up to the airport. When I get home, I'm going to take care of the scraps of James' letters. I'm still planning on burying them in one of my flowerbeds. Maybe the one right under the stained-glass window.

Then I'm going to make some phone calls, to arrange home health care for my mother. If I can get someone to come to her home a couple of times a week, that will take a huge load off my shoulders.

Mom won't like that idea. She'll have a few choice words to say about it. But I'm going to put my foot down with her. Yes, you heard that right. Meek little Edith Clemens is going to put her foot down hard.

And after that, I'll call Margaret and reserve a spot in her class. The more I think about it, the more excited I get.

Sam and I agreed on something tonight. Next weekend, no one is coming over. We won't be babysitting any of the grandchildren. We won't even have the kids over for Sunday dinner. It'll be our time.

FRANCES: I was so tired out, I went to bed early tonight, maybe 7:30, 8:00 o'clock. Sleepin' like a log, I was. But just a minute ago, I woke up all of a sudden. And the sweetest feelin' come over me. Like an angel of the Lord done passed through the room. And I couldn't help but call out in the darkness, "God is good." Yup, that's all I could think to say. God is good.

AUTHOR'S NOTE

I grew up, along with my eight siblings, in rural Brown County, Indiana. My father was the minister of the Bean Blossom Mennonite Church mentioned in this novel. It is because of my enduring affection for and fascination with that part of the country that I chose Brown County as the setting for this story.

My childhood home was on Gatesville Road, one half mile east of the tiny village of Bean Blossom, fifty miles south of Indianapolis. Our shabby little house, surrounded by the vegetable gardens that sustained us, was set against a backdrop of wooded hills that were incredibly beautiful when the leaves turned colors in the fall.

Back then, the farther east from Bean Blossom one traveled on those narrow, winding roads, the sparser the population became. As a child, I endowed those remote wooded parts of the county with an aura of mystery. Thus, I found it satisfying to locate the Rafferty family homestead "way out in the middle of nowhere."

For the most part, the locales and businesses mentioned in this story currently exist or have existed in the past, and were part of my childhood experience. Sprunica Elementary and Brown County Junior and Senior High are real schools. However, the Rafferty homestead, Frances Rafferty's mobile home, the country church where Martin Rafferty preached, the cemetery where he is buried, the church and parsonage in Greenwood, and Margaret Brown's studio in Nashville are entirely products of my imagination.

Lois Jean Thomas

OTHER BOOKS BY LOIS JEAN THOMAS

Me and You—We Are Who? (The Sambodh Society, Inc., 2006)

All the Happiness There Is (The Sambodh Society, Inc., 2006)

Johnny and Kris (The Sambodh Society, Inc., 2013)

Daughters of Seferina (Seventh Child Publishing/ CreateSpace, 2013)

Days of Daze: My Journey Through the World of Traumatic Brain Injury (Seventh Child Publishing/ CreateSpace, 2014)

Rachel's Song (Seventh Child Publishing/CreateSpace 2014)

A.K.A Suzette (Seventh Child Publishing/CreateSpace, 2014)

Blessed Transgression (Seventh Child Publishing/ CreateSpace 2015)

CPSIA information can be obtained
at www.ICGtesting.com
Printed in the USA
LVOW13s1602300317
529063LV00012B/685/P

2

9 780997 644500